Tom Derringer

and the

Aluminum Airship

OTHER NOVELS BY LAWRENCE WATT-EVANS

Vika's Avenger
One-Eyed Jack
The Chromosomal Code
Touched by the Gods
The Rebirth of Wonder
The Nightmare People
Among the Powers
Shining Steel
(with Esther M. Friesner) *Split Heirs*
(with Carl Parlagreco) *The Spartacus File*

THE FILES OF CARLISLE HSING
Nightside City
Realms of Light

THE FALL OF THE SORCERERS
A Young Man Without Magic
Above His Proper Station

THE ANNALS OF THE CHOSEN
The Wizard Lord
The Ninth Talisman
The Summer Palace

THE OBSIDIAN CHRONICLES
Dragon Weather
The Dragon Society
Dragon Venom

THE LORDS OF DÛS
The Lure of the Basilisk
The Seven Altars of Dûsarra
The Sword of Bheleu
The Book of Silence

LEGENDS OF ETHSHAR
The Misenchanted Sword
With A Single Spell
The Unwilling Warlord
Taking Flight
The Blood of a Dragon
The Spell of the Black Dagger
Night of Madness
Ithanalin's Restoration
The Spriggan Mirror
The Vondish Ambassador
The Unwelcome Warlock
The Sorcerer's Widow
Relics of War (forthcoming)

Tom Derringer
and the
Aluminum Airship

Lawrence Watt-Evans

Misenchanted Press

Takoma Park

This is a work of fiction. None of the characters and events portrayed in this novel are intended to represent actual person living or dead.

Tom Derringer & the Aluminum Airship

Published by Misenchanted Press
www.misenchantedpress.com

Cover design by Lawrence Watt-Evans & Connie Hirsch

Frontispieces by Kyrith Evans

In memory of my mother,
Doletha Watt Evans

J. Thomas Derringer, Jr.

Miss Elspeth Vanderhart

TOM DERRINGER

Chapter One

I Discover My Heritage

I was eight years old when I found my father's journals. They were neatly arranged on a shelf above the harmonium, not concealed in any way, but I had not troubled myself to explore that particular collection until one rainy day in 1874, when I tired of my customary amusements and clambered atop the polished wooden top of the instrument to see just what lay within those brown leatherette bindings.

I did not immediately recognize my father's handwriting; he had been dead for some four years at that time, so I had not had much occasion to encounter it. I did see immediately that these were hand-written works, rather than printed books, but it took me considerably longer to grasp that they were not fiction and that my late parent was the author.

Eventually, though, after glancing at first one volume and then another and flipping through pages as my whimsy took me, I decided to start at the beginning, and there, upon the first page of the first volume, I found the inscription, *My Journal, by John Thomas Derringer, Age Twelve*, and the date, the third day of March, in the Year of Our Lord 1854.

Needless to say, that captured my attention, and I began reading.

I cannot overstate my astonishment at what I read therein, at this sudden discovery that my father had led a life of excitement and adventure in the years before my birth.

My mother found me there, sprawled across the harmonium, some three hours later. I was well into the second volume, covering the autumn of 1854 and the winter of 1855, enraptured by my father's adventures.

I received a stern admonishment for climbing on the furniture, but was permitted to continue my reading. Indeed, Mother was kind enough to lift down all twenty-two volumes and help me carry them to my room, so that I might peruse them at my leisure.

I shall not describe at length the contents of those journals to my readers; I trust everyone who has taken an interest in this account is familiar with the general outline of Jack Derringer's career as the young companion of the famed adventurer Darien Lord. Nor do I think it difficult to imagine the effect those books had upon me. My father, an adventurer? What a revelation for a lad such as I was. I could scarcely contain my excitement. I read through all twenty-two volumes in a great rush, and when I had finished I returned to the beginning and read through them again.

Once again, I was enthralled. The realization that the bold and beautiful Arabella Whitaker described in the later volumes was my own dear mother added to the delight I found in my father's narrative.

I took some time to absorb what I had read, to ponder on its significance, and then, perhaps a fortnight after that original discovery, I went to my mother with a head full of questions and began asking her for every detail she could recall that my father had not thought worth preserving.

There were, it seemed, a good many, and my mother answered my questions directly and honestly. That may surprise some readers, as many parents go to great lengths to protect their progeny from the less pleasant facts of life, but my mother was a remarkable woman.

She did ask, though, that I say nothing of any of this to my playmates, and I took that request to heart. Indeed, it pleased me to keep my father's life a secret; I feared that if I were to boast of his exploits, my friends would remind me that their own fathers were still present, while mine was not. While there is much to recommend knowing that one's father was a hero, it seemed to me at that age that there is even more to be said for having a father still among the living.

I did speak of it to my sister, Mary Ann, who was three years my junior, but I am not sure how much she grasped. She scarcely seemed to understand that we had ever had a father, for he had died two months before she was born.

It is in the nature of boys to wish to emulate their elders, and so it was for me. The more I learned of the life my father had led, the more I hoped that I might someday follow in his footsteps. I kept this desire to myself for some time, but at last, one night, as Mother and I conversed at the supper table, it slipped out.

When the words had escaped my lips, and I realized that I could by no means call them back, I stared at my mother in horror. I thought she would dismiss my wish as nothing but a childhood fancy, or perhaps proclaim it far too dangerous a profession for her only son. I thought she would object. I thought she might chastise me for my presumption in thinking I might be capable of such a life.

I had misjudged her.

Instead of any of those unfavorable responses, she gazed at me coolly for several seconds, considering the situation, and then said, "If you are to be an adventurer, Tommy, you must be trained for the role. An adventurer must not only be strong and brave, but must also know how to fight, and when not to fight. He must be familiar not only with the arts of combat, but also with the arts of persuasion. He must know not only all the common affairs of mankind, but also as much as he can learn of the secret histories and hidden ways of the world. He must be adept with mathematics, knowledgeable in every science, and alert to the possibilities of the supernatural. To fall short in any of these fields is to tempt Fate.

"You have read my dear Jackie's journals; you know what became of Ebenezer Dawes, and the Fancher brothers, and the crew of the *Iapetus*. Rest assured, my son, that there were many others in the adventurer's trade besides these who died inglorious deaths through some tiny slip, some minuscule gap in their education, some tragic shortcoming in their skills. You are my beloved son, and it would please me to see you live a long and quiet life, untroubled by any extraordinary risk, but you are your father's son, and blood will tell. If I were to attempt to keep you at home one moment longer than you choose, I am sure you would find some way to elude me. I knew, when I allowed you to read dear Jackie's journals, how you might react, and although I felt many a pang, I knew I could not keep the past hidden from you, and that you might respond to this knowledge in the very fashion you have. So be it. If you are determined upon a life of adventure, I know I cannot prevent it, and indeed, I would not ask you to forego it. I remember well the delight your father took in his travels and accomplishments, and how can I refuse you a chance at similar satisfactions? Why, as you have read, I participated in some of those adventures myself, and I can scarcely deny that I enjoyed them. So I will not hold you back, but I will see to it, Tommy, that before you set forth upon the trail, you will be prepared in every fashion I can devise. Would that suit you?"

I stared at her in astounded delight and exclaimed, "Oh, most wonderfully, Mother!"

"Then it is done," she said. "And may Heaven smile upon us in this!"

Chapter Two

My Education Begins

My education in the adventurer's arts began the very next day, when my dear mother brought forth several things I had not known we possessed: my father's pistols and cutlass, several training swords made of birch, and an assortment of other weapons. I was not permitted to shoot or cut anything, but only to familiarize myself with these tools of the trade.

I was also sent to the post office with a thick handful of letters my mother had written the night before – had, in fact, stayed up very late to finish. Only later did I learn that these were directed to various instructors and suppliers, arranging for every aspect of my training.

For the next six years, Mother saw to it that I received the most complete training she could devise. I learned to fence and shoot – not only with sword and pistol, but with dagger, spear, halberd, rifle, bayonet, and musket. I was trained in archery in the English, Indian, and Asian styles, and even learned the proper use of the crossbow. As I gained sufficient stature I was taught boxing, and savate, and several curious Eastern forms of hand-to-hand combat, as well as the use of a variety of sticks and staves.

I should make clear that Mother did not handle most of this herself; though she did, in fact, know the rudiments of a surprising number of martial skills. She hired a variety of tutors to ensure that I mastered the techniques I might someday need, and these worthies paid regular visits to our home. Some instructed me in and about our own modest property, while others insisted that it was important to deal with unfamiliar surroundings and would take me to various other locations to train.

I was also tutored in a variety of more subtle and less aggressive fields; I learned the essentials of chemistry and physics, with emphasis on identifying and treating various poisons, improvising explosives, calculating leaps and throws under adverse conditions, and so on.

And history – ah, I despaired of ever learning all the history that my books and tutors tried to cram into my poor head! I was expected to know not only the facts every schoolboy learned, such as English kings and American presidents and the dates and victors of important battles, but also the secrets behind those facts – the true role of the Freemasons in various events, the identity of every spy and traitor who altered the course of events, the genealogies of the noble families that lived in exile hoping for eventual revenge or reinstatement, and all the other miscellanea that might someday be crucial in understanding an intrigue or conspiracy.

My studies in geography included not just those nations found on every modern map of the world, but also the known appearances of the Lost City of the Mirage, the suspected location of entrances to the tunnels of the lizard people said to live beneath the deserts of southern California, the true location of Shangri-La, the best guesses on where El Dorado might lie, the dimensions and mystic significance of each pyramid and temple in Egypt and the Yucatan, and other such lore.

I acquired a basic understanding of several languages; fortunately, I had a certain talent for them and learned Latin, French, and German readily enough. Russian, Greek, and Hebrew gave me more difficulty; I did not take readily to their unfamiliar alphabets.

Naturally, I could not hope to learn every language I might encounter; the best I could do was to develop a general set of linguistic skills that I hoped would allow me to pick up other tongues as needed. For the present I settled for those six languages and a study of the known dialects of English, since the ability to identify a speaker's origins could prove valuable.

I kept a journal, as my father had, though I had nothing to enter therein one-tenth as exciting as his own experiences. He had been caught up in adventuring by chance in that long-ago winter of 1854, when he had taken shelter from a blizzard in the same cabin that Mr. Lord and his entourage had claimed as their base of operations against the supposed werewolf of Newfield. He had been flung into the adventurer's river to sink or swim, as it were, while I was still on the shore learning the currents and training my limbs. Even so, I thought record keeping was a good habit to develop, and so I forced myself to make a daily entry, however tedious it might be. I amused myself and enhanced some of my other lessons by writing in various languages, not limiting myself to my native English.

When I was fourteen my mother's ingenuity in devising useful lessons was exhausted, and I took charge of my own education, using her extensive connections in the adventurers' brotherhood to find the men and women who could train me in more esoteric disciplines. In every case, we made contact with these individuals by mail or telegram and invited them to our home. If they were not willing to attend me there I made do without their services, but most were quite coöperative.

And finally, in the spring of 1882, when I was sixteen, we agreed that it was time I should travel to New York City, to introduce myself to certain persons there.

Until then I had always lived in a pleasant little town I shall not name, inasmuch as my mother and sister still reside there, and I do not wish to give any clue to their location. I had ventured into the Adirondacks to master the skills of wilderness survival in the course of my training and had learned the basics of seamanship on Lake Erie, but had in general stayed close to home and had not yet set foot in any great city.

This was in part due to my mother's natural caution, aided and abetted by several of my tutors; my father had, like every adventurer, made enemies, and the possibility that some old foe, or even just an over-enthusiastic rival, might strike at my family could not be ruled out. Yes, my father was long dead, but that might well be insufficient to slake the bitterness in some cases, and in other circles his death might be thought a hoax. Certainly, false reports of an adventurer's death were not uncommon; any number of adventurers said to have passed beyond this vale of tears had later turned up alive. Further, we had always lived off the income from investments that had been purchased with some of the treasure that had been my father's share of his journeys in company with Darien Lord, and that wealth might be sufficient to tempt malefactors who bore us no animus, but who thought those funds might better serve them than us.

Accordingly, my mother had lived quietly in our small town and had kept my sister and I close. She had maintained a correspondence with several old friends, though, largely through a single trusted agent in New York City - our family banker, a gentleman named Tobias Arbuthnot. I was to take the train into the city and introduce myself to Mr. Arbuthnot, who would in turn, I was told, acquaint me with certain services the city offered and present me to certain individuals who resided there.

It was not intended that I should set out upon some great adventure at this point; rather, this was to be the next phase in my training, moving from the abstract to the real, and from the general to the specific.

My mother and I had both sent letters to Mr. Arbuthnot, who had acknowledged them. I had also written for reservations at a modest hotel on Lower Broadway. Thus prepared, I packed my trunk, kissed my mother farewell, and boarded a train bound for the late Commodore Vanderbilt's Grand Central Depot.

This was my first experience of the New York Central & Hudson River Railroad's main line, and I was quite impressed by the luxurious appointments of the cars. I sat on maroon velvet cushions, surrounded by polished brass and gleaming crystal, as one of America's finest steam engines pulled us along at high speed. The ride was astonishingly smooth, with scarcely any jouncing or rattling, and I found myself marveling at this magnificent display of modern machinery. In fact, I was so struck by the experience that I went so far as to remark aloud, "This is really something, isn't it?"

Although there were a dozen other passengers in the car, I had not directed my comment to anyone in particular and was rather startled when it was greeted by girlish laughter. I turned to find a well-dressed young lady, who I judged to be no older than myself, smiling at me from the next seat back.

She was a petite creature, wonderfully turned out. Her face was a perfect oval, framed by a cascade of golden locks; her red bow of a mouth was turned up toward her pert little nose. I had rarely met so beautiful a girl.

"Can I help you, Miss?" I said.

"Oh, I think you already have," she replied. "I had just been thinking what a tedious journey this was, and you have reminded me that not everyone sees it that way. I suppose I should count my blessings."

"Tedious?" I gestured toward the countryside streaming by outside the window. "Look at that! Why, we must be traveling at fifty miles in an hour!"

"I suppose we must," she agreed with a grin.

"Why, it's a miracle of modern science," I insisted. "Surely, you can't find it *tedious!*"

"I assure you, sir, anything can become tedious with sufficient repetition, and it seems to me I have spent the better half of the past year upon one train or another, racing about the countryside on my father's behalf."

"Have you?" I glanced out the window at the Hudson sparkling in the sun and at the green fields beyond. "I can certainly think of worse fates."

"I can scarcely argue with *that.*"

We smiled at one another, and I held out a hand. "I'm Tom Derringer," I said.

She hesitated, then offered her own; I bent and brushed her fingers with my lips. "Betsy," she said. "Betsy...Jones."

The slight pause before offering a surname led me to surmise that she might be recently married and not yet accustomed to her husband's name – but then, where was this fortunate fellow? And I saw no ring.

"Are you traveling alone?" I inquired.

"I am," she said. "And you?"

"I am, as well," I replied. "I'm bound for New York City. On business."

"As am I," she said. "Perhaps we'll see one another there."

"I would be delighted if that were to happen," I said, while wondering what sort of business a girl like this might have in the city and why she was traveling unchaperoned. "I am given to understand that New York has become quite a metropolis, though, so the odds that our paths will cross seem slight."

"Given to understand? Oh, have you never been to New York before?"

"I have not," I admitted.

"I am living in the city at the moment," she said. "With my parents."

Ah, she was going home! Then I had obviously misunderstood her. "As am I" had only meant that she was bound for New York, not that she was traveling there on business.

It was still curious that she was unescorted. She spoke of her parents as still alive; why would they allow something so inappropriate?

Whatever their reasons, I had no immediate reply to her words; it seemed as if our conversation had reached its natural conclusion, and I was about to make my excuses and depart when she said, "Did you say your name is Derringer?"

"Yes," I said, dreading what was to come. "J. Thomas Derringer."

"Are you related – ?"

I had heard this question a hundred times and did not bother to let her complete it. "To the late Henry Deringer, the acclaimed Philadelphia gunsmith?" I said. "No, Miss, I am not; my family spells the name with a double R, while he used only a single consonant."

"Ah," she said, though she gave me a very odd look.

I realized that I had been rude to cut her off as I had, so I sketched a quick bow and retreated. "A pleasure to have met you, Miss," I said, and then I turned and left the car, making my way to the platform at the back of the train, where I stood for several minutes watching the landscape rush past and the rails stretch out behind us, and letting the fresh air clear my mind.

When I returned to my seat Miss Jones had vanished. I rather regretted that, but I settled in and pulled out a book I had brought with me. Not so very much later we arrived at Grand Central Depot, where I disembarked, collected my luggage, and hailed a hansom cab to take me to my hotel.

Chapter Three

A Meeting with Tobias Arbuthnot

My first view of the great city was all that I might have hoped for. I had seen pictures, of course, but those scarcely did justice to the scale and vitality of the place. Buildings grew to astonishing heights, and the streets bustled with life – people and horses on every side.

I had business to attend to, though, and was tired from the long ride, so I wasted little time in sightseeing. Oh, I took a stroll along Broadway, but I made no attempt to seek out any of the famous landmarks of the metropolis. I dined in the hotel and made an early night of it.

Mr. Arbuthnot's offices were located on the second floor of a rather grand building on Madison Avenue near 34th Street, and my appointment was for nine o'clock on the morning after my arrival in the city. I arrived at roughly a quarter before the hour and waited in a pleasant little antechamber for perhaps ten minutes before being summoned into the banker's office.

Tobias Arbuthnot did not fit the popular image of a banker, as presented by Mr. Nast and the other artists who adorned the papers with their etchings. He was not a fat man in a waistcoat bedecked with a gold watch–fob, but a short, thin fellow, scarcely taller than my sister and probably weighing rather less. He wore a black coat of severe cut, the elbows shiny with wear, and neither vest nor waistcoat. His cheeks were clean-shaven, but a long, thin black beard adorned his chin; his hair was likewise black, dead straight, parted in the middle, and long enough to reach his collar.

His secretary ushered me into the office, then departed quickly, closing the door as he went. The latch had scarcely clicked into place when Mr. Arbuthnot leapt up from behind his desk and came around it to greet me, smiling broadly, with both hands extended.

I raised my own hand, and he took it firmly in both of his, pumping it enthusiastically. "Tommy Derringer!" he exclaimed, in a rapid, high-pitched tenor. "At last we meet. I have read so much about you in your mother's letters. You have much of your father in your features, but I must say, I would never have expected Jack Derringer's son to be so tall! I suppose it's your mother's blood; she was always a fine figure of a girl, was dear Miss Whitaker. Was your journey pleasant? Is your hotel suitable?"

"Quite suitable, thank you," I said, somewhat overwhelmed by this verbal torrent.

"You're at the Robertson Hotel, I believe? I'm sure we could find you more luxurious accommodations, should you choose."

"No, the Robertson is fine."

"Good, good. Is your mother well? I know she always says in her letters that she is in the very pink of health, but I'm quite sure that she could have any numbers of agues and fevers and not think it worthy of mention; she has never thought it necessary to trouble others with matters they are not equipped to improve. And your sister? How is her education proceeding?"

"Mother is well, sir; she has not omitted anything that might say otherwise in her letters, I assure you. Mary Ann is also well and has been studying relentlessly." Indeed, my sister had become an avid reader on any number of topics and was developing a startling level of expertise in several academic disciplines.

"Excellent! Here, sit down, sit down, and let us get down to business." He gestured toward a chair, and I settled into it as he dashed back behind his desk and resumed his own seat.

He opened a drawer and pulled out a ledger, then turned it about and set it before me on the desk. "Your family accounts," he explained. "I trust you will find everything in order."

"I'm sure I will," I said, placing a hand on the ledger but making no move to open it. "But I am not here to go over the books with you; I told you my reasons in my letter."

"Indeed you did, indeed you did! And I – "

He stopped in mid-sentence, as if the clockwork that had driven his frenetic speeches had abruptly run down. He blinked at me across the desk. He swallowed. Then he sighed.

"I have done my best to oblige you, Mr. Derringer, and I will continue to do so," he said, speaking much more slowly than before. "But I must tell you, I would counsel you against pursuing your intentions."

"Oh? And why is that?"

He glanced at the closed door, as if concerned that someone might be eavesdropping, then leaned forward across the desk and spoke more quietly.

"An adventurer's life, young man, is not an easy one. You understand, I hope, that much of my business comes from people like yourself and your father – adventurers and their families. Far too often, this means their widows and orphans. Oh, I know that dear Jack died of natural causes – or at least, so I have been told...?"

"That has always been my understanding," I said. "I was too young to have any first-hand awareness of the circumstances, but my mother has always said that he died of a fever."

"Ah, but what fever? It might have been one he contracted years before, traveling in some godforsaken foreign land. If it was, in fact, an entirely natural death, an unavoidable fever of domestic origin, then he was one of the fortunate few. Most of my clients die in far more spectacular fashion. I have lost customers by gunshot and bowshot, by sword and stick, in falls and fires and floods. They have perished in earthquakes and landslides, blizzards and hurricanes, tornadoes and torrents. They have been found frozen to death, or drowned, or dead of heatstroke or of thirst. All too often they aren't found at all, and their heirs must wait seven years before petitioning the courts to have them declared legally dead. And those who survive – Tommy, my lad, sometimes I think they would have been better off if they had not. Some of them are broken men, incapable of caring for themselves or taking any pleasure in their lives. Some are simply mad, their minds shattered by experiences Man was never meant to know. And some are still sane, whole in mind and body, but penniless, having spent their every cent upon their machines and expeditions. Are you sure you want to join this unhappy brotherhood?"

It hardly seemed a sufficient response to so impassioned a diatribe, but I replied simply, "I am."

He sat back, shaking his head. "I expected no other response from Jackie Derringer's son, but I had to try." He took a deep breath, then let it out. "You wanted to meet any of your father's old companions who might be available. I am afraid the list is quite short, which rather illustrates the point I was making a moment ago. Mr. Darien Lord, the leader of the band, died several years ago – shot in the back by a thief, I believe, though I am unclear on the details."

"He was rather elderly," I pointed out.

"Yes, he was. He was seventy-four. And while that is a respectable age, Mr. Lord might have lived to be a hundred had he chosen a safer line of work. He broke the thief's neck before he succumbed to his wounds, did you know that? He was strong and fit right to the end."

I did not reply. I merely said, "Go on."

"Ashton Darlington disappeared in the wilds of Africa," he said. "Ichabod Tunstall was poisoned in Shanghai. Joshua Brown died of exposure in the hills west of Vladivostok. Philippe de Burgh was eaten by dingoes – the wild dogs of Australia."

"I know what dingoes are," I said.

"Peg Armstrong was murdered by serpent cultists in Istanbul," he continued. "And of course, I'm sure you know that Calvin Sweet died at Chickamauga."

I had indeed known that Captain Sweet had died fighting for the late Confederacy; most of the others were news to me.

"Besides your mother, I have only found one survivor of all those I know to have accompanied your father," he said.

I had already run through the names I remembered from my father's journals and noted only a single omission.

"William Snedeker," Mr. Arbuthnot said.

"Mad Bill," I said.

"Mad Bill," Mr. Arbuthnot agreed, smiling. "Though I'm pleased to say that I don't believe he really *is* mad. He retired from adventuring some years ago and now owns an establishment downtown. I have spoken with him, and he is expecting you to join him there for luncheon at one o'clock."

"Excellent!" I said. "Thank you, sir."

He opened the drawer that had held the ledger and pulled out a letter.

"I took the liberty of writing this, as well," he said. "It is a letter of introduction, attesting that you are indeed your father's son and that I will vouch for you in matters of both reputation and finance. You will want to have it with you when you visit Dr. John Pierce this afternoon."

I frowned. "John Pierce?"

"New York's foremost consulting archivist. You may find his services invaluable if you persist in becoming an adventurer."

I did not entirely understand how an archivist could be helpful, but I supposed it would become clear in time.

After that, we went over the family accounts together. I was startled and dismayed to see how much Mother had paid for my various tutors and for some of the equipment I had used in my preparations for a life of adventure, but pleased to discover that Mr. Arbuthnot had been a worthy steward of our funds, and the very considerable principal was intact.

"Your father was lucky," he said, when we had concluded our review. "Many adventurers spend their entire fortunes on supplies and travel and never show a return on that investment. Mr. Lord's little band was unusually successful in that regard, and at least half of that success came from capturing the Golden Dragon's treasure ship."

"I read about that," I said. "Volume Seventeen."

Mr. Arbuthnot s hand flew up, and he pressed a warning finger to his lips. "Hush!" he said, as he looked around, clearly worried. "Hasn't your mother taught you that no place is safe from spies and informants?"

"Of course she has," I said, startled. "What of it?"

He leaned close and whispered, "Tommy, the very existence of your father's journals is a secret. If it were known, there are any number of parties who might be interested in obtaining them. There is undoubtedly a great deal of information in them that might yet lead a clever and determined individual to various valuables."

"But – but Mother made no attempt to conceal them; they were openly displayed."

That seemed to startle him, but he recovered quickly and said, "Your mother is a clever woman; she doubtless guessed that anyone seeking them would assume they were hidden and that anything displayed as you describe must be of little value."

"And...aren't they? Doesn't *every* adventurer keep a record of his travels and accomplishments?" I asked.

Mr. Arbuthnot straightened up. "Oh, by no means! Many rely entirely upon their memories. Others make records well after the fact, carefully omitting anything that might aid a rival. Even those who do keep records often make extensive use of codes, ciphers, and cryptic references; Jack Derringer's habit of writing out everything in plain English was *most* unusual. Dr. Pierce will explain this to you at length, I am certain, and he will also be able to give you a good estimate of the current value of your father's journals."

"Dr. Pierce? The archivist?"

"The very soul. I would be surprised if he does not make a generous offer for those journals, or at least for the right to copy them for his archives.

This was all surprising and a little puzzling for me. "But why?"

Clearly, my ignorance was just as surprising to Mr. Arbuthnot. "Tommy, don't you see?"

"No, sir, I do not."

"Well, let us suppose, then, that you were tracking an ancient artifact, and you learned that in 1855 it fell into the possession of Rudolfo Grassi."

"Grassi? The axe murderer?"

"Yes. The first man your father ever killed."

"Darien Lord led the party that tracked Grassi, and of course, as you say, it was my father who shot him, but I still don't see what this has to do with the journals."

He sighed. "Tommy, is there enough information in the journals to recreate Grassi's route through the mountains?"

I considered that question carefully and finally answered, "I'm not sure. Parts of it, perhaps."

"And if you were searching for something that Grassi had possessed at the time of his death, is there any better source of information for where he might have hidden it?"

"Ah..." I tried to remember the details. The party that pursued Grassi had been composed of Darien Lord, Big Josh Brown, Mad Bill Snedeker, Calvin Sweet, and my father. "Mad Bill might know more," I said.

"How much would he remember after more than twenty years? But you, my boy, have a detailed account of the pursuit written *while it was taking place*. Who knows what significant clues might be contained in that narrative? And that's just one incident in two dozen thick volumes."

"Twenty-two volumes," I corrected him. "But I believe I see your point." I blinked, then asked, "Is your example entirely hypothetical, or did Rudolfo Grassi have some interesting artifact with him?"

"Well, actually, he had left it with his sister in Milan – a jade brooch that had reportedly belonged to the Chinese emperor Kublai Khan and was said to grant the wearer prophetic visions. Sarah Tolliver recovered it in 1862; I understand it to be in the secret collection of the British Museum now."

"Is there anything *known* to be of value in my father's journals, or is this entirely speculative?"

"You'll have to speak to Dr. Pierce about that. That is *precisely* the sort of information that constitutes his stock in trade. What I would advise you to do, my boy, is to make a deal with Dr. Pierce – unlimited access to his services, as needed and without further payment, in exchange for a copy of the journals."

"I will take that under advisement," I said.

He nodded, glanced down at the ledger, and then looked me in the eye. "Tommy," he said, "you've seen the numbers. You don't need to go adventuring to earn a living; with only the slightest care, you could easily live off your father's share of the Golden Dragon's treasure ship for the rest of your life. Are you *sure* you want to continue?"

"Absolutely," I said.

"You don't need the money."

"I need to be able to look myself in the mirror every morning, Mr. Arbuthnot, and respect the man I see there."

"And you can't do that in some less dangerous occupation?"

I shook my head. "I've been training for this since I was eight, sir; I am far more prepared than my father was, and he died quietly in bed." I smiled. "Besides," I said, "it'll be fun."

Chapter Four

Mad Bill Snedeker

New York City smelled of horses. By the time I reached Snedeker's Tavern & Billiard Emporium on Perry Street, I was glad to substitute the scents of cigar smoke and spilled beer.

In a way, it was when I stepped through the front door of that establishment that I first realized just what a sheltered life I had lived in our quiet little town. Despite my training, I had never before set foot in such a place. I had read of them, but never experienced the reality.

The floor was covered in sawdust, and the windows were covered with thick draperies of badly stained velvet, so that even at half-past noon the gaslights were ablaze. A long, ornate bar ran along one side, and three billiard tables were ranged on the other; in between were half a dozen tables and half a dozen patrons.

That simple description does not begin to convey the sordid atmosphere of the place. Everything in it seemed battered and stained, and much of it had been cheap to begin with. The customers were all male, and all of unsavory appearance – no respectable woman would set foot in such an establishment, and the other sort would not be out so early in the day.

I stood in the doorway for a moment, taking it in, and then realized that the man behind the bar, who had been polishing a glass when I arrived, was taking *me* in – his gaze was firmly fixed on me.

I saw no reason to delay or dissemble; I crossed to the bar, put one foot on the brass rail, and said, "I'm looking for Mr. Snedeker. I believe he's expecting me."

The bartender put down the glass and jerked a thumb toward an open door at the back. "Through there," he said.

I thanked him and strode to the back room, unsure what to expect.

What I found was a fat old man with an immense beard, bent over a table, working sums with the stub of a pencil. He looked up at the sound of my entrance and flung the pencil aside.

He stared at me, then leapt to his feet with surprising agility for a man of his years and girth. "You're early," he exclaimed.

"A little," I admitted. I held out my hand. "I'm – " I began.

"Jackie Derringer's boy – "

From this point on, I beg my readers' indulgence. In order to give an accurate representation of Mad Bill Snedeker's speech, I fear I must forgo restraint; to resort to the customary devices by which authors avoid giving offense would utterly destroy the flavor of his conversation. To present a true picture of the man, I must risk disturbing delicate sensibilities.

So –

"Jackie Derringer's boy – Well, damn me to Hell if you ain't just like him; I'd know those eyes anywhere. No question who your daddy was, is there? But you're a good foot taller'n he was, ain't you?" He grabbed my hand in his own and pumped it vigorously, then all but dragged me to the table. "Sit down, sit down. Dobbs! Dobbs, get your lazy backside in here and fetch this boy a goddamn beer – "

"Mr. Snedeker, I don't – "

"Don't you Mr. Snedeker me, boy. You call me Bill – Uncle Bill, if you like, for God knows I tried to be the big brother your daddy needed to look after him. Damn fool kid wa'n't afraid of anything in this world, I swear. You know he once took on a mountain lion with his bare hands, when it caught him while he was shaving? Damn fool dropped his razor. Had to beat the cat senseless against a tree. Said later he wouldn't have wanted to ruin the razor's edge in any case, and wasn't he glad he hadn't put on his shirt yet? Didn't want it clawed up, nor to get his blood on it. I was the one that bandaged him up, damned if I wasn't, and he had me tell a dozen bloody lies to his pretty Arabella so she wouldn't know what he'd done. Didn't want her to worry. Dobbs! Where's that damned beer? A man could die of thirst here!"

Mr. Snedeker's account of the incident with the mountain lion accorded reasonably well with the version I had read in my father's journals, but being asked to lie to my mother was a detail I had not encountered heretofore, nor had the undamaged shirt been mentioned.

By this point I was seated at the table, with my host seated opposite me, and the much-maligned Mr. Dobbs was bringing a tray. Mr. Snedeker paid no attention to his employee as Mr. Dobbs set down the tray and poured two beers from the pitcher thereon.

I was not familiar with the juice of the barley and did not consider this an ideal time to make its acquaintance, but I did not think it wise to refuse the offer. I accepted a mug and hoped Mr. Snedeker would not notice that I wasn't drinking.

"So you're Jackie's boy," he said. "Toby said he was sending you, but I wasn't sure I believed him. Didn't see what you'd want with a washed-up old bastard like me and thought maybe it was some young jackanapes had fooled old Toby and come looking for my hidden treasure." He let out a bark of laughter. "Treasure! Damn my eyes, if I'd managed to hold onto any of that treasure, would I be here, selling beer and sandwiches to a bunch of scoundrels who barely know which end of a cue to hold? But there are stories, I know there are, that I've got an idol's eye hidden under the bar, or a chest of gold in the cellar." He shook his head. "Took every penny I could find to buy this damned miserable saloon."

"But...but my father left my mother, my sister, and me reasonably comfortable," I protested. In truth, we were very comfortable indeed, but I thought it unwise to boast of it.

"Your father, my lad, was a sensible fellow, not like me. He took his share of our loot and invested it in banks and mills and railroads, where I spent half of mine on wine, women, and song, and invested the other half in Dr. Pettigrew's Elixir of Life, or Baltimore Gurney's Galvanic Light Beam, or the like, and not a damned one of them panned out, save the tavern, which God knows hasn't made me rich, but I'll tell you that it has kept food on the table." He cocked his head as a thought struck him. "*Are* you reasonably comfortable, then, or have you come to your Uncle Bill for a hand up?"

"Our finances are in fine shape, Mr. Sned...Uncle Bill. If you doubt my identity, I have a letter from Mr. Arbuthnot..."

He held up a hand. "I don't need your damned letter. Your face is all the proof I need that you're who you say you are. You're the very image of the Pistol."

Taken aback, I asked, "Of...of what?"

"The Little Pistol. That was what we called your daddy, by way of a nickname – you must know that. Jackie Derringer, the Little Pistol." He smiled. "Which makes you, laddie my boy, a true son of a gun."

There are times, I confess, when I regret bearing the name Derringer and curse Henry Deringer for linking it so thoroughly to his infernal little devices. I could not think of a single thing to say in reply to Mr. Snedeker's words, and even as I started to wonder why there was no mention of any such nickname in my father's journals, I realized that most likely he had preferred to avoid any reminders.

"Well, then, if you've not come for money, why *are* you here?" he asked. "Can't be sentiment, surely, or why in Hell would you have waited so long?"

"Well, sentiment is a part of it," I said. "My mother did not think New York City a fit place for me when I was younger."

"A part, eh? What's the rest of it, then?"

"Why, I've decided to follow in my father's footsteps and take up a career of adventure, and I hoped you might assist me in getting started."

He stared at me silently for a moment, then leapt to his feet so violently that he upset the table, spilling both mugs of beer and sending his papers flying. He stood over me, fists clenched at his sides. "Are you mad, boy?" he demanded.

Astonished, I looked up at him. "I do not believe so, sir," I said.

"Then why on God's green earth would you consider such a god-damned piece of hare-brained folly?"

"I...I wish to lead a useful life, Mr. Snedeker, and not simply sit at home living off my father's accomplishments. Why would I not follow his trade?"

"Because it's bloody dangerous, you damned fool!"

"Well, of course..."

"Darien Lord is dead," Mr. Snedeker exclaimed. "Big Josh is dead. Candy Cal is dead. The Little Pistol is dead, and Dead-Eye Peg, and Smoky Ash, and Frenchie de Burgh, and Ike Tunstall –

they're all dead. *I'm* only alive because I wasn't worth killing once the rest were gone and I'd retired. And we weren't any unluckier than most; the Crimson Colonel was eaten by crocodiles, for God's sake!"

"But...but there are others..."

"And they're all fools! They called me Mad Bill, but compared to most of the current lot I'm sane as houses. It was bad enough in my day, battling serpent cults and lost tribes and the like, but we were up against six–guns and poisoned daggers; nowadays you'll find you're facing Gatling guns and electrical fences and God knows what else! Who can tell what nightmares Tom Edison and Alfred Krupp are building in their damnable foundries now? When I was one of Lord's men we used to talk about conquering some little principality in Europe someday where we could retire as kings, but Bismarck and Garibaldi and the rest have turned all those little states into a handful of empires, and God forbid you offend the Kaiser or the Tsar! Queen Victoria's fleets and armies patrol the globe, and ever since the war Washington's power has been growing. The scale of it all – I'm not sure the bloody world still has room for adventurers."

"Nonetheless, Uncle Bill, I am determined to give it a try," I said, trying to keep my voice steady. "I had hoped you could introduce me to others in the brotherhood, perhaps suggest some little escapade I might undertake to get my hand in and to begin making a name for myself."

He stood silently for a moment, but then the estimable Mr. Dobbs, with much clattering and thumping, righted the overturned table, distracting Mr. Snedeker. He looked at the table, at Mr. Dobbs, and then back at me. He sat down abruptly.

"Listen, Junior," he began.

"My name is Tom," I interrupted.

"I...it is?"

"Of course it is!"

He looked genuinely puzzled. "You don't have your father's name?"

"John Thomas Derringer? Yes. But I'm called Tom. I'm not my father, Mr. Snedeker."

"You're not trying to be? Then why in Hell do you want to be an adventurer?"

I sighed. I had given this subject a good deal of thought in those years since I first read my father's journals; my mother had never hesitated to tell me that I did not need to continue my training if I did not want to, and I had long ago sat down and asked myself why I was resolved to stay the course. "Uncle Bill," I said, "my father left me enough money to live on, so I have no need to earn my daily bread by the sweat of my brow. I do not have the temperament to be a man of leisure, though; I feel the need to make myself useful. I have no talent for the arts, nor for politics, but I have no reason to think myself unable to follow in my father's footsteps. I find myself drawn to the excitement and strenuous activity. The idea of aiding innocents in trouble appeals to me. It may be that once I have tried it, I shall find, assuming I survive, that the life does not suit me so well as I expected; in that case, I shall reconsider my options."

"You're saying it sounds like fun."

"Well...yes."

He shook his head. "It's not what it used to be, and it was never as much fun as those blasted dime novels made it sound. I told you, it's dangerous. If I send you off on some goddamn fool's errand and you get yourself killed, your mother will never forgive me."

"It was always dangerous, and my mother knows better than to blame anyone but me."

"That's true enough." He sighed. "What do you want of me, then?"

"Introductions," I said. "Contacts."

"Seems to me Toby could give you those."

"Mr. Arbuthnot was never an adventurer himself. He cannot provide the same sort of first-hand insight you can as to who can be trusted, who is best avoided, and so on."

Mr. Snedeker shrugged. "Most of the younger ones I don't know any better than he does. You know the old gang broke up in 1861, when Candy Cal insisted he'd fight for the bloody rebels, don't you? That's more than twenty years; there's a whole damned new generation since then."

"I know that Darien Lord's band was dissolved, and my father retired from the field, but *you* didn't retire then."

"Damn right I didn't. I fought under Phil Sheridan, and after the war I signed on with Prince Gorchakov and ran a few errands for the Tsar." He grimaced. "If I'd stayed there, maybe the old boy wouldn't have been assassinated last year – I had a hand in saving him back in '66." He shrugged. "Or maybe the damned Nihilists would have blown me up along with the rest. But I was retired by then. I bought this place and settled down in '74. That's eight years ago, plenty of time for a new crop of rowdies and troublemakers to establish themselves and for half the old guard to die off."

"But you still know the other half."

"And you want me introduce you to someone who's looking for a junior associate?"

I shook my head. "I told you, Uncle Bill, I'm not my father. I'm not going to be anyone's lackey. My father may have been content to be Darien Lord's underling, but I intend to be my own man."

For a moment Mr. Snedeker didn't reply; then a big, crooked grin spread across his countenance. "Good for you, by God! You know, that was one reason your father gave it up – he'd been Darien's man so long that no one could take him seriously as his own, so when the gang broke up, that was it, and there was damn-all he could do about it."

"He implied as much in his journals," I said. "I'm determined to learn from his experience and avoid that particular mistake."

"You're bound and determined to do this?"

"I have trained for it since I was eight," I replied.

His eyes widened. "Trained?"

"Yes, of course."

He shook his head. "Tommy boy, nobody *trains* to be an adventurer! It's just something you *do*."

"It seems to me, Uncle Bill, that if it's as dangerous as you say, I'd be a fool not to prepare as best I can. That's why I'm here."

He leaned back in his chair and stared at me over his beard. "Damn me if you aren't as smart as your father, and with your mother's common sense, to boot! Very well, then – I'll tell you what I know about the current crowd, and you'll tell me about this training of yours, and what your mother and sister have been up to. Agreed?"

"Agreed."

He turned. "Dobbs! We have a guest for lunch, damn your eyes – where's the bloody food? And bring another pitcher, I've spilled the beer."

Chapter Five

A Visit to the Archives

I fear I cannot in good conscience praise Mr. Dobbs' cooking, but otherwise my luncheon with Mad Bill Snedeker went quite well. I found Mr. Snedeker to be much as my father's journals described him, though perhaps a little more world weary, and I could easily understand my father's professed fondness for him.

Our meal was punctuated with orders and abuse directed at the unfortunate Mr. Dobbs, and at one point, when Mr. Snedeker was out of the room, I asked him why he tolerated his employer's shabby treatment. He looked at me in astonishment and said, "Why, bless you, sir, he don't mean nothing by it. He pays a fair wage, and I love to hear him talk about his old adventures."

When we had eaten our fill and finished our conversation, it was resolved that Mr. Snedeker would escort me to the premises of Dr. John Pierce, New York's foremost consulting archivist, to ensure that I was favorably received. I suggested that he need not trouble himself, that Mr. Arbuthnot's letter would prove adequate, but he would not hear of it. "Old Pierce isn't exactly the trusting sort," he said. "The walk will do me good." He glanced at the clock. "I shan't be able to stay long, damn it. I need to be back here when the workmen start coming in off the goddamn docks. I can make sure you get in the door, though, and that the snooty son of a bitch knows he's to treat you with respect."

I argued no further, and the two of us set out through the city's crowded streets. Dr. Pierce's curious establishment stood on the east side of Lafayette Street a few blocks north of the Astor Library, at the top of a flight of stairs above a haberdashery – and above several other shops, as well. I was startled by the broad vista that lay behind the frosted glass of his door, behind the gilt letters spelling out "J. A. Pierce, Archives." It appeared almost the entire second floor of a very large building was devoted to his enterprise.

Upon stepping inside, I found myself facing the longest counter I have ever seen, made of good dark wood and equipped with dozens of green blotters. On the near side were arrayed at least a score of wooden stools, perhaps half of them occupied by a motley assortment of customers peering at various books and documents; on the far side of the counter, stretching from floor to ceiling, were the closely spaced and overflowing shelves from which those books and documents were apparently drawn. Several small ladders stood ready to provide access to the highest shelves, which were beyond the reach of even the tallest man.

"What *is* all this?" I asked.

"This is the Pierce Archives," Mr. Snedeker said. "Now, hush a moment while we find Pierce." He craned his neck, looking for the proprietor, and finally spotted him in the depths of that vast scriptorium. "Hey, Pierce!" he bellowed.

Several of the clients raised their heads to glare at us, and Dr. Pierce himself came hurrying over.

He was extraordinarily tall. I am of above average height myself, scarcely short of six feet, but Dr. Pierce towered over me. His hair was gray and reached past his collar, and a magnificent set of side-whiskers adorned his face. He leaned across the counter toward us. "So it's you, Snedeker," he said with a nod. "And who is this?"

Mr. Snedeker leaned forward until his nose was only inches from Dr. Pierce's chin. "This is John Thomas Derringer the younger," he said. Then he leaned even closer and whispered, "He has his father's journals. Twenty-two volumes – and they're not in any goddamn cipher!"

"Ah." He looked at me. "And what does the young gentlemen want for them?"

"I'm not interested in selling," I said. "However, I would be willing to loan them for copying." I confess, I still did not fully understand the nature of Dr. Pierce's business, but I knew this was what Mr. Arbuthnot had suggested.

Dr. Pierce frowned thoughtfully. "On what terms?"

I looked to Mr. Snedeker for guidance.

"Full membership," that worthy said on my behalf. "One year per volume." He looked at me and added, "If you're still alive and adventuring twenty-two years from now, you'll be able to pay your own damn fees."

"I would need to see these journals, but that seems fair."

"They're at..." I began, but Mr. Snedeker cut me off. He clearly considered it unwise to say they were at my hotel, in my trunk.

"They're safe," he said. "He'll bring them next time."

Dr. Pierce nodded. "Very well. Was there anything else?"

Mr. Snedeker looked at me, and I decided the time had come to admit the truth. "Dr. Pierce," I said, "I don't understand any of this. What *is* this place?"

Dr. Pierce blinked at me in surprise. "Why, this is my archive!" he said.

"Archive of *what?*"

"Of adventure!" He saw the look of incomprehension on my face, and said, "Oh, dear. Well, Mr. Derringer, I take it you, or someone you know, is planning a career as an adventurer?"

"I am," I agreed.

Dr. Pierce nodded. "Excellent! It is a proud and honorable tradition, dating back centuries to the knights-errant of old. Adventurers like your father, or Mr. Snedeker, roam the world in pursuit of fame and fortune, righting wrongs and battling injustice – or not, as the case may be; not all adventurers have such pure motives. When a monster is to be slain, or a tyrant overthrown, that is an adventurer's proper employment – but there are also ruined cities to be looted, tombs to be robbed, lost tribes to be exploited. It is a dangerous occupation, and one in which the old saying that forewarned is forearmed is very true indeed. A competent adventurer will want to know as much as possible about his foes and fellows before he sets out – and that's where I come in. I keep records of every adventure I can, successful or not. I pay adventurers for their stories. I keep copies of every treasure map, every mysterious prophecy, every secret blueprint that I can get my hands on, and I make them available – for a price. I seek these documents out and annotate them – a treasure map to a treasure that has already been recovered is relatively useless, after all. A set of directions that has led some poor would-be paladin to his death cannot be relied upon. I therefore do my best to cross-reference every document, every grimoire, every map, every cipher in my collection." He turned and gestured toward the shelves. "This collection goes back more than three hundred years; I am following in my grandfather's footsteps, as it was he who brought it to America, and my family has also acquired and incorporated several older archives." He pointed to one nearby shelf. "If you want to know when and where the Lost City of the

Mirage might next appear, for example, I have accounts and maps of every known manifestation since the sixteenth century, along with various calculations of the pattern these appearances seem to be following."

"I see," I said, as I finally grasped the significance of the archive. I hesitated, then asked, "Why have I not heard more about this place? Why is it not mentioned in my father's journals?"

"Ah, your late father was not one of our clients. His employer, Mr. Lord, was."

Mr. Snedeker nodded. "I didn't sign up myself until after that bastard Cal showed his true colors and broke up our band. Wasn't any point in paying for more than one of us. I'm not sure Jackie ever knew where we got some of our facts, but old Darien always came here to study up before we'd ever go out on some damned errand or other. Hell, half the time he found out there was something worth doing by coming here."

I gazed at the shelves curiously. "That's fascinating," I said. "Dr. Pierce, you mentioned the Lost City of the Mirage – then it's a real city? And it's the same one every time?"

Dr. Pierce frowned, then said, "I really ought to wait until I have verified the existence and value of your father's records, but I suppose I can extend a certain amount of credit." He leaned forward across the counter and lowered his voice. "Yes, it is indeed a real city, and Peter Kirk, the only man known to have visited it twice, swears that it was the same city both times he saw it. Maps and sketches from its other manifestations also would seem to indicate that it was the same city in each of its known appearances. On the other hand, if that is the case, there is something very peculiar about it. In the earliest reports the city was ruinous, the buildings little more than shells, the streets gone to sand and weeds, but in each subsequent appearance it has been somewhat less damaged. The reports I have from the most recent expedition describe it as surprisingly intact – most of the houses have roofs and some furnishings, and the pavements are largely whole. Wherever it is between its visits to our world, it would seem someone or something is gradually restoring it."

My eyes widened. "I should like to see that," I said.

Dr. Pierce shook his head. "Not any time soon, I'm afraid," he said. "The most recent appearance was in the Arizona Territory scarcely two years ago. The Hammerschlag hypothesis would put the next in 1887, and the most likely location in central Australia."

"Hammerschlag?"

"Dieter Hammerschlag is a mathematician who has studied various esoteric phenomena. His theory is generally considered the most reliable in predicting where the Lost City will next appear."

"But there are others?"

"Oh, yes. The Barnstable-Gomez theory puts the next appearance on an island in the South Pacific late in 1884, while Giuseppe Spinelli's estimate agrees, at least approximately, on the date, but puts it somewhere in the Andes Mountains."

"I take it the pattern of its appearances is not a simple one, then."

"Not simple at all. Nothing about it is simple. It is one of the world's most enduring mysteries."

I shook my head. "I had no idea," I said.

Dr. Pierce glanced along the counter. "As it happens, one of the men who visited it in Arizona is right here; shall I introduce you?"

I hesitated, as I thought about it for a moment. I was not, in truth, so very concerned with the Lost City; it was interesting, but not of any great importance, and I did not intend to wait until at least 1884 to begin my adventuring. On the other hand, I had come to New York largely to meet other adventurers and to begin the process of joining their brotherhood. Any opportunity to speak with an active participant in recent adventuring was not to be scorned. "I would be in your debt, sir."

Dr. Pierce smiled. "You are *already* in my debt, Mr. Derringer, and I expect to collect at your earliest convenience. But for now, step this way, and meet a man who has visited the mirage." He beckoned, and I followed. A moment later we were standing beside a heavy-set fellow in a worn sheepskin coat who was bent over an old leather-bound volume, his forehead resting upon one hand, his elbow on the counter. Dr. Pierce cleared his throat.

The reader looked up. "Yes?"

"Herr von Düssel," Dr. Pierce said, "allow me to present John Thomas Derringer the younger."

The man turned to look at me. I held out my hand.

"I do not know you," he said.

"Tom Derringer," I said, still offering my hand. "I'm pleased to make your acquaintance."

He sighed and took my hand briefly in a rather limp grip, then glanced longingly back at his book. He looked up to see Dr. Pierce frowning at him, then turned back to me. "Gerhardt von Düssel," he said. "How can I help you?"

"Dr. Pierce tells me that you visited the Lost City of the Mirage two years ago."

He cast Dr. Pierce a look that made it clear he would have preferred not to have this known, then acknowledged, "I did."

"I would take great pleasure in hearing about it," I said. "Perhaps I could take you to dinner at a restaurant of your choosing this evening? Just the two of us?"

He eyed me thoughtfully, glanced at Dr. Pierce and Mr. Snedeker, then nodded. "Yes. We will do that. Now I have work to do."

And with that he turned back to his book.

Chapter Six

The Lost City of the Mirage

I shan't describe my dinner with Herr von Düssel in detail. I can't say I found him very pleasant company. The restaurant he chose, a place called the Heidelberger, seemed to serve nothing but beer and sausage, though they carried dozens of varieties of both. It was decorated in dark wood and moth-eaten hunting trophies and furnished with massive wooden tables. Their prices came as a shock to an innocent country boy such as myself but did not seem to be reflected in the quality of the food.

Or rather, I did not think so; Herr von Düssel clearly savored every bite of sausage and every gulp of beer and consumed so many of both that I feared my traveling funds would prove inadequate.

He did, however, live up to his end of the bargain and gave me a brief account of how he had managed to put himself on the wrong side of both the Hohenzollerns and the Habsburgs, so that upon the Prussian king's elevation to the position of Emperor of Germany he found it expedient to cross the Atlantic and seek his fortune in the New World. He went on to describe in much greater detail his journey to Arizona and what he found there.

He had not been alone; rather, he had been one of a motley assortment of adventurers and opportunists who had, by one means or another, learned that the Lost City was likely to appear in the desert about forty or fifty miles south of a railroad town called Flagstaff. Not all of them had reached the Lost City during the four days between its discovery and its disappearance; they had been spread over a considerable expanse of desert, as the predictions of the city's location were not very exact. Herr von Düssel had been one of the fortunate ones, arriving on the second day after discovery, and departing at the first sign of instability.

Not everyone who went in got out; two men and a woman had overstayed and had vanished with the city.

He described the city itself – broad, straight streets lined with towers of stone and crystal that gleamed brightly in the desert sun; strange machines everywhere, none of them functional, so far as the adventurers could determine. The whole place seemed so alien, as he described it, that one wondered whether the builders had been human, or some other race entirely.

The entire reason to visit the city, of course, had been to loot it. Herr von Düssel had been only modestly successful in that, coming away with a handful of jewelry and some coinage that had appeared to be silver, but assayed as worthless alloys of base metals.

"I had not a wagon brought," he explained. "I had only my pockets and a saddlebag. Still, this paid for my efforts."

"Did anyone else do better?" I asked.

"Oh, yes," he said. "McKee had not one wagon brought, but a dozen, and two traction engines to pull them when the mules would not."

"McKee?"

"Hezekiah McKee. You know this name?"

I shook my head. "I do not."

He shrugged. "He did not take jewels or gold. He took metal, but not gold or silver; I know not what it was. A gray metal, very light – it was everywhere. The lampposts were made of it, and fences, and many things. McKee and his men filled all their wagons with it and took several tons of it."

"*Tons?* Why?"

He shrugged. "Who knows? Perhaps he thought it would be valuable. Perhaps he was right."

"How very curious."

Von Düssel shrugged. "I have stranger things seen."

We continued our conversation long after the meal was over; when he could think of nothing more to tell me about the Lost City he went on to other adventures, and he listened politely as I spoke of my own plans and aspirations.

When at last we prepared to depart, he paused, and clapped a hand on my shoulder. "Listen, Thomas," he said. "You are a good boy. Go home and forget adventuring. It is no way for a good boy like you to live. Go home, take care of your mother, find a pretty girl, forget all this."

I thanked him for his advice, and he thanked me for his dinner, and we went our separate ways – I to my hotel, and he I know not whither.

The following day I attempted to visit the Order of Theseus, that famous club frequented by adventurers of every sort, but I was turned away – I had no sponsor, nor could I name any adventures I had participated in that might qualify me for membership. My father had been an associate member once upon a time, yes, but that was almost twenty years earlier, and his membership had lapsed, all accrued benefits forfeited. My initial welcome when I returned to the Pierce Archives was little better; I had no specific subject to research, and I had not yet paid my fee. When I brought forth the first volume of my father's journal, though, my reception warmed greatly.

Still, until Dr. Pierce had had the opportunity to properly assess the journal, my membership remained probationary, and I was asked not to distract the paying customers.

I paid a visit to the telegraph office, and to more than one of the city's newspapers, to arrange for certain reports to henceforth be forwarded to my home as swiftly as possible – an adventurer needed to know what was happening in the world if he was to intervene in events in time to accomplish anything. I also stopped into some of New York's better bookshops and purchased several volumes to be added to my library back home.

Over the next two days I made a few further calls and did what I could to familiarize myself with the metropolis, but finally I concluded that I had done enough and had fulfilled my immediate mission. I checked out of the hotel, had my baggage forwarded, and returned to the station to catch the next train home.

Upon arrival at the family threshold I was greeted like a returning hero; my mother and Mary Ann welcomed me with enthusiasm I thought quite unwarranted. When I remonstrated that I had only been to New York, not China or Patagonia, Mother retorted, "That, Tommy, is why we're so pleased."

My puzzlement was plain, and she elaborated, "We had no idea when you might return. We thought it likely that you would sign on with some globe-trotting expedition on the spur of the moment, or follow some clue into an exotic mystery halfway across the continent."

"But...why would you think that?"

She laughed. "You're planning to be an adventurer, are you not? You've read Jack's journals; you know he was always ready to dash off at the drop of a hat. Indeed, I think that's the very heart of adventuring – a willingness to seize the moment, to leap into action, ready or not, when called upon.

"I suppose it is," I said.

Indeed, her words had struck home, probably far more so than she intended. I had just spent three days meeting adventurers young and old and speaking with them, and while they had all praised the virtues of planning and preparation, their accounts of actual adventures all seemed to involve a great many spur-of-the-moment decisions and desperate improvisations.

I, on the other hand, had spent half my life in planning and preparation and had never yet leapt into action. For the first time since the age of eight I began to wonder whether I really was cut out to be an adventurer. I might have the physical skills necessary, but did I have the heart? Messrs. Arbuthnot, Snedeker, and von Düssel had all advised me against a career in adventure, and I had dismissed their concerns, but perhaps they were right.

That night, despite the rigors of my journey, I lay awake, staring at the ceiling and thinking about my future, for quite some time before falling asleep.

Two days later I received the first of the telegraphic reports I had ordered, alerting me to the latest political, military, scientific, and mystical developments. The following week I began receiving the "Adventurer's Edition" of the *New York Post*. From then on I spent every morning reading these through and considering whether there was anything in them that should inspire me to action. That nothing leapt out at me worried me and increased my doubts. By the first of June I was seriously considering simply choosing some situation at random and throwing myself into the middle of it, to test my mettle.

And then I saw it.

It was only a brief item, wired from a town called Phoenix, somewhere in the Arizona Territory. Just two days earlier, on the thirtieth of May, a large object, far too large to be any sort of bird, and far too dense to be a natural cloud, had passed over the town from north to south. This mysterious flying thing was said to have cast a shadow so vast that entire streets were darkened.

I turned to the atlas – not my father's rather battered old one, but the most up-to-date one I had been able to find during my visit to the city – and located Phoenix on a map. I observed that it lay almost directly south of Flagstaff and noted that the gigantic flyer, whatever it was, had been moving steadily southward. I read the descriptions of the mystery object as gray, but gleaming like metal where it caught the sun.

"The Lost City," I murmured. "Hezekiah McKee."

"What was that, dear?" my mother asked, as she puttered about the sideboard, arranging fresh flowers in one of the vases.

I rose and bent to kiss her cheek. "Mother," I said, "I think I need a flying machine."

She straightened and turned to look at me.

I did not speak, but merely handed her the newspaper, pointing to the relevant item. She read it, then looked at me. "A flying machine?" she asked.

"Whatever this thing is," I said, "I think I had best be prepared to meet it in its own environment."

"But do you mean a balloon, then?"

"A dirigible balloon, yes. The French have been doing excellent work in developing them, and the Germans are not far behind."

"We are in neither France nor Germany, Tom, and this...this thing was seen in the Arizona desert, not above the plains of Europe."

"Oh, but surely," I protested, "we Yankees have not let the Europeans get so far ahead of us in any field of scientific endeavor as that! While we may not be as advanced as the Tissandier brothers or Herr Haenlein, we must have something capable of controlled flight..."

"I'm sure I wouldn't know," she said. She glanced at the paper again, then met my gaze with her own. "Why are you so concerned with this? Of all the strange reports and curious sightings, why does *this* one interest you?"

I was at a loss for words to explain myself; I simply knew that I *must* investigate this. Still, I struggled to convey what I could.

"Herr von Düssel told me about a man named Hezekiah McKee who took a great quantity of an unknown metal from the Lost City of the Mirage two years ago," I said. "This mysterious object – I'm sure it's McKee's doing."

"After two years?"

I nodded. "He could scarcely build it overnight."

"Build it? Then you think this was a flying machine?"

"I do, yes."

"Even if it is, why do you think it requires your attention?"

"It just...it..." I stopped, took a deep breath, then let it out. "Mother," I said, "I don't know why. I just know it does. Unless you can tell me a quicker way to find an airship, I'll be leaving for New York this afternoon."

She looked at me for a moment, and I could tell that she wanted to protest further, to try to talk me out of haring off in this fashion, but she didn't. She had been an adventurer's wife, and she knew me as only a mother can. She did not protest; instead she said, "I'll help you pack."

Chapter Seven

The Reverend Hezekiah McKee, and Professor Aloysius Vanderhart

I was at the door of the Pierce Archive at a quarter to eight the next day, waiting eagerly until Dr. Pierce opened for business, shortly before the hour. I had two topics to research – airships and Hezekiah McKee. Allow me to tell you what I learned separately, and beginning with the latter.

The Reverend Hezekiah McKee had been born and raised in South Carolina, the son of a dealer in slaves. Upon his home state's secession in 1861 he had enlisted in the Confederate Army, and he had fought bravely for the South, distinguishing himself in several battles, and rising to the rank of captain shortly before General Lee's surrender.

He had accepted the South's defeat and had gone into the Baptist ministry, but had then been involved briefly with the Ku Klux Klan – the exact nature of his involvement was unclear, the accounts in the archive vague and contradictory, but by 1872 the result had been the loss of his congregation, and his exile from South Carolina. He had gone West, but as neither settler nor preacher; instead he had been a hired gun and sometime adventurer.

That last, of course, was why some of his biographical details were included in the archives. He had been reasonably successful in his new career, and by 1879 he was the leader of a small band of mercenaries, men from a variety of backgrounds – one was even said to be a Scottish laird.

Then in 1880 the Lost City had appeared outside Flagstaff, and the Reverend McKee had joined in the rush to loot it. He had survived the city's disappearance, according to several witnesses, but had then vanished, along with his men. They were not dead; every so often one of them would turn up in Flagstaff to re-provision. Except for these supply runs, though, they were never seen again. No one had gone looking for McKee, so far as the records in the archives could tell me – and why *should* anyone do so? McKee was not a particularly pleasant fellow and was not wanted for any serious crimes. To the best of my knowledge, no one had any compelling reason to seek him out.

As for airships, I knew, of course, about Thaddeus Lowe and the other aeronauts who had ventured upward during the Civil War, providing reconnaissance and signaling capability, but those were tethered balloons, not dirigibles.

The first truly practical dirigibles were built by the French, beginning with Monsieur Henri Giffard's 1852 steam-driven ascent from the Hippodrome, and the only serious challengers to French dominance in the field were the Germans. Both nations had experimented with various forms of motive power, but to date only steam engines seemed practical. There were rumors that Gaston and Albert Tissandier were developing an electrically driven dirigible, but it had yet to fly.

Americans, it seemed, had been surprisingly slow to take to the air; one Solomon Andrews of Perth Amboy, New Jersey had reportedly demonstrated a series of innovative devices he called Aereons some twenty years ago, but none of these were still functional, the methods employed appeared to be of severely limited utility, and financial reverses had forced Dr. Andrews to abandon further experimentation in the field. In the present day my options on this side of the Atlantic appeared to be severely limited, but Professor Aloysius Vanderhart of Rutgers College, in New Jersey, was said to have recently constructed an aerial vehicle of some sort. That seemed to be my best option if I wanted a craft capable of following this mysterious intruder through the skies of the Arizona Territory.

Professor Vanderhart maintained a townhouse in his native New York City, but for most of the year was more often to be found at his place of employment. Accordingly, I set out for New Jersey, bound for the Rutgers campus. A hansom to the station, a train to New Brunswick, directions from the station-master, and I was able to walk up to Geology Hall, a rather fine stone building of relatively recent construction, where Professor Vanderhart's office might be found.

Alas, while his office was there, the gentleman himself was not. I inquired after him with little success, but eventually encountered a suggestion that he might be at a certain shop on Hamilton Street.

He was not, but the shop's proprietor suggested another establishment, and a clerk at that one suggested a third, and finally, as daylight faded and lamps were being lit on all sides, I located him at a carpenter's workroom, where he and the owner were bent over a table, studying a set of plans. I felt confident in my identification of the two men; the carpenter was a stocky fellow in a leather apron, with sawdust in his curly hair and a well-used chisel in his left hand, while his right remained available to point at whatever detail of the schematics might currently be under discussion.

As for the professor, he had been described to me, and I thought it extremely unlikely that there would be two such men in the vicinity. He was of medium height, but must have weighed at least three hundred pounds. A Bowler hat perched on a tangle of yellow hair above a woolen jacket that had undoubtedly been expensive when new, but which was now rather the worse for wear.

They paid no attention to me, and I stood quietly amid the sawdust on the plank floor, waiting until such time as one or the other might chance to look in my direction.

After several minutes of intense muttered debate neither had yet looked anywhere but at the plans or each other. I cleared my throat loudly.

They still paid me no attention whatsoever. I tapped my fingers on a handy column and shuffled my feet in the sawdust, to no avail. At last I ventured to say, "Excuse me, gentlemen."

They continued their conversation, oblivious to my presence.

I decided desperate measures were called for. "Professor Vanderhart!" I called.

The carpenter threw me a quick glance; then the two returned to what appeared to be an intense discussion of the relative virtues of varnish and shellac and the best way to apply those substances to a particular mechanism.

I was preparing to call again when the door behind me opened, and a well-dressed woman stepped in. She glanced at me in surprise, then said, "Al?"

The professor straightened up abruptly and whirled on one heel to face us. "Mary!" he said. His gaze passed between us to the darkness beyond the open door, and he said, "Is it as late as that?"

"I'm afraid so, dear," Mary replied.

"Well, well. I suppose we got rather caught up in our discussion. Who is this with you, then?"

Mary glanced at me. "I don't know him, dear; he was here when I arrived."

"He's the one was making all that dreadful racket," the carpenter volunteered. "Shuffling his feet and clearing his throat and who knows what all."

"Indeed, I am," I agreed. "If I could have a word with you, Professor?"

He frowned. "Are you one of my students?"

"No, no," I hastened to say. "I am an outside party with an interest in your work."

"What work?"

I was somewhat baffled by this; what other work could I mean? "The construction of airships," I said.

"*Pfah* - I suppose you...no, you're too young. Who do you represent, then?"

"No one," I replied. "Save myself."

"Then what the devil do you care about airships?"

"I...wish to investigate aerial phenomena in the Arizona Territory."

"A telescope and a tethered balloon won't serve?"

"No, Professor, they will not."

"And you want me to assist you in building an airship? I am - "

I cut him off quite rudely, I fear. "No, no, Professor," I said. "I have no intention of building one; I cannot afford the time. I was hoping I might borrow, or rent, or if necessary purchase outright, one that you have already built."

He stared at me for a moment, while his wife and the carpenter exchanged glances and shrugs.

"You're just a boy," he said at last.

"I'm sixteen," I replied.

"The Arizona Territory, you say?"

"Yes, sir."

"Purchase, you said. Have you sufficient funds?"

"That depends on your price."

He named an amount, and I cringed inwardly; it was a very substantial sum of money. It was within my means, however.

"And what would I receive for this?" I asked.

"An airship. The only one I have constructed to date that was actually functional."

I was not happy to hear that there was only a single option. "I would need more specifics," I said.

Mrs. Vanderhart spoke up then. "Al," she said, "your supper is getting cold. Perhaps this young man would join us at our lodgings, and you might discuss this over the meal?"

"That would suit me," the professor said. "What do you say, young man?"

"I would be honored," I replied.

Twenty minutes later we were seated around the table in a modest house a few blocks away, where Mrs. Vanderhart and three of her children were serving out a generous meal of pot roast, boiled potatoes, and succotash.

"It occurs to me," Professor Vanderhart said from his place at the head of the table, "that I never got your name."

"Tom Derringer, sir."

"Ah! Any relation to the gunsmith?"

"Henry Deringer? No, sir; the spelling is different."

"And is your family in any similar trade?"

"No, sir. We live on investments my late father made."

"Very fortunate!"

"Yes, sir."

"So you pursue no particular occupation, but you find yourself in need of a dirigible balloon?"

"Yes, sir."

He waited for further explanation, but I did not provide any; instead I fell to eating the very fine meal the Vanderharts had provided. When it became plain that I was not going to volunteer more information, Professor Vanderhart demanded, "How much do you weigh?"

I blinked, startled by so direct and personal a question, but I could see how it might be relevant. "About a hundred and seventy-five pounds, I believe. Perhaps a trifle more – my mother tells me, based on how my clothes fit, that I'm still growing."

"Have you any experience in the operation of steam engines? Perhaps you have handled a traction engine?"

"No, sir, none. I understand the theory, though, and am told I'm a quick study."

"Ha!" He sat back in his chair and helped himself to a chunk of beef.

A moment later, when we had both enjoyed more of the excellent repast, the professor said, "I became interested in airship design because the concept of making objects lighter fascinated me, not because I had any great obsession with flight. I built a prototype machine to test my theories and demonstrate that I had grasped the underlying science. I named this contraption the Vanderhart Aeronavigator, but that title may be over-reaching; while it functioned adequately as proof of concept, the machine is of only limited practical use. It measures some ninety feet long and uses a steam engine of my own design, weighing in the neighborhood of four hundred pounds. It has a top speed of eleven knots in still air, fully loaded. You say you want to use it in the Arizona Territory?"

"Yes, sir."

"Then you'll need to find a way to get it there. At present it is housed in the town of Lakehurst, some forty miles from here."

"Can it be disassembled for transport by rail?"

"It can be disassembled to some extent, yes. Whether it can be crammed onto a rail car, I can't say. I would think something can be managed." He paused. "It will undoubtedly be expensive," he warned.

"Undoubtedly," I agreed.

"There is one further complication," he said. "There is only one person alive qualified to operate it."

"Al – " Mrs. Vanderhart began.

He held up a hand to quiet her. "You will need to hire this person as your driver and mechanic. I cannot allow you to operate it yourself; the risk is too great, and I refuse to have your death on my conscience."

"I see no problem – " I began.

"Al!" The professor's wife had set aside the platter she had held, and was now glaring furiously at her husband. Her hands were on her hips.

"Yes, my dear?" the professor said, feigning innocence.

"The Arizona Territory?"

"It will be most educational, I should think."

"Educational! I should say dangerous."

"Oh, nonsense, my dear. It's not as if the Apache are still raiding every settlement in sight."

I bit my lip and held my peace; the Apache most certainly *were* still active in the region, though I believed they mostly operated to the east and south of my intended destination. Mrs. Vanderhart clearly took a personal interest in the welfare of whoever my driver and mechanic was to be, though, and I did not want to give her any further cause for concern.

"Al, I must protest. The Arizona Territory is a desert at the far end of the continent, home to more scorpions and rattlesnakes than it is to honest citizens!"

"Your protest has been duly noted, my dear, but should we not leave it up to the party under discussion to decide the matter?"

"I think we must *all* discuss it before we make this fine young man any rash promises!"

The professor sighed. "My wife," he said to me, "sometimes allows her maternal instincts to rule. While I would very much prefer that you leave steering the Vanderhart Aeronavigator to experienced hands, that may be impossible. Do you think, given written instructions, you could learn to operate the device yourself?"

"Oh, I believe I could, Professor," I replied hastily, before he could reconsider.

"Well, I hope it won't prove necessary, but in that case, I will allow you to purchase my machine – honestly, I don't have any other use for it. If you wish to transport it to the Arizona Territory for reassembly and launch there, you may make the arrangements, and I will see that either the engineer will join you there, or you will have the best written instructions I can manage."

"That's more than fair of you, sir!" I exclaimed.

"Good, good," he said, smiling. "Then it is agreed."

Mrs. Vanderhart was clearly not entirely happy with this, but she put on a brave front and forced a smile. "It seems to be time for dessert," she said. "Ice cream, anyone?"

I happily accepted a generous portion of that frozen concoction, which more than adequately capped a very satisfactory meal.

Chapter Eight

The Vanderhart Aeronavigator

The following day I delivered an alarmingly large bank draft to Professor Vanderhart and then set out for Lakehurst armed with assorted papers providing the necessary instructions, directions, permissions, and authorizations to take custody of the Vanderhart Aeronavigator and send it on its way to Flagstaff, in the Arizona Territory.

I confess that my first view of the craft did not impress me. It was stored in an immense barn that had apparently held dairy cattle not so very long ago, and which still retained a certain bovine odor. When I arrived at the designated building and presented the two guardians of the place with my letters, they slid open a door and allowed me a glimpse.

I had envisioned it as looking something like an inverted boat, perhaps with a windmill's blades at either end to propel it. I had expected it to be sleek and modern. That was not quite what I saw. In fact, at first glance I was not entirely sure whether I was looking at the famed Vanderhart Aeronavigator, or at a trash heap.

"That's it?" I said to the man who held the door.

"That's it," that worthy replied.

"Aye, there she be," his companion affirmed.

I stepped in and took a closer look, and my initial misgivings faded somewhat. I could see now that there was indeed a substantial framework here; it was merely folded down for storage. There were at least a dozen curving strakes running the full length of the contraption, which did appear to be approximately the ninety feet the Professor had claimed for it – I had played a few games of base-ball, where the first base lies ninety feet from the batsman's box, so I had some feel for such a distance. These strakes, or struts, were of fine bamboo, richly varnished to a golden brown. Naturally, the professor had been unable to obtain single stems of such a length, so each strake was woven from several pieces of bamboo and securely bound at several points with what appeared to be first-quality hemp. The strakes were connected to one another with ropes of a material I did not immediately recognize, but finally identified as white silk. Beneath the bamboo struts lay a great mass of fabric, all of it covered with a gray sealant of some sort. This was clearly the inflatable balloon that would carry the whole thing aloft. Beneath *that* was a structure largely hidden from me by the fabric, but which I took to be the motor and passenger compartment of the aerial vehicle. I was somewhat dismayed that this concealed portion seemed rather small; I had not actually enquired as to how many passengers the Aeronavigator could carry, or what tonnage of supplies, but I had expected a larger carrying capacity than anything implied by the mass beneath the balloon. Well, I told myself, perhaps it folded out somehow when the balloon was inflated.

In truth, I did not see that I had much of a choice. This unprepossessing tangle of bamboo and silk was said to be the finest airship on this side of the Atlantic. If I intended to pursue that mysterious thing that had flown through the skies above Phoenix, this was my best hope of success.

The possibility that I *had* no real hope of success did occur to me, but the successful adventurer does not yield so easily as *that* to difficult circumstance! I could recall half a dozen instances in my father's journals when he had faced seemingly impossible situations and somehow won through – tracking the Carolina banshee, retrieving the Darlington Covenant, and so on. If this device proved inadequate to my task, it might lead me to a better approach.

"Will this fit on a railroad car?" I asked.

The two men beside me exchanged glances. "How the devil should *we* know?" one of them asked.

I had no good answer for that question. I sighed.

Still, getting the craft to Flagstaff was no great obstacle compared to some of the difficulties my father had faced. I began a closer inspection, measuring tape in hand, and recruited the two guardians to aid me in assessing the situation.

In the end, I found it necessary to hire several other able-bodied men and two large wagons, as well. I feel no great need to go into all the tedious details; suffice it to say that three days later I was aboard a train headed west, and the component parts of the Aeronavigator occupied the entirety of a freight wagon some two cars behind me. It had been necessary to partially unweave the long bamboo strakes in order to get them into the car; everything else had fit without serious difficulty. I hoped that reversing the damage would not be too difficult, nor excessively costly in either time or money, once I reached Flagstaff.

I had been in contact with the Vanderhart family by telegraph and was assured that my engineer would be following on the next train and would meet me in Flagstaff with the necessary tools and supplies to get the Aeronavigator restored to full functionality – or at least, as close to full functionality as it had ever been. Professor Vanderhart admitted that it was not the equal of some of the aerial vehicles reported to have plied

European skies of late, and even the best of those had severe limitations regarding lifting capacity, range, and the ability to drive against the wind.

I had sent my mother a brief telegram of reassurance as well, but most of my electrical communications had been with the professor and his family. I noticed that the Vanderharts had carefully avoided telling me my engineer's name; at first I had thought it merely an attempt to save the cost of added words in their telegram, but eventually concluded the omission was deliberate. I had supposed this engineer to be a member of the family – perhaps their oldest child, or a sibling of either the professor or his wife – but why they felt themselves unable to trust me with this individual's specific identity I could not easily imagine.

I did not allow it to trouble me unduly as I made my way across the continent, a journey that would have required the better part of a week under the best of conditions. Conveying the Vanderhart Aeronavigator meant that my traveling conditions were *not* the best, and I felt myself to have done well when I arrived in Flagstaff some ten days after departing Lakehurst.

The voyage was uneventful – uneventful to the point of tedium, in fact, so that I soon came to appreciate the attitude of the young Miss Jones I had encountered en route to New York City those several months before. I began to wonder whether this was a normal part of adventuring, whether the undoubted moments of excitement were not the whole of an adventurer's career, nor even the bulk of it, but only an occasional spice.

My father's books had often referred to one journey or another as boring, but had never devoted more than a few words to this, so I had dismissed it as the impatience of a young man accustomed to vigorous activity and frequent danger. Now, though, I began to realize that the travels necessary to an adventurer's career surely must include many tiresome days of sitting aboard one conveyance or another, doing little of significance. I did take the opportunity to read and study, but I cannot say my days held much interest.

I had thought I might pass the time by writing in my own journal, but I found I had nothing to say that seemed worthy of recording – or at least, no more than I have said here. I wondered whether my father had experienced similar sentiments.

I did wire reassurances of my continued good health to my mother every few days, when an opportunity to do so presented itself, and occasionally chatted briefly with my fellow passengers, but all in all, the trip was tedious.

However dull the journey, though, I must say that the scenery was spectacular. I had never been west of the Mississippi before, and the vast western landscape impressed me greatly. Even in the middle of Flagstaff, as I disembarked, I could see mountains looming to the north that made the Adirondacks where I had trained look insignificant in comparison.

I had no time to waste on sight-seeing, though, if I was to catch the mysterious flying object that had passed over Phoenix two weeks before. I set about my preparations immediately.

I was overseeing the unloading of the Aeronavigator when a lad trotted up, a sheet of paper in his hand. "Are you Mr. Derringer?" he said.

I turned, startled – surely, this youth could not be my engineer? He was younger than I was myself!

"I'm Tom Derringer," I admitted.

The boy thrust the paper at me. "Telegram," he said.

"Ah," said I, accepting it.

The boy waited expectantly, and I fished a nickel from my pocket for him; the moment the coin touched his palm he whirled and scampered away, without a word of thanks. I watched him go, taking note that he wore neither the cap nor jacket I was accustomed to see on Western Union's messengers. Perhaps such niceties were not observed out here on the frontier, or perhaps this outpost of civilization was served by a different telegraph company. Given the boy's haste to be elsewhere, the possibility of mischief also occurred to me, but I could not see what form it might take.

When the lad was a hundred yards away I turned my attention to the telegram. I was pleased to see that the telegrapher had a good clear hand. The message was from Professor Vanderhart, and read, "Forgot to tell you. Engineer our eldest daughter, Elspeth Vanderhart. Should be there soonest."

Daughter! Ah, the mystery was explained! "Forgot," indeed – I did not for a moment believe that the Vanderharts' failure to identify my engineer was the result of any sort of lapse whatsoever; indeed, it was obviously a conscious and deliberate act, intended to keep me ignorant of the sex of my engineer until I was in a position where I would be unable to make any effective protest. I smiled.

This subterfuge had not been necessary. Oh, I was, and am, well aware of the idea that women's minds are not equipped to understand machinery, or to comprehend the science that makes lighter-than-air flight possible. I likewise knew that many considered the weaker sex unsuited for the rough physical labor involved in operating engines. Doubtless Professor Vanderhart thought I would be appalled at the thought of trusting myself to his daughter's skills.

I, however, was the son of Mrs. John T. Derringer, the former Arabella Whitaker, and had observed in my mother capabilities far beyond those of most men. Whether such abilities were truly exceptional, or whether we men are simply in the habit of underestimating our female compatriots, I cannot say with any assurance, but I had little doubt that this Elspeth Vanderhart would live up to the trust her father placed in her. If a man sent his son out to do a job that proved to be beyond the young man's capacities, that would surprise no one – we expect boys to face challenges bravely and to confront adversity, so that they might learn from the experience. Our modern society in this nineteenth century is more protective and less demanding of our daughters, though, and we do not willingly thrust them into situations where there might be an expectation of failure. If Professor Vanderhart was sending a girl, then he must be quite thoroughly convinced that she was up to the task at hand.

I folded the telegram and stuffed it into my pocket, then turned my attention back to getting the Aeronavigator safely off the train. I trusted that when Elspeth Vanderhart arrived she would find me readily enough; I had left my name with the stationmaster, and with the telegraph office, and given them both the name of my hotel.

At least, I told myself, the telegram had ensured that there would be no embarrassing scene caused by my natural expectation that my engineer was to be male. Indeed, that might have been the reason the professor finally relented and revealed her identity.

By this time the unloading had begun to draw the attention of some of the locals. The steam engine had attracted no great interest, but when the balloon and its woven–bamboo frame began to fill up the platform, several passersby stopped to watch. I paid them no heed; I was too busy ensuring that no further damage was added to the indignities already inflicted upon the machine by its long journey.

I was rather startled, therefore, when a woman's voice called, "Mr. Derringer!"

But then I realized that this most likely must be Miss Elspeth Vanderhart. I turned to look for her, and at first I saw no one. Then I lowered my gaze, and to my astonishment saw a familiar face. "Miss Jones!" I exclaimed, recognizing my companion from my first train ride to New York. "Whatever brings you to the Arizona Territory?"

"The Atchison, Topeka and Santa Fe Railroad," she said, smiling at my obvious surprise.

"Well, yes," I said, my pleasure at seeing her now somewhat tempered by the playfully over–literal reply. "I meant rather, what are you doing here? I last saw you in the Hudson Valley, bound for New York – you said nothing of any plans to venture to the far west!"

"I believe I told you that my father's business sends me traveling all over the country."

"Indeed you did, but I had not thought you meant it as literally as that! Why, this is delightful and quite staggeringly unlikely that we should meet again here, thousands of miles from the location of our last encounter."

"Oh, it is perhaps not so great a coincidence as all that!"

"You think not?"

"Has it not occurred to you that we might be here on the *same* business?"

I glanced at the empty sky to the south. "You read of the strange object that passed over Phoenix, then?"

She blinked at me. "What?"

"Well, that is why *I* am here," I said. I gestured at the Aeronavigator. "And that is the purpose of this – to allow me to pursue that mystery!"

"Ah," she said. "Well, it is not the mystery that brought me. I came because of *that*." She waved at the Aeronavigator.

At that, I finally understood. The airship, errands for her father – it all fell together. "You told me your name was Jones!" I protested. "And if I am not mistaken, you said it was Betsy, rather than Elspeth, as well."

"I'm as much Betsy as you are Tom," she said. "Really, do you think I want to be called *Elspeth*? Half my friends can't say it without spitting."

"That's as may be, but Jones is hardly a common abbreviation for Vanderhart."

"And Vanderhart is hardly a common name. I prefer to remain incognito when traveling; my father does have enemies who would not hesitate to strike at him through me."

I blinked. "Does he? How would a college professor come to have such ruthless foes?"

"If you thought him nothing but an ordinary classroom lecturer, we would hardly be standing on this platform beside one of his inventions."

I could scarcely argue with that. I looked at the disassembled airship and then back at Miss Vanderhart. She was, I noticed, wearing a fine gown of blue silk, with French lace at the throat. "So you are to be my engineer?" I asked. "I cannot say you look the part."

"I cannot say I like walking the public street in my working attire," she retorted. "If I want to be treated like a lady here, I must dress the part. Rest assured, I will not be wearing silk and lace when we're aloft."

It was at that moment that I recognized for the first time an impediment to my plan. "When *we're* aloft? You and I?"

"Yes. That *was* your intention when you purchased the Aeronavigator, was it not? To fly in it? It's rather large and expensive for a lawn ornament."

"And not particularly decorative in its present state, but I think you mistake my point. Of course I intend to fly in it, and I agreed with your father that he would provide me with an engineer to assist in its operation. However, when I made that agreement, I was unaware of your sex and of the rather limited confines of the craft. There is no room for a chaperone, is there?"

"*Space* is not the problem, Mr. Derringer; lifting capacity is. The Aeronavigator can only carry approximately four hundred pounds in addition to itself if you wish to achieve any notable altitude – five hundred at the outside. My father built it mostly to determine just how large a device would be required to support his own weight, which is considerably more than yours or mine – quite possibly more than both of us together – but still not so tremendous as all that. He chose me to train as its operator because I am the smallest person he could find who he felt he could trust with the job. Only if we were to go aloft without any supplies – no food, no water, no additional fuel – might we accommodate a duenna."

"That would hardly be practical," I said.

"I would agree with that assessment."

"You do not consider it inappropriate for the two of us to isolate ourselves in the device?"

"I assume you to be a gentleman, Mr. Derringer, and I take it that my father gave you that same credit when he chose to trust you with my presence unescorted. What's more, I have been aloft in the Aeronavigator, and I cannot imagine a less salubrious environment for any sort of inappropriate activity. Finally, should I have misjudged you, should my father have been derelict in his parental duties, and should you find your amorous intentions unhindered by the precarious nature of an airship's compartment, rest assured, I may be small, but I am capable of defending myself."

"I cannot begin to doubt it," I acknowledged. If the young lady was as good with her hands as with her tongue, I was certain she could indeed fend off unwelcome advances.

In any case, I had no intention of making any such advances. I found Miss Vanderhart unquestionably charming in both her appearance and her unorthodox manner, but our relationship was, first and foremost, a matter of business, and I was determined not to allow my baser appetites to interfere with my quest.

"I was concerned," I said, "not so much with any genuine risks, but with the appearance of impropriety. I would not wish to sully your reputation."

"Very commendable, I am sure, but I can attend to my own reputation. Your concern does you credit, but is quite unnecessary."

I raised my hands in surrender. "As you please. Then would you like to begin assembly of the Aeronavigator immediately, or are there matters we should attend to first?"

She turned to study the device and assess its condition. "I will need my tools," she said. "And of course, we cannot get it off the ground without the hydrogen generator, which I have stored at Beckman's Stables." She pointed eastward along Main Street.

"Then let us be about it," I said. "Lead the way, Miss Vanderhart!"

Chapter Nine

My First Flight

By the following afternoon the Vanderhart Aeronavigator had been transported, by means of hired wagons, to a stretch of open land a few miles south of Flagstaff – the town was located in the rolling foothills that separated the mountains I had observed to the north, and a vast desert plain to the south, so that it was to the south that open space was most easily found. Miss Vanderhart had also delivered to the site a great deal of additional equipment. The largest part of this was the complex coal–fired boiler that would generate the hydrogen gas to fill the Aeronavigator's balloon, but there were also supplies of fuel and water and camping gear so that we would have no need to return to town at night, the better to devote every moment of daylight to getting our airship aloft.

I had not realized, when I first determined to acquire an airship, just how massive an undertaking it was to put such a machine into the sky. I found myself wondering how the Reverend McKee had managed it, if that mysterious object seen passing over Phoenix was indeed an airship of his design – though of course, it might have taken him as much as two years to build it. Miss Vanderhart seemed constantly in motion, fitting bamboo shafts together, setting ropes to the proper lengths and tension, adjusting valves and levers, and directing the workmen in laying out the various components, fueling the various engines, and generally setting the contraption to rights. It was sometimes hard to credit that so small a frame was capable of such energetic feats.

By nightfall the Aeronavigator had been reassembled, but not yet inflated. The hydrogen generator's iron flue was heated red-hot, ready to begin separating lifting gas out of steam, and the boiler beneath was filled and heated. The men we had hired to assist us to this point had all ridden back toward town, but we were by no means ready to take to our beds. Indeed, the machines had developed much of the required heat and pressure, so we could not shut down operations at that point without having to start them over from scratch in the morning. It was perhaps an hour after sunset when, working by lantern light, Miss Vanderhart began to pump hydrogen into the airship's gas-bag, while I provided what assistance I could.

Miss Vanderhart, I should say, had been as good as her word in every particular. She had demonstrated a complete mastery of the many machines involved and displayed a strength of body and mind belying her diminutive stature. As promised, she no longer wore silk and lace, but had instead spent the day in a sturdy outfit of canvas, leather, and linen quite unlike anything I had ever seen before. Her outermost skirt was divided in two, to allow for freedom of movement, but each half was voluminous enough to provide for feminine modesty. Drawstrings at either ankle kept this curious garment in place even when she was clambering about the airship's frame. Her high-collared blouse was more traditional, but equipped with a startling number of pockets and cloth loops where tools could be secured. A broad leather belt sported additional loops of both leather and metal. When occasion called for it, and the sun's heat did not render it unbearable, she wore a smith's leather apron over all, and a railroad engineer's billed cap on her bound hair. A pair of goggles protected her eyes when she was working with anything that carried a risk of explosion.

This costume was not very ladylike, but it was extremely practical for the task at hand. Our hired men may have found it curious, perhaps even worthy of mockery, but none dared disparage it where either Miss Vanderhart or I might hear. Despite her small size, Miss Vanderhart had clearly impressed our hirelings as someone not to be crossed. Practical as this attire was, I entirely understood why she would not have dressed in this manner back in Flagstaff.

By mid–evening the gas production had settled down to a steady flow, and Miss Vanderhart suggested I take a rest, saying that she could manage without me for a while. I remonstrated against this, but she assured me she would wake me immediately should occasion arise. Reluctantly, I yielded, and settled down upon my bedroll, intending only to rest my eyes for a moment before resuming work.

I awoke to find the sun well above the eastern hills, and the Vanderhart Aeronavigator inflated to its full magnificence. I sat up and stared at it. In this, its proper condition, it scarcely resembled the mess I had seen in Lakehurst.

It was comprised of two major sections. The upper section was a great cylinder with rounded ends, rather resembling a sausage – but a sausage almost a hundred feet long, and perhaps twenty feet in diameter, its shape maintained by a framework of shellacked bamboo strakes, hempen ropes, and silken netting over the gas–bag itself. The framework gleamed a rich golden brown in the morning light, while the gas–bag itself was a very pale gray, almost white.

Beneath this immense cylinder hung the much smaller compartment that held the steam engine and provided space for what few passengers and small freight the mechanism could transport. This compartment was framed in gleaming brass and floored in blue-enameled steel, but the sides were largely open, and where safety required some sort of barrier beyond the brass rails, Professor Vanderhart had installed flimsy looking wickerwork. I understood the necessity of keeping weight within limits, but I confess that openwork cage did not fill me with confidence.

The lower section was perhaps twenty feet long, half that in width, and perhaps seven feet in height. The engine's boiler occupied the exact center, with fuel stores and water tanks carefully balanced along the sides, and the engine itself was mounted atop the boiler, where it drove a long wooden shaft. This shaft ran the full length of the compartment and extended a dozen feet from either end before terminating in triple screw propellers; these somewhat resembled the familiar sails of windmills.

A labyrinth of exhaust pipes, relief valves, and other plumbing extended out from the steam engine on either side, and an assortment of ropes, hooks, and sandbags added to the clutter. I could hear steam hissing somewhere, and two brass governors were turning steadily.

The amazing thing about this contraption, the feature that made me wonder if perhaps I might still be asleep and dreaming, was that the entire machine was hovering a foot or so off the ground, held in place not by the natural pull of gravity, but only by half a dozen strong ropes that were secured to ordinary tent-pegs.

Miss Vanderhart was leaning over a brass rail into the lower compartment, tinkering with something I could not see on one side of the boiler. I watched for a moment, and in time she straightened up, wiped her brow, and noticed me.

"Ah, Mr. Derringer," she said, raising her goggles. "Are you ready for your first flight?"

I did not hesitate. "Of course," I said.

"I have steam up in the boiler," she said. She pointed to a jointed pipe that connected the airship to the hydrogen generator. "I transferred it under pressure from the gassing furnace, to save time and fuel. We can go up as soon as you like." She glanced up. "The weather seems ideal."

"Indeed," I acknowledged. "Then we can set out for Phoenix immediately?"

She blinked. "Phoenix?"

"A town approximately a hundred and fifty miles south of here."

"Is that where you intend to go?"

"Yes. It is where the mystery object was last seen."

"Oh - of course. You did mention that." She glanced up at the Aeronavigator's gas–bag. "I must confess, Mr. Derringer, that I am not certain we can make it so far as that. The engine is a superbly efficient one of my father's own design, but we have never flown it more than thirty miles, and I am not certain how far it can go without refueling. Much depends on the winds." She frowned thoughtfully. "I would suggest we make a test flight, so that I can adjust the machinery. It might also be advisable to hire someone to follow on the ground with a wagon of supplies."

I glanced around and saw an obvious requirement. "Including the hydrogen generator?" I asked.

"I think that would be wise, yes."

"Is there any way we can take the hydrogen generator aboard the Aeronavigator? I do not like the notion of being so thoroughly dependent upon a piece of equipment we are not carrying with us."

She shook her head. "That would be quite impossible. The generator is built of cast iron. Even without fuel and water, the machine weighs more than the Aeronavigator can lift."

That was disappointing. I was further disappointed that we could not set out in pursuit of the mystery object that very minute, but I could hardly argue with her reasoning. As Messrs. Arbuthnot and Snedeker had both repeatedly warned me, foolhardy adventurers generally don't live long.

"Let me fetch a few things, then, and we can take a test flight," I said.

"Excellent! I'll disconnect the hydrogen generator."

I turned away while she clambered down from the airship and set about separating it from the other machine. I hurried to take care of my morning ablutions and quickly to down a cup of cold coffee left from the night before. Since this was to be only a short test flight I did not try to bring a full set of luggage, but I remembered incidents in my father's journals where some vital piece of equipment was left behind because it shouldn't have been needed, so I did fetch a bag of tools and emergency supplies that I had prepared. I made sure that my Colt revolver was in its holster on my belt, with five rounds in the cylinder and the hammer resting on the empty sixth chamber, and I slung my Winchester rifle on my back. Then I once again turned my attention to the Aeronavigator.

It was still hanging from nothing, a foot or so off the ground. Only two loops of rope still held it down; the other lines had been released and coiled up. The pipes and hoses that had connected it to other machines had all been detached and withdrawn. It was a very curious thing to see that great machine floating in air. There was an almost dreamlike quality about it. I had seen pictures of balloon ascents, but the reality was rather different.

Miss Vanderhart was standing in the lower compartment, holding a lever and waiting for me. "If you are ready, Mr. Derringer, then come aboard," she said.

I hurried to the machine and clambered aboard, lifting myself over a brass rail onto an open patch of steel flooring. That platform was strangely unsteady and swayed beneath my weight – not as a railroad carriage might sway as it rattled around a curve, but more gently, more slowly, rather like a porch swing. I stood and looked out at the surrounding countryside, and at our encampment, aware that beneath my feet a foot or so of empty air separated the Aeronavigator from the ground.

"If you would be so kind as to release that rope?" Miss Vanderhart said, pointing. I looked where she indicated and realized that the two loops holding the machine down were secured in a single connection – a rope ran from either end of the undercarriage, out through an eye–bolt set into the ground, then back into the Aeronavigator, where these two lines were fastened to one another with a pair of hooks. It appeared a simple matter to unhook them.

It proved not quite as simple as it looked; the two ropes were drawn taut, and getting enough slack to separate the hooks required more strength than I had expected. I managed it in the end, though.

While I had been grappling with the ropes, Miss Vanderhart had thrown the lever, and with a hiss, steam vented from somewhere atop the boiler. Machinery jerked into motion, the governors accelerated, and the long shaft began to turn the multiple screw propellers.

The hooks came free and were snatched out of my hands, flung rattling off to either side, and with a surge the Aeronavigator rose into the sky. I grabbed the brass rail for dear life as the world fell away on all sides. The trees and hills surrounding our campsite were dropping – or so it appeared; I knew that in truth the landscape was not moving, *we* were.

The speed with which we were rising was astonishing. While I felt no sensation of movement in the usual sense, the floor seemed to be pressing me upward, and I could *see* how quickly we were ascending. Within seconds, we were well above the treetops.

"Good heavens!" I exclaimed.

Miss Vanderhart did not reply to my outburst; she was busy at the controls, her hands on the valve-wheels while her eyes were fixed on the nearer set of screw propellers. My own gaze followed hers, and I saw that the screws were spinning rapidly, so rapidly as to be all but invisible. Only then did I realize that I could feel the rush of air from our machines and observe that we were moving horizontally as well as vertically.

"Mr. Derringer!" she called. "Where would you like us to go?"

I had not given the matter any thought. This flight was to demonstrate the machine's capabilities, not to achieve a specific destination, but if we were to test its dirigible properties, we needed a goal to aim at. Phoenix was too far away for this initial excursion, and there was really only one other place I knew to suggest. "Flagstaff," I said, shouting to be heard over the chuffing of the engine. "Take us over the town. See how close you can bring us to the railroad station."

She nodded and looked around, orienting herself. Then she reached for an overhead cord and tugged. A panel that I had thought was merely a part of the compartment swung around, acting like a sail or rudder, deflecting the stream of air the forward screws were driving toward us. The entire world seemed to swim for a moment and then began turning around us – or so it seemed. I knew that in fact it was the Aeronavigator that was turning, but from our vantage point it did not look or feel like it.

In fact, the airship's motion was unlike anything I had ever experienced. In some ways it resembled a boat's, but the medium in which it floated was so very much more attenuated than water that the sensations were quite different in detail.

As we turned, I looked down at the trees and hills, and it struck me that I was looking down at some fairly significant hills and could see for what must be several miles in every direction. "How high up are we?" I asked.

Miss Vanderhart had been struggling with the cords and levers of the steering mechanism, but she glanced at me over her shoulder as I spoke, then looked out at the world around us, at the great open expanse of empty sky and at the vast landscape laid out below us. She briefly studied a set of gauges, then said, "I would estimate it at twelve hundred feet, Mr. Derringer."

My eyes widened, and I swallowed hard. "Twelve *hundred* feet?" I asked.

"About that, yes."

"How high *can* we go?"

She frowned. "I don't know, Mr. Derringer, and I have no intention of experimenting to determine that."

"No, of course not." I leaned over the rail and looked down...and down...and down! I had never seen the world from such a vantage point before. It was enlightening, to look down on it all as if I were one of Heaven's angels. I recognized our campsite; it was little more than a smudge on the landscape from so far up. I could see the road, no more than a line across the countryside. I let my eyes follow that road northward and located Flagstaff, which looked like a child's toy. The railroad was like a silvery thread stretching across the entire world, from horizon to horizon, and the town was a collection of buildings, no larger than salt cellars, that clustered along that thread for a brief interval. The tree-covered mountains to the north provided a dramatic backdrop.

"It's amazing," I said.

"It's science," Miss Vanderhart replied. "But yes, it's amazing."

"It's wonderful. I'm surprised that more people haven't built dirigibles."

She made a rather unladylike noise that I can best describe, uncomplimentary though the term may be, as a snort. "It isn't particularly cheap or easy to do, Mr. Derringer. Striking the proper balance between the buoyancy of the vehicle and the power of the engine is very difficult. The more weight you want to lift, the larger the balloon must be, but the larger the balloon, the greater both the weight of the vehicle itself, and the resistance of the air that the vehicle moves through. The engine must overcome that resistance, so the larger your vehicle is, the more powerful the engine must be, which once again adds to the weight. When you figure in the fuel you must burn, and if you are using steam, the water for the boiler, you have still more weight. Building a working dirigible is a challenging piece of engineering; so far as we know the Aeronavigator is the best anyone has done on this side of the Atlantic, and you see how little carrying capacity it has."

I looked around and saw her point. The tiny patch of steel floor on which we stood made the cramped quarters of a railroad carriage appear a veritable mansion by comparison.

"You do realize that the reason my father trained *me* for this job is that I weigh scarcely a hundred pounds? Every additional pound of engineer is one less pound of fuel."

"I had not given the matter much thought," I admitted.

She gave me a curious look. "You had not wondered why your engineer is a girl?"

"I had assumed your father had chosen the most suitable candidate for the job, regardless of sex," I replied. "I had not considered that suitability would include size, but of course I can see how it would." I looked at the boiler behind us, which occupied most of the Aeronavigator's lower compartment and surely made up more than half the vehicle's weight. "Is steam really the most practical propulsion system in such an application, then? The pressures involved require quite a mass of metal."

"The Tissandier brothers are said to be working on an electrically driven dirigible," she said, "but the batteries for such a device are necessarily fairly massive and limited in capacity. Several of the German experimenters have used internal combustion engines of one sort or another, and eventually those may well show themselves to be superior, but my father was more comfortable with the proven reliability of steam."

I nodded, then glanced over the rail again. We were perhaps halfway from our campsite to Flagstaff. "I think I have seen enough for now," I said. "Shall we descend and prepare for our flight to Phoenix?"

"As you please," she said, turning her attention to the controls.

It took better than an hour to return to our campsite and spiral down to a landing; venting enough hydrogen to allow gravity to regain its hold on us without sending us plunging to our doom was a delicate and time-consuming process. I did what I could to assist Miss Vanderhart, but she was intimately familiar with every aspect of our craft's operation, while I could scarcely tell one valve from another. In the end, though, we were drifting along perhaps two feet off the ground, and I was able to vault over the rail, catch one of the trailing lines, and secure the Aeronavigator to its anchorage.

Chapter Ten

We Fly to Phoenix

I had hoped to make all necessary preparations quickly and see the Vanderhart Aeronavigator southward bound that same day, but that proved impossible; not all the workmen who had been eager to help us get the machine to our campsite south of town were willing to make the long journey to Phoenix, and some of the supplies Miss Vanderhart wanted to have on hand were not readily available in Flagstaff. It was not until the morning of the third day that we were finally able to take once more to the air and turn the dirigible's nose southward. We watched carefully as we ascended and began our journey, making very sure that our half-dozen hirelings were following in the three mule-drawn wagons – the possibility that some or all of them might decide not to undertake the trip, or might abscond with our belongings, had occurred to us both.

All three wagons did roll southward after us, though – one wagon loaded with the usual supplies required for any travel in the western wilderness, one holding additional fuel, water, and parts that Miss Vanderhart wanted to have on hand in case the Aeronavigator needed repair, and the third and final one hauling the hydrogen generator, so that we should be able to get the dirigible back in the air after bringing it down to earth.

The weather was quite coöperative – clear and sunny, as it most commonly is in the western deserts. It might have been oppressively warm had we stayed down on the ground, but a thousand feet up in the steel-and-wicker carriage, shaded by the gas-bag and cooled by the breeze, we traveled in comfort. Sometimes we stood; at other times one or both of us would sit upon the steel floor with legs thrust under the brass rails, dangling in open space. We had no furniture to allow more dignified seating, and I mused to myself about devising some sort of lightweight sling-chair or hammock. For the present, though, the compartment edge was sufficient.

Although we spent much of our time simply admiring the scenery, and Miss Vanderhart did need to give regular attention to our altitude, our course, and the operation of the steam engine, we had time to talk at some length. I do not pretend to remember every word we said, or even the precise order in which various topics were discussed, but I do recall several interesting moments in that long conversation.

The matter of an unmarried couple traveling unchaperoned came up and was quickly dismissed - there was no privacy to be had on that open platform, with scarcely four feet of floor between the boiler and the rail, and we were in plain sight not merely of our own hirelings, but of anyone for several miles in every direction who happened to notice the Aeronavigator while in possession of a spyglass or binoculars. Our chastity was scarcely in any danger under such circumstances.

I also explained something of my own history to Miss Vanderhart. She found this amusing.

"You know, when we first met, on the train to New York," she said, "I had no intention of asking whether you were related to Henry Deringer. I had wanted to inquire whether you were related to *Jack* Derringer - as indeed you are. Certain friends of my father are adventurers, and he has been a guest of the Order of Theseus, and your father's name had come up. When you cut me off and informed me that you are no kin to the gunsmith, I concluded that you had not even *heard* of Jackie Derringer, the Little Pistol. Now it turns out that you are his son, and deliberately following in his footsteps!"

"And *you* told *me* your name was Betsy Jones," I reminded her. "It would seem neither of us gave an entirely truthful impression."

I explained that I had chosen to investigate the mysterious flying object seen over Phoenix as my first step in a career of adventuring, but I did not immediately tell her the story of Reverend McKee hauling several wagon-loads of a mysterious metal out of the Lost City of the Mirage.

Our most common subject, though, was the state of the art in dirigible design. Miss Vanderhart was thoroughly knowledgeable in this area and was able to explain to me every problem that had hindered the development of useful aerial coaches and every hope for possible solutions.

"Engine design is the obvious place to look for improvement," she said, "but there are also some interesting prospects for new materials. As I'm sure you see, if we had stronger, lighter materials, we could build better aerial vehicles. My father used bamboo and hemp and silk because they are strong and light, but in fact bamboo is not as strong as one might like. No wood is really ideal for airship construction; every one Father tried proved too flexible, too fragile, or too heavy."

I nodded and encouraged her to say more. She went on at some length about varnishes and shellacs that might provide better seals, about exotic woods that might be useful, and finally about the possibilities of using other metals than the usual iron, steel, brass, and tin.

"Iron, lead, and most of the others are simply too heavy," she said. "Tin and zinc aren't strong enough. Steel and brass are the best we have, but chemists say there are other metals that would serve far better if they were available in quantity."

"Oh?" I said. "What might those be?"

"Well, the most obvious one is aluminum," she said. "It's lighter than tin, but almost as strong as steel, and its ores are fairly common. The only problem is that refining aluminum is almost impossible. Chemists have managed to produce tiny quantities of pure aluminum in the laboratory, but the difficulty in doing so is so great that it is more precious than gold. If someone were to find an inexpensive way to create metallic aluminum, it would change the world! I think we would see dirigibles of a size and efficiency today's experimenters would find incredible."

"Aluminum?" I said. "What does it look like?"

She turned from reading the pressure gauges to look at me curiously. "What an odd question! I have never seen it, of course, but I understand it to be of a silvery-gray color, rather like nickel."

I remembered Herr von Düssel's description of the metal Hezekiah McKee had hauled out of the vanishing city – a gray metal, very light. If it was not aluminum, I thought, it must be something very similar, and the Reverend McKee had collected several tons of the stuff. I looked up at the gas-bag over my head. Professor Vanderhart had built this flying machine with ordinary materials – silk, hemp, bamboo, and so on. One didn't need a vast supply of aluminum merely to get off the ground – but Miss Vanderhart said that the available materials limited the *size* of any possible dirigible. Aluminum would allow the construction of a much larger one.

It might seem as if I was drawing conclusions from very sparse evidence, and in fact, I was, I admit it. All the same, I felt quite certain that the thing seen flying over Phoenix had been a large aluminum dirigible, built to McKee's specifications.

But the next question was, what was he *doing* with it? Why fly south from Flagstaff, instead of taking it east to Washington or New York? Other than Phoenix, there wasn't anything south of Flagstaff except a few scattered settlements and hundreds of miles of desert, stretching all the way to the Mexican border. If he had indeed created this scientific marvel, this engineering triumph, why fly it out where no one could see it? Why not announce it, demonstrate it, and bask in the admiration of the civilized world? I remembered that Reverend McKee had been commanding a small mercenary company, which despite his calling to the clergy did not indicate a humanitarian nature. What did that imply about his possible motives?

Mercenaries fought for money, but there were other ways to make money, safer and more certain ways; from what Miss Vanderhart told me, McKee could have simply sold the aluminum to bring in a very substantial sum. Using it to build a giant dirigible instead hinted at interests beyond mere wealth.

Fame did not seem to be his primary goal; if he sought fame, he need merely fly his creation, his airship, over New York's Fifth Avenue.

Neither money, nor fame – perhaps knowledge? Was there something in the southern deserts that he thought could best be found from the air? Some secret treasure? He had been an adventurer, after all, and searching for lost treasures was a common undertaking for members of the adventurous brotherhood. I considered that for a few moments before discarding the idea. No, he would not have required an oversized dirigible for that; an ordinary tethered balloon would have served just as well.

Not wealth or glory – power, then? He had been not just a mercenary, but a commander of mercenaries, and I knew from my studies of history that mercenary commanders have sometimes wound up as rulers, overthrowing their employers or carving out their own little kingdoms. Did Reverend McKee hope to build himself an empire out in the desert?

I could not see much *point* in that – it was, after all, *desert*. But beyond the desert lay Mexico; was that his destination? Could he have some notion of overthrowing Porfirio Diaz, the Mexican dictator, and taking the country for himself?

He very well might, I thought. Though just how a dirigible figured into such a scheme I could not quite see. Did he think that he could terrify the Mexicans into surrendering simply because he could fly? Did he hope to be taken for a pagan god, as Cortez had reportedly been? Somehow, I did not think the modern–day people of our southern neighbor were as gullible as their distant ancestors had been.

"We'll need to land soon to refuel," Miss Vanderhart said, interrupting my reverie. She was standing behind me, studying the gauges. I turned to look up at her.

"How fast can the Aeronavigator travel, Miss Vanderhart?" I asked.

She looked down at me and cocked her head. "We have been moving at our best safe speed, Mr. Derringer," she said. "I know my father claimed eleven miles an hour, but if it's possible at all, that would require straining the boiler to the maximum and increase the risk of fire or explosion beyond the level I'm willing to accept. It would also mean landing to refuel much more often. Unless we should happen to catch a strong following wind, I think you'll have to settle for the seven or eight miles an hour we have achieved thus far."

"Of course," I said. "Thank you." At eight miles an hour it would take at least a week, flying day and night, to reach Mexico City, and that assumed ideal conditions. I wondered how fast McKee's dirigible, if it actually existed, could fly. Was it already there, hovering over the city that had once been the Aztec capital?

"Mr. Derringer," she added warningly, "even a steady eight miles an hour will most likely outrun our supply wagons. As indeed we have."

"Oh. Yes." I felt slightly foolish for not considering that. Without the hydrogen generator and other equipment, we would be very limited indeed in what we might hope to accomplish.

"Shall I descend, then?"

I looked around, at the vast, empty landscape below us. Our wagons were faintly visible, far to the north; they would need some time to catch us up. "Yes, please, Miss Vanderhart," I said.

She tugged her goggles into place and began to operate the venting apparatus.

As anticipated, we had the Aeronavigator down almost to ground level and tethered to some of the desert scrub long before our train of wagons arrived. In time, though, they did reach us, and we set about renewing the craft's stores of fuel and water. By the time that was done the sun was scarcely clear of the western horizon, and we resolved to spend the night just where we were and resume our southward journey in the morning.

"Have you any idea how far we have come?" I asked Miss Vanderhart, as we made a simple supper over a campfire. I had been composing the night's journal entry in my head and thought that recording our progress would be appropriate.

"I would think the wagon drivers would be able to give you a better estimate than mine," she said. The hired men had their own fire a few yards away; I finished my meal before consulting them.

Harry Deerfield, our crew chief, gave the matter serious consideration before replying.

"We darn near killed the mules trying to keep up with you," he said at last. "I'd say it's better'n fifty mile."

"I ain't never gone so far in one day before," a fellow named Abner Fries offered.

That was encouraging – but on the other hand, I had hoped to reach Phoenix in a day or two, and at fifty miles a day we could not hope to achieve that. I had been spoiled, it seemed, by the speed of modern railroads.

And so it proved. On the second day we covered a good distance, it seemed to me, but even so, it was not until late in the afternoon of the third day that I finally saw signs of civilization to the south of us. I pointed the settlement out to Miss Vanderhart, and she altered our course accordingly, directing the Aeronavigator toward the collection of buildings I assumed to be Phoenix.

That was the highlight of the day, as it happens. The wide-ranging conversation of the first day had burned itself out by midday of the second, and the scenery, impressive as it might be, had begun to pall. As I had on the train, I found myself once again forced to acknowledge that extended periods of travel, no matter how marvelous the method of transportation might be, could become tedious. By the middle of the third day I was already bored with the miracle of flight and regretted that the Aeronavigator's limited lifting capacity did not allow me to bring my library with me, so that I might have spent my time aloft reading. I resolved to carry at least one or two books with me in the future, while leaving the rest in the wagon.

I did have a charming companion, of course, but our interests and temperaments were sufficiently disparate that our conversation had dwindled to little more than an occasional comment on an unusual bit of scenery. She was more interested in the machinery than in me, and I could not intrude upon her attention without being rude or forward.

The temptation to be forward was certainly there, as her golden hair caught the sunlight and her peculiar attire failed to disguise her slender waist, but I was firmly resolved to be a gentleman and to give no affront, so I kept my attention focused on the landscape beneath us, rather than the beauty beside me.

We did not reach the town that third day; instead we set down in the open desert a few miles to the north, thinking to ride into town by wagon in the morning to resupply before once again taking to the air. Mr. Deerfield and company did not catch up to us until well after dark; fortunately, the huge fire–lit mass of the Aeronavigator made an excellent beacon to lead them to our campsite, so they had little difficulty in locating us.

Nor, it turned out, were they the only ones. We were still eating breakfast and warming up the hydrogen generator the next morning when an unfamiliar voice hailed us. Startled, I turned to see a surprisingly well–dressed gentleman on a fine bay gelding.

"Can I help you, sir?" I called.

"Well, I hope you might," he said. "I'd like to know what the devil that thing is, and what's holding it up!" He pointed at our airship.

"Ah," I said. "That's the Vanderhart Aeronavigator. It's a dirigible balloon, and it's supported by hydrogen gas."

"Is it yours?"

"It is."

He studied the Aeronavigator for a moment, then looked from the machine to me, and then back to the machine. "Would you be this Vanderhart, then?"

"No, sir; I purchased it from the inventor. My name is Derringer, Tom Derringer. And yours?"

"Coats, he said. "George F. Coats. City Councilman for the city of Phoenix. You said Derringer?"

"Yes, sir, I did."

"Any kin to the fellow that invented those little guns?"

"No, sir; my family spells it differently."

"You ever been in Phoenix before, by any chance?"

"No, sir."

He waved at the dirigible. "Has *that* ever been in Phoenix before, then? Before you bought it?"

"No, sir, it has not. I brought it out from New Jersey just last week."

"So it wasn't this that flew over a couple of weeks back?"

"No. It was sitting in a barn in Lakehurst, New Jersey at the time. But I did hear that something was seen flying over your community; that's why I came."

He cocked his head and looked me over carefully. "How's that, son?"

"I read the reports of something flying over Phoenix, and the incident caught my fancy. I decided to come and investigate, and obviously, if I hoped to catch this mystery object, I would myself need some way to fly. Thus, the Aeronavigator."

He stared at me. "Son, are you saying you went out and bought yourself this...this thing, just so you could come out here and chase our mystery object around the sky?"

"Yes, sir, that's it exactly."

"You're an adventurer, then?"

I smiled, pleased that he had recognized this. "I hope to be, yes."

He looked from me to Miss Vanderhart, who fortunately had not yet donned her working attire and was wearing a rather ordinary cotton dress; I would not have cared to explain her flying costume. His gaze then moved on to Mr. Deerfield and the others.

"I don't suppose you would care to come to town with me, Mr. Derringer, and explain this to some other folks? Because if I go back and tell them that without any proof, they're going to think I've been out in the sun too long."

I looked at Miss Vanderhart, and then at Mr. Deerfield.

"I think we can manage our resupply without you," Miss Vanderhart said. "Wouldn't you say so, Henry?"

Mr. Deerfield nodded.

I confess I was curious to see more of Phoenix and to talk to her citizens regarding what they had seen in the skies. I yielded to that temptation. "I should be glad to accompany you, Mr. Coats," I said, "just as soon as I have finished my breakfast. Would you care for a cup of coffee?"

Chapter Eleven

An Interview in Phoenix

The gathering was held in the lobby of the Bank Exchange Hotel, an establishment that would have been unremarkable in New York, but was rather grand for so small and isolated an outpost as Phoenix. About a dozen men and a handful of women were present, and they listened to Mr. Coats with attitudes ranging from astonishment to obvious skepticism as he relayed my explanation.

As with Mad Bill Snedeker, I beg the reader's indulgence regarding the rough language that follows; I wish to keep the flavor of the conversation, which lacked the refinement one would find in the parlors of New York. This was, after all, the frontier, far from the civilizing influences of the East.

"The boy's too young to be an adventurer," protested the possessor of a remarkably fine beard, when Mr. Coats had completed his introductory remarks. "Leastways, by himself."

"I prefer to think otherwise," I replied.

"Seems a dang fool thing to do, though, to set out after that thing we saw without a clear idea what the devil it *is*," said another man.

"I have a theory," I said.

Several members of my audience exchanged glances. *"Do you?"* someone said.

"Indeed I do. I believe that a fellow by the name of McKee got his hands on a supply of metallic aluminum and used it to build himself a dirigible."

"Metallic what? Built a what?"

I smiled. "If I may, gentlemen – did any of you personally observe the mysterious aerial phenomenon?"

"Of course we did!" the bearded man exclaimed. "Danged hard to *miss* it!"

"I believe we *all* saw it, Mr. Derringer," Mr. Coats remarked.

"Could you describe it, then? Can you give me any reason to think it is *not* the Reverend McKee's dirigible?"

"This McKee's a preacher?"

Someone hushed the fellow who asked that, and another man said, "Describing it isn't all that easy, Mr. Derringer. We only saw the underside, and that from a considerable distance."

"Well, let's start with the obvious," I said. "How big was it? The reports I saw didn't say."

"That's because it isn't easy *to* say. Wa'n't nothing up there to judge it against but the sky."

"It was big," another man offered. "*Really* big."

"Bigger than yours," Mr. Coats offered. "*Much* bigger."

I frowned at him. "Then why, sir, did you ask whether the Aeronavigator had been here before?"

"Well, it's like Alvin here says," Mr. Coats explained. "It was powerfully hard to judge the size of the thing. I'd have said, just as John does, that it was a good bit larger than your machine, roughly a dozen times larger, but it might be that it was far closer to the ground than I'd thought, and nowhere near as big. While your machine doesn't bear much resemblance to the one I remembered, I wanted to be sure; a fellow's eyes can play tricks on him."

"Wa'n't anywhere near the ground, that's for dang sure," said the man Mr. Coats had called Alvin. "It was *way* the hell up there!"

"Now, you can't be sure," a woman said.

"I know what I saw!"

"If it was really as high up as it looked, it'd have to be *huge!*"

"Then the dang thing was huge! I tell you, I looked at it up there, and I looked at its shadow on Camelback, and that thing was *miles* up, and hundreds of feet long!"

"Is Camelback that hill I saw on the way here?" I asked Mr. Coats. I had noticed an oddly shaped formation rising from the desert north and east of Phoenix, and the name fit it. He nodded.

"What was it shaped like?" I asked. "Not Camelback; the flying thing." That stopped the argument about its size; the men exchanged glances, looking for a spokesman.

"Like a badly rolled cigar," someone offered at last.

"With...bits sticking out here and there," a woman added.

"Badly rolled," the first man repeated. "As I said."

That did not give me as clear an image as I might have hoped, but it would do.

"It had parts that shone in the sun," said the bearded fellow. "But it wasn't *all* shiny."

"That's right."

"How fast did it move?" I asked.

Again, glances were exchanged.

"Not so very fast," Mr. Coats said.

"It took darn near all day to get across the valley," someone else said.

That was interesting. "Did it make any sound?"

That one got me a chorus of answers. Unfortunately, they were a roughly equal mix of yes and no.

"It hummed," someone said.

"It dang well did not!"

"More of a hiss."

"It didn't make any sound at all! You all are imagining it."

"It could have been bellowing like a mad bull, and we wouldn't have heard it," Mr. Coats said. "It was too far away."

"Which way did it go?" I asked. "Due south?"

"A little east," said the bearded man.

"Towards Tucson," Alvin said.

I was vaguely aware that Tucson was a town further to the south; I knew little about it. I had thought it too small to matter.

"You think you can catch it, Mr. Derringer?"

"I intend to try, sir."

"It's got quite a head start on you. Nigh on a month."

"Indeed it does, but I think I may have the faster machine."

"Where do you reckon it's bound?"

"I don't know," I said, "but if I had to guess, I'd say Mexico City."

The good folk of Phoenix traded looks. "You think this McKee is working for Diaz?" someone asked.

That possibility hadn't even occurred to me, but I didn't care to admit that. "He might be," I said. "Or he might be working with the enemies of the regime."

"What would *they* want with this flying machine?"

"Yes, what good is it?"

"I don't really know," I admitted. "I suppose it's impressive."

"Could be, if he flew it low enough so you could *see* the darn thing!"

"Mr. Derringer," someone asked, "your machine needs to land regularly for fuel and supplies, does it not?"

"It does," I acknowledged.

"Did you know some of us followed that thing you say is this McKee's dirigible? On horseback. And it didn't land, not in all the three days we kept it in sight. We finally lost it when it flew straight over Tortolita Mountain; we couldn't keep up with it in that terrain. How is that possible, if it's a vessel like yours?"

"I don't know," I admitted.

That was the truth; I had not realized that the mystery dirigible had not landed. How *had* McKee managed that, if it really was McKee? What was he using for food, and water, and fuel? I didn't see a better way to answer those questions than to find him and ask.

"Another question, if I may," Mr. Coats asked.

"Yes, sir?"

"You've come all the way from New York to see this thing that flew over Phoenix last month, is that right?"

"It is."

"Might I ask *why?*"

I opened my mouth, and then closed it again as I realized I didn't have a ready answer. I looked around at all those faces, men and women alike, staring at me and waiting for my reply.

"I'm an adventurer," I said at last.

Some of them exchanged glances.

"That ain't an answer," someone said.

"We ain't never heard of you," said another.

"Well, I'm...I'm trying to make a name for myself," I said, "and it seemed to me that finding this mysterious flying machine might be a way to do it."

More looks were exchanged.

"Mr. Derringer," Mr. Coats said, "seems to me that most of the adventurers I've heard of have some *reason* for setting off after a mystery, or hunting a legend. Usually it's to make money – I mean, it's pretty obvious why a fellow would go hunting El

Dorado, as it'd be a bigger strike than Sutter's Mill. Sometimes it's to right a wrong, such as when Jim Carstairs fetched the Ballester girls out of the sand monster's lair caverns last year. But you're saying you got yourself a flying machine and came all this way just because you were *curious*?"

When he put it in those terms, I had to admit that it sounded absurd, but I gathered my wits and said, "Gentlemen, ladies, it's a gamble, I admit it, but it seems to me quite possible that finding this flying machine – if it *is* a machine – might be very profitable. What's more, what I know of the Reverend McKee does not impel me to trust him. I think he might be dangerous, and if he is, the sooner he's found and stopped, the better. Now, if it should prove that there's no money to be made, and McKee's not up to anything nefarious, well, I'll have wasted my time, but that's my own concern, and maybe I'll know better next time."

"Seems a dang fool thing to do," Alvin said.

"It may be," I admitted.

"If the boy wants to waste his time and money, it's no skin off *my* nose," someone said.

"I'd be glad to know what that thing *was*," a lady ventured.

"Adventurers are all crazy," someone muttered – I could not say whom. At other times and in other places I might have protested, but then and there I was not entirely certain I disagreed.

After that we spoke for perhaps another half-hour, but nothing of much interest was said, and at last I said my farewells, and after a brief stop at the telegraph office to reassure my mother that I was alive and well, I headed back to the Aeronavigator.

I found that Miss Vanderhart and my hired men had taken care of all the necessary preparations, and caught up in a sudden enthusiasm that I confess might have been enhanced by a sense that my visit to Phoenix had not been without its embarrassing moments, we quickly put the dirigible back in the air and set out for Tucson.

Chapter Twelve

On McKee's Trail

I will not weary you with every detail of the journey. We did reach Tucson that night, but only after the sun was down, which made landing the Aeronavigator more of an adventure than I really desired it to be. The following day was spent in town, where I spoke to some of the locals and determined that the mysterious flying object had indeed passed within sight of the town two days after it had left Phoenix, still heading south by southeast – presumably bound across the border into Mexico.

I was still resolved to follow it, of course. I wired my mother, then paid off Henry Deerfield and the rest of our crew from Flagstaff – they were not prepared to continue the journey into Mexico. I was able to hire five others in their stead, however, who all had the added virtue of being able to speak at least a little Spanish.

I regret to say that I did *not* speak any Spanish. I had, of course, studied other languages in the course of my training and could read French, German, and Latin fluently. I could write and speak them with somewhat less facility, and I had a little Russian, Greek, and Hebrew, as well. Spanish, unfortunately, had not been included in my curriculum; I could not learn *every* language, after all. I was beginning to regret this; even in

Tucson it would have been useful, and once we were in Mexico – well, I told myself I would make do somehow.

In Tucson we had learned that the mystery object was flying south by southeast. Accordingly, we set out in that direction, following the road across the Mexican border to a town called Nogales. There, we were informed that no such monstrosity had been observed, but upon further questioning – alas, I can give no details, as it was one of our hired men, a handsome fellow by the name of Joshua Herrington, who coaxed the tale out of a drunken woman in a tavern, and I was not present – we heard that the Indios to the east had spoken of a flying mountain that had passed overhead. Clearly, we were too far to the west. We adjusted our course accordingly and resumed our southeasterly flight.

From that point on, our journey slowed significantly. The terrain became so rough, and the roads so poor, that I was tempted to abandon our supply wagons entirely, but Miss Vanderhart reminded me that without the hydrogen generator we would soon be unable to fly. We struggled on, buying supplies and new draft animals where we could, as the occasion arose.

We learned a few tricks to make the journey more comfortable. Miss Vanderhart taught me how to use the boiler's heat to brew coffee and cook food, so that we were able to eat hot meals while aloft, and we both grew adept at using the gas-bag's shade and the breeze from the screws to keep cool in the heat.

On those rare occasions when it rained we remained airborne; the gas-bag kept us dry, for the most part, and after some discussion we concluded that the winds were less likely to damage our craft in open air than on the ground, where it might be blown onto rocks, trees, or buildings. These storms sometimes threw us a few miles off course, but we were able to recover once the weather had cleared. For the most part water simply ran off the Aeronavigator.

We had made our way perhaps two hundred miles into Mexico when I finally discovered that Miss Vanderhart knew Spanish – nor did she tell me; rather, I realized her ability when I saw her blush spectacularly at a comment by a shopkeeper during one of our landings. When I inquired as to why she had not mentioned this sooner, she put her nose in the air and said, "You never asked. Besides, you hired me as an engineer, not a translator."

While this response was the simple truth, I did not think it adequately explained why she had not been more forthcoming. Still, she was entitled to her privacy, and I had not asked. I therefore made a point of asking, politely, just how much Spanish she knew and whether she had any other hidden talents I might want to know about.

She admitted to moderate fluency in Spanish, but declined to volunteer any further information.

The journey had grown extremely tiresome, and as I had been even so early as the flight from Flagstaff to Phoenix, I was constantly reminded of my observation on the train to Flagstaff that a great deal of adventuring could be tedious. That aspect of the trade was almost never mentioned in the stories, and I began to wonder why; surely, I could not be the only adventurer prone to boredom when trapped for hours or days on end in a small conveyance?

Still, I was not ready to abandon my quest; I had come prepared to face guns and monsters, and to yield instead to boredom would hardly speak well for my character. We continued on.

Miss Vanderhart and I found less and less to say to one another as we spent so many long hours crammed into the tiny compartment of the Aeronavigator, and I marveled anew that even something so miraculous as flight could become so very tiresome so quickly. I began to wish I had brought a more extensive library; I had perhaps a dozen books with me, but no more, and would generally carry only one or two aloft at a time, to save weight. There were few bookshops to be found in the wilds of Mexico, of course, and the books I did encounter offered for sale were in Spanish.

I did acquire a map of the country at one of our provisioning stops and spent some time studying it, trying to plot our course on it, with mixed success.

We lost one of our wagons on a mountain road somewhere in Zacatecas, but fortunately, not the one that held the hydrogen generator, and the driver managed to spring clear and suffered only a few bruises.

I continued to wire messages of reassurance to my mother when circumstances permitted, but for much of our journey our stops were in towns that did not have access to anything so modern as a telegraph. I posted a few letters from some of these villages, but held very little confidence in their arrival. Naturally, since we never knew from one day to the next where we would be, I did not expect, nor receive, any responses to my communications; I could only hope that my mother and sister were well.

I believe Miss Vanderhart also wired her parents occasionally, as well, but cannot say so with any certainty.

We followed the reports of the mysterious aerial phenomenon, whether it was called a flying mountain, or a solid cloud, or by some other fanciful name. This often led to shifting our course further to the east, and upon studying maps

I had acquired at our various stops I eventually concluded that we were *not* heading for Mexico City. Unless the mystery object greatly altered its course, we would miss the capital by at least fifty miles. What's more, our quarry was veering even further to the east.

"Is he heading out to sea?" I mused.

"If he does, we can't follow," Miss Vanderhart said. "Or not very far, in any case."

We had lost some ground in the central highlands, but now, as we moved down out of the mountains toward the coast, we began to gain on what I still believed to be McKee's dirigible. We had been flying for about five weeks when I first caught the glint of sunlight on water on the horizon and realized we were indeed within sight of the Gulf of Mexico.

That afternoon we landed on a beach a few miles southeast of Alvarado, within sight of the coastal highway, and as the sun set behind us we waited for the wagons. Our hired hands had instructions to resupply in Alvarado, as usual, but we expected them to need extra time, as Alvarado was on the northern side of a large inlet, and we were on the south. We had seen a ferry in operation as we passed over, so we were reasonably certain they would reach us eventually.

I sat by the Aeronavigator, a mug of coffee in my hand, and looked out over the calm blue waters of the Gulf of Mexico, trying to convince myself that McKee, or whoever was piloting the mysterious craft, would not have simply headed out to sea.

I could not quite manage it. Our quarry was somehow able to stay airborne indefinitely and might therefore be bound for one of the Caribbean islands, or even for Africa, on the far side of the Atlantic. I did not understand how McKee, or whoever it was, could possibly have carried sufficient supplies for a journey of this length! Food, water, fuel – how could *any* airship, even one constructed of the miracle metal called aluminum, carry so much?

I was beginning to think that my first attempt at adventuring was going to be a complete failure and was about to say as much to Miss Vanderhart when we heard the rattling of a wagon approaching. I rose, and saw that I was indeed one of ours, the wagon carrying the hydrogen generator. It was driven by Joshua Herrington, accompanied by a fellow named Leonard Raymond. We had hired both these in Tucson, and they had come with us much farther than I had expected. Both Mr. Herrington and Mr. Raymond gave every appearance of being quite excited about something; the instant they spotted me, Mr. Herrington began waving frantically.

Startled, curious, and eager to hear whatever had so disturbed his equanimity, I hurried up the slope.

"Mr. Derringer!" he called as I approached. "They were here!"

While that was good news, it hardly seemed sufficiently surprising to justify Herrington's behavior. Puzzled, I walked up as he brought the wagon to a halt beside the highway. "Yes?" I said. "The airship was seen passing near here?"

"More than that!" he said. "The locals say that four *gringos* came into Alvarado, asking questions and buying supplies."

That *was* startling – and encouraging. It meant that McKee was not enough of a miracle worker to have created an entirely self–sustaining airship. I glanced at Mr. Raymond, who nodded vigorously. I looked up the road behind them.

Noticing my gaze, Herrington explained, "The other wagon's on the next ferry. Couldn't fit both at once."

"Ah," I said, relieved that there was an explanation for its absence. "Tell me your news then, gentlemen!"

Herrington handed the reins to Raymond, then jumped down and began his tale.

A mere three days ago, it seemed, four men had arrived in Alvarado. They were clearly *Norteamericanos*, from their accents – all four spoke Spanish, but none of them spoke it very well. They purchased large quantities of salt beef and salt pork, several barrels of corn meal, and four tons of coal, and ordered it all to be delivered to a particular stretch of empty land just outside town. They had also inquired about the situation in Yucatan – were the Maya still in rebellion? Had Diaz' troops managed to subdue Chan Santa Cruz?

At that point I interrupted. I knew who General Diaz was, of course, and I knew something of the history of the Maya, but I had never before heard of Chan Santa Cruz. I asked for an explanation.

Neither Herrington nor Raymond knew very much about the matter, but it seemed that a cult called the Talking Cross had sprung up among the rebellious Maya, centered on a vision of a cross that somehow conveyed the word of God, providing divine encouragement for their resistance to Mexican rule. Thus inspired, one Maya faction had seized control of a fairly extensive area and set up their own capital in a town called Chan Santa Cruz – "Little Holy Cross," in English.

"Why would they ask about *that?*" Miss Vanderhart asked from behind me. Until she spoke, I had not realized she was there.

"I haven't the slightest idea, Miss," Raymond said, taking off his hat in acknowledgment of a lady's presence.

"But we're just getting to the *good* part, ma'am," Herrington said, smiling boyishly.

"Go on, then," I told him.

"Well, these four men asked all these questions and ordered their supplies, and then had everything delivered to a patch of land near the lagoon, and some of the townspeople were mighty curious about why they were putting it in that spot, seein' as how they hadn't any horses or wagons, not so much as a dog cart. So they went to watch. And while they were there, a great shining thing like a silver ship came sailing through the air and lowered ropes, some of them with big baskets on the end. The four men attached the ropes to the barrels and boxes and heaved the bags of coal into big baskets, and then climbed into the baskets on top of the coal, and the whole lot of them – barrels and baskets and men – were hauled up into the flying ship, which sailed away to the south."

I realized that my mouth had fallen open during this recitation. "Ropes!" I said. "*That's* why they never have to land!"

"Four tons of coal!" Miss Vanderhart said. "Their lifting capacity must be *astonishing!*"

"They were asking about the rebellious Maya!" I exclaimed. "That must be their destination!"

"And Mr. Derringer, they're only three days ahead of you!" Raymond said.

"Why, that's right!" I said. "We should be able to catch up to them soon."

As I said that, though, I noticed that the smile had vanished from Mr. Herrington's face. "Ah, Mr. Derringer," he said. "You want us to go to Chan Santa Cruz?"

"If that's where McKee's taking his airship, indeed I do!"

Herrington shook his head. "I won't do it, sir."

"What?"

"I won't do it. I won't go a mile farther east than Merida. They say there isn't a white man left alive within fifty miles of Chan Santa Cruz – the Maya have killed them all."

That was rather disconcerting, to say the least. I turned to Mr. Raymond.

He shook his head. "I won't go there, either, Mr. Derringer. *I'm* no adventurer."

I looked from one to the other, baffled. As a would-be adventurer, *I* could scarcely turn back at this point, but how could I insist these men risk their lives on my behalf?

Behind me, Miss Vanderhart cleared her throat. "We'll just have to catch up to your Reverend McKee before he gets that far," she said.

"Exactly!" I said, relieved by this suggestion. We were not yet in Yucatan, and I understood from what Mr. Herrington and Mr. Raymond had said that most of the peninsula was probably still under the control of the Mexican government. "Let's have a look at the map, shall we?"

Our other three employees arrived while we were consulting the map, and one of them, a Texan named John Schwerin, turned out to have some knowledge of the war being fought in the territory – or at least, he had heard and retained more of the local gossip than had any of the rest of us. He indicated that roughly two–thirds of the Yucatan peninsula, the north and west, was in Mexican hands and that we could travel safely in this area. The cities of Merida and Campeche, and the great henequen plantations surrounding them, were no more dangerous than many of the areas we had already traversed.

The other third of the peninsula, however, was Maya territory, where any white man who set foot there was risking his life – though the British, operating from their base at Belize Town in British Honduras, traded with the Maya, selling them the guns and powder they needed to resist any Mexican advance. I could not in good conscience ask any of my five drovers – nor, for that matter, Miss Vanderhart – to accompany me into those jungles.

Not all of the Maya were followers of the Talking Cross cult, according to Mr. Schwerin; the Cruzob, as they were known, were by far the largest of the tribes or states within the Maya territory, but there were also factions known as the Ixcanha and Icaiche who did not follow the new faith, recognizing neither the authority of Chan Santa Cruz, nor that of Mexico City. It all sounded quite complex – and quite dangerous.

If McKee, or whoever was piloting the great airship, was headed into that unhappy land, then this pursuit might well be an adventure worthy of the name.

Of course, we did not know his destination. Perhaps he was bound for Merida, or the area around Valladolid that Mr. Schwerin said had been in dispute at one time years ago but was now fairly secure, and his inquiries had only been intended to ascertain whether the situation had changed since he had last received word.

"We will continue the pursuit," I said, "until such time as we reach hostile country. At that point the six of you will go no further, and I will proceed alone."

Miss Vanderhart put her hands on her hips and demanded, "And just how will you do that, without my assistance and without the hydrogen generator?"

"My dear Miss Vanderhart, I have watched you operate the machinery for more than a month now; I would be a sorry excuse for a man if I had not learned the basics. I think I can fly the Aeronavigator myself. The hydrogen generator does present a problem, I admit, but I think I can improvise – I will stay aloft as long as possible, using as little fuel as possible, and following our quarry's example, I will lower myself down on a rope, rather than landing the craft, when I need food or water. Am I correct in assuming that if I do not vent any of the hydrogen, the Aeronavigator can stay airborne for several days?"

She stared at me, and if I read her expression correctly she thought me a fool, but she did not say so in so many words.

"I don't know," she said at last. "There is some seepage, as you may have noticed."

Indeed I had; by late afternoon our altitude was always significantly lower than when we first set out in the morning, despite the consumption of coal, water, and food. I had, I thought, taken that into account; I estimated that with care, I should be able to keep the Aeronavigator above the trees for eight to ten days. I hoped that would be enough. I nodded. "Nonetheless," I said, "I would venture to try it."

She did not reply, but glanced around at our hirelings. I followed suit, and discovered that all five were now staring at me as if I was quite mad.

"I *am* an adventurer, after all," I said. "I expect to take some risks."

Mr. Schwerin was the first to react. He shrugged, and said, "No skin off my nose. I'll stop when the locals warn us, and what you do from there, Mr. Derringer, is entirely up to you."

Mr. Herrington was not quite so calm, but in the end his reaction amounted to much the same decision. Likewise Mr. Raymond, Mr. Lopez, and Mr. Murphy.

Miss Vanderhart was not as immediately agreeable. "I have no desire to see you wreck my father's flying machine," she said.

"It is *not* your father's machine," I pointed out. "It's mine. I paid him handsomely for it."

"It is my father's *creation*, whoever may presently hold title," she insisted. "I would prefer not to see it destroyed."

"I have no intention of destroying it."

"No, you're just going to fly it into a wilderness occupied by bloodthirsty savages, alone and unsupported, inadequately supplied, without the proper training!"

I smiled at her. "At our present rate of speed I believe you have three or four more days to train me before we reach the frontier – assuming we do reach it and don't find the Reverend McKee hovering over Merida."

"I never agreed to train you!"

"But you did say you don't want to see the machine destroyed."

She glowered at me. "*Mister* Derringer – I will do as I see fit, and whether that includes training you to operate the Aeronavigator remains to be determined. Whether it includes accompanying you into rebel territory is also not your decision to make, nor is it a decision that has been made – I will judge the situation when the occasion arises and will act accordingly, whether *you* like it or not."

"After getting to know you these past several weeks, Miss Vanderhart, I would scarcely expect otherwise."

She glared at me with an even greater intensity and seemed to swell with outrage, but said nothing. I confess I did not entirely see why she should be outraged, but I had spent enough time with her to know what I was seeing and to have expected this reaction, senseless though it might be.

If the truth be known, I found her anger oddly attractive, though of course I would never be so foolish as to tell her that. Our relationship was a purely professional one, and I was determined it would remain so; anything more than that was more likely to be due to our constant proximity than any true sympathy of spirit.

"That's settled, then," I said. "We will continue the pursuit, with the understanding that the wagons and their drivers will stop at the first sign that we are entering dangerous ground, and I will continue, leaving the equipment behind, while Miss Vanderhart comes with me or not, as she sees fit. I hope, Miss Vanderhart, that you will condescend to teach me how to handle the Aeronavigator properly, but I cannot compel you to do so."

"Good enough," Mr. Schwerin answered. The other four men nodded as well, accepting the plan with only a little grumbling.

Miss Vanderhart was clearly not satisfied, but said nothing.

In fact, she said nothing more to me for the next two days.

Chapter Thirteen

Above the Jungles of the Yucatan

I had hoped that our quarry would follow the coast, turning at the port of Coatzacoalcos, the most southerly point of that portion of the Gulf of Mexico, from a southeasterly course to east and then north once more, rounding the Gulf to head for Campeche or Merida, but that was not to be. Reports from locals in Coatzacoalcos indicated that the mystery craft was continuing east by southeast, following the road toward what the map called San Juan Bautista de la Villa Hermosa, but which the natives referred to as simply Villa Hermosa. We were still gaining on it.

A look at the map gave me the notion that perhaps McKee, or whoever it was piloting the other airship, was headed for Belize Town. Could he be working with the British, perhaps? But in Villa Hermosa they told us the metal cloud had headed due east – directly toward Chan Santa Cruz.

I sent my mother a telegram from Villa Hermosa warning her that I would probably be incommunicado for some time, as we were heading into areas where neither telegraph nor post were likely to be found.

We flew on, but our progress slowed – the roads were deteriorating as we headed inland, so that the wagons were not able to keep up our customary pace. There were days when we did not pass over a single town, but only scattered farms amid vast expanses of jungle.

Finally, we reached a village where we could find no one who spoke decent Spanish, let alone English, and where no one would accept either American dollars or Mexican pesos for the supplies we wanted to buy. These people were not openly hostile; rather, they were curious about both the airship and the wagons, eager to communicate with signs and scraps of broken Spanish, and happy to barter. They did not seem surprised by our coloring or features or clothing, so I believe they had seen white people before, but obviously not often.

They had no coal to sell us for the boiler or the hydrogen generator, which was, to say the least, inconvenient.

John Schwerin proved to have a knack for making himself understood despite the language barrier; I believe he had somehow picked up a few words of Maya. He inquired whether they had seen another, larger airship, and they confirmed that yes, they had, two days before. It had passed over without stopping, heading east – or according to my compass, east by northeast. I found myself wishing that the talented Mr. Schwerin might accompany me into the eastern wilds, but he had repeatedly made it plain that he had no interest in doing so.

Indeed, that night Mr. Schwerin, Mr. Herrington, and the others informed me that they would go no further and intended to turn back in the morning. They demanded their wages.

"Give me one more day," I said. "Help me get the Aeronavigator fully stocked and off the ground tomorrow, and I will give you your full pay and send you home with my blessing. You can sell the wagons in Coatzacoalcos and book passage home by sea, if you like."

Herrington snorted. "Can't get to Tucson by sea!"

"You can get to Corpus Christi, in Texas, and get the train to Flagstaff," I said. "Or there may be some better route, I can't say."

"It's something to talk about," Mr. Raymond acknowledged.

"How will *you* get home, sir?" Mr. Murphy asked. "Assuming, of course, you live long enough for that to be an issue."

"I'll manage," I said. "I appreciate your concern, but I'm sure I'll be fine."

Miss Vanderhart snorted. I turned to her.

"Will you be accompanying these men back to civilization, Miss Vanderhart?" I asked.

She looked the lot of them over disdainfully, then turned to me and said, "You offer me a choice between traveling with five cowards, or with one lunatic."

"I scarcely think anyone who has come this far with us can rightly be called a coward, Miss Vanderhart," I remonstrated. "I believe that was uncalled for."

"I notice you make no protest to being labeled a lunatic!"

"I am hardly in a position to judge my own sanity."

"At least you recognize that much!" She glared at me. "Better one fool than five," she said at last. "I will stay with my father's machine and trust to your claims of expertise and education to see us somehow safely out of this wilderness." With that, she stormed off to her tent.

When she had gone, I told the others, "My sincere apologies, gentlemen, for allowing her to impugn your bravery. You have all been exceptionally helpful for all these past two months, and I appreciate it very much, even if Miss Vanderhart does not."

"Oh, we don't mind," Mr. Herrington replied. "She's just scared, and that makes her mad."

"Scared?" I said, startled.

"'Course she is. We all are. She just doesn't want to admit it."

That analysis caught me entirely by surprise, and I could not immediately form any estimate of its accuracy. I looked thoughtfully at Miss Vanderhart's tent. Only a few seconds later did it strike me that Herrington had admitted he and his companions were scared, and none of the others had objected.

"Do you think there is cause for fear here?" I asked.

"Mr. Derringer, we are out in the middle of the Mexican jungles, maybe no more than a few miles from a bunch of savages who are said to kill any white man they meet, and that's without considering panthers or giant snakes or any other creatures that might be lurking out there in the dark. The folks in this village seem kind enough, but for all we know they're just waiting until we're asleep before they slit our throats. I'd say there's plenty of grounds for...well, a goodly caution, at the very least."

I could not argue with that. It occurred to me that in fact, these five had shown far more courage on this journey than I had. While I had floated safely above all the dangers, they had made their way through hundreds of miles of unfamiliar territory, facing the risk of bandits, beasts, and a myriad other hazards. I had not really appreciated the situation.

"True enough," I said. "Thank you." I yawned. "I believe I'll turn in, then."

"Good enough," Herrington said. "Murphy's got the first watch."

I nodded and retired to my tent.

The night passed without incident, and in the morning we set about jamming as much food, water, and fuel into the Aeronavigator as we could reasonably expect it to lift. When that was done we fired up the hydrogen generator, planning to burn all the remaining coal and inflate the gas-bag to its greatest possible volume.

By mid-afternoon the bamboo strakes were beginning to creak warningly, and the tie-down ropes were stretching badly as the craft struggled to rise. The hydrogen envelope had expanded to a larger size than I had ever seen, and Miss Vanderhart was eyeing it worriedly.

At last she said, "I don't think it can hold any more."

I agreed – indeed, I had been waiting for her to say so for some time. "Good," I said. "Then let us be off."

"This late in the day?"

"The plan, Miss Vanderhart, is to stay airborne night and day from now on, so does it really matter when we ascend?"

She had no good response to that, and we set about disconnecting the hydrogen generator and making a final check of our preparations. Our hired men assisted us this one last time, and then waved farewell as we boarded the Aeronavigator. They would be spending one more night in the village, and then heading west in the morning. Messrs. Raymond and Murphy cast off the final lines, and with a lurch our airship shot skyward.

The heavy load combined with the distended gas-bag to distort the craft's usual behavior. Rather than its usual gentle motion it jerked and swayed like a staggering drunk, but it did rise, carrying the two of us into the afternoon sky.

The platform was so jammed with supplies that we could scarcely move; we had less than half our usual space, and the vehicle had never been spacious to begin with. Miss Vanderhart had positioned herself at the controls, of course, while I had taken up a post where I could feed coal into the firebox. We had a good head of steam, so as soon as we were clear of the trees around the village she threw the lever that unlocked the airscrews and set them spinning.

The added weight and increased size meant that the Aeronavigator's movement was far slower and less agile than our usual, but it did move, pressing slowly eastward.

I believe I have mentioned more than once that even something as wondrous as powered flight can grow tedious through excessive familiarity. Add in our restricted movements, our slower progress, and the dull sameness of the jungle canopy below us, and you can imagine that this part of our travels was not exactly delightful. Add further our worries that we had overstrained our craft, and that we might not be able to locate the mystery airship before our own reached its limits, and you will see that we were unlikely to take much joy in our circumstances.

The truth is, though, that the excitement of our situation was not entirely unpleasant. One way or another, we were now committed, and our long expedition would soon be reaching a climax – either we would find our quarry, or we would be forced down somewhere in the wilderness beneath us when the Aeronavigator gave out.

I had given some thought to what we might do should we fail in our quest. If we found no sign of the mysterious flyer ahead, we could turn either north, and head for Merida, or south, and try for Belize Town. If we were forced down before choosing a destination, and had to make our way through the jungles, I thought Belize Town might be the safer choice, since the Maya were not actively fighting the British as they were the Mexicans; their southern border should be less heavily guarded.

Of course, if we did not find the mystery craft, I had wasted a great deal of time and money. Flying an airship across most of Mexico was interesting, in its fashion, but it did not really accomplish much. I doubted it would qualify me for membership in the Order of Theseus.

And if we *did* find our quarry, it might prove to be a complete anticlimax. Whoever was flying it had not kept it entirely secret, after all; it had been seen everywhere from Phoenix to Villa Hermosa. It might be merely a test flight. Or perhaps it was being delivered to a buyer in Belize Town for eventual transport to England. Just what I intended to do upon finding it was not clear.

Chasing it had seemed a good idea back in New York, but here in the Yucatan the benefits were much less obvious. I had, perhaps, gone off half-cocked in my eagerness to begin my career as an adventurer.

But it was too late for doubts. I was here.

As was Miss Vanderhart. I regretted allowing her to accompany me, but I was unsure how, short of physical violence, I could have prevented it. I had no right to tell her what to do, and she had made it perfectly clear that if I tried, she would still do as she thought best. I owned the Aeronavigator, so in theory I might have forbidden her access to it, but on the other hand I had promised her father, as part of the purchase agreement, that I would entrust flying it to her.

Accordingly, the two of us flew on to the east, into the rebellious Maya territory, and I did not question her presence.

Night fell, and the splendor of the tropical night spread across the sky, the stars blazing unhindered by the smoke and mist of my northerly home, or the lights of human habitation. A few faint fires could be seen here and there below us, like tiny sparks in the black carpet of jungle, but for the most part the world below was dark, while the sky above was strewn with the glories of heaven. We had never flown by night before, and at first the experience was thrilling, an awe-inspiring change from the drab routine of daytime flight, as we hung in empty space surrounded by stars.

Neither of us was eager to sleep, but exhaustion did finally overtake me, and I dozed for some time. Miss Vanderhart awakened me some time later, while it was still full dark, so that I could take a turn at the controls while she rested, and I did my best to keep the craft steady and to make good speed. The stars made navigation easy; I am not sure what we would have done had the night been overcast. I needed merely keep us headed east.

We did not know with any certainty whether the mystery airship was still proceeding eastward, but we had no reason to think otherwise, and what other course could we take?

I regret to say that I was dozing at my post by the time the eastern sky began to brighten, lulled by the steam engine's steady chuffing; I told myself that should anything go wrong that rhythmic sound would change, and that change would bring me alert. I could have awakened Miss Vanderhart, but I had lost track of time – I had somehow not thought to check my watch when she awoke me, so I did not know how long I had been on duty, nor whether I had yet done my fair share. Besides, I wanted to see the dawn. I told myself that I would wake her once the sun was up.

Thus she was still sleeping, and I was not fully alert, when the sun's light burst over the horizon, flooding the sky with color and light, and transforming the unbroken blackness below us to a deep, dark green. In my mazy state it took me a few moments to realize, when my eyes opened again, that a new day was upon us.

At last, though, the situation registered upon my consciousness, and I decided that I had done my share. The time had come to wake Miss Vanderhart and snatch a few hours of sleep. I checked the gauges, heaved a bucket of coal into the firebox, adjusted the valves, and then scanned the horizon to make sure there was nothing she need worry about.

And that was when I saw it, far off in the distance – not directly ahead of us, but slightly to the north of our present heading. It was a tiny black speck edged with silvery brightness, far, far away over the jungle.

I sucked in my breath.

That was it. That *had* to be it. If I was anywhere remotely close to the truth in my estimate of its location, it was much too big to be a bird, and it did not move like a bird, in any case – in fact, it did not appear to be moving at all.

"Miss Vanderhart!" I called. "Miss Vanderhart, come and see!"

There was no response, and I turned to see her still slumped by the rail, sound asleep.

"Miss Vanderhart!" I called again. "*Betsy!*"

She stirred at last and opened her eyes. Then, remembering where she was, her head snapped up and she called back, "Is something wrong? Are we losing altitude?"

"No, no," I said. I glanced down, and judged that we were still a thousand feet or so up – something, I guiltily realized, I had not checked in hours. "No, it's not that. Look ahead! Just a little to the left, way out there!"

She clambered to her feet, brushed a little coal soot from her clothing, and then let her gaze follow my finger out to the patch of sky I indicated. She thrust her head forward slightly, and although I could not see her face from this angle, I guessed she was probably squinting.

"What *is* that?" she said.

"That," I said, "is our quarry. *That*, if I am not mistaken, is Hezekiah McKee's aluminum airship."

Chapter Fourteen

The Aluminum Airship

We adjusted our course and boosted the boiler pressure as high as we dared, to coax the maximum speed from the Aeronavigator. Since we were no longer limited by the need to keep within sight of our wagons, we were able to drive forward at a higher velocity than we had customarily maintained.

At first I steered us directly toward the other craft, but after an hour or so I realized that it, too, was moving, and that we would miss it if we continued on a straight line toward where we had first seen it. Instead we shifted our heading slightly to the south, so that our courses would converge.

The other airship was moving, but we were moving faster and gaining on it. That black speck grew ever so slowly larger.

The morning wore on, and we chugged steadily across the sky, trailing steam and coal smoke. Due to the sustained high speed our stocks of water and fuel dwindled faster than hydrogen escaped our gas–bag, and as the day progressed the sun warmed the remaining gas, so we were rising gradually higher into the tropical air as we flew. I hoped that our reserves would hold out long enough to intercept McKee's vehicle. It appeared certain that we could stay airborne, but our continued ability to maneuver was more questionable.

As we drew nearer to the other vessel it became even more doubtful that we would have enough fuel to overtake it, because we began to realize just how big it was, and how far ahead of us. When we had first seen it, it had seemed a mere speck, and I had judged it to be perhaps five or six miles away. In making that calculation, I had horribly underestimated its size; when more details became visible I increased my estimate to twenty miles distant, and then to fifty – though by then we were steadily reducing the gap.

The day wore on, and we continued to approach the mystery craft. The sun rose to its zenith and passed overhead, into the west, so that the shadows that had hidden our quarry's features slid away. While Miss Vanderhart kept the steam engine burning, I found my Porro–prism binoculars and studied the strange vessel.

Most of its volume was a gigantic gas–bag, one that dwarfed our own ninety-foot device, that was indeed shaped something like a cigar, just as the witnesses in Phoenix had said. It was more bluntly rounded fore and aft than the Aeronavigator's balloon, and much larger in every dimension. Where ours was white silk – somewhat discolored now – theirs was some drab gray material. Where ours was caged in shellacked bamboo, theirs was caged in gleaming silvery metal – aluminum, I assumed. The framework was arranged very differently, as well; the Aeronavigator's bamboo struts ran fore and aft, meeting in a rounded point at either end, and bound by ropes at five points along the way, while the other airship's gas–bag was bound by at least a dozen gleaming metal vertical bands and one long horizontal bar running its full length.

As for the rest of the structure, the Aeronavigator had only the single compartment slung beneath the gas–bag, holding the steam engine, the driveshaft, the steering mechanisms, our supplies, and ourselves, with the triple airscrews protruding at either end. The other vessel was more complex. It had an undercarriage that presumably held the crew and cargo – an undercarriage that was, incidentally, larger than the entirety of the Aeronavigator – but it also had three gigantic engines arranged around the gas–bag, one at the top and one on either side, their airscrews turning too rapidly to be seen as anything but faint blurs. These engines were steadily puffing white vapor, so I concluded that McKee was relying on ordinary steam engines, rather than any more exotic propulsion. There were huge vanes at the rear of the gas–bag that were plainly intended to aid in steering and stability, rather like a fish's fins. And there were four other relatively small compartments, two fore and two aft, of no obvious purpose, projecting from the sides of the gas–bag.

When I say "relatively small," you must understand that the more important word is "relatively." When we got close enough to make out more detail, I determined that each of these four side compartments was a half-cylinder perhaps eight or nine feet high and seven or eight feet across, with its flat side against the gas–bag, and a slit running around its curved exterior perhaps halfway up.

The main undercarriage, which I judged to be at least a hundred feet long, thirty feet wide, and two or more stories in height, was mostly enclosed, rather than being openwork like our own. There were, however, small open galleries at the stern, on the lower deck at the prow, and midway along either side. I occasionally glimpsed figures moving in these galleries, which gave me a way to measure the size of the thing.

All of the major components appeared to be constructed of that same gleaming metal, or of gray fabric. Combined with its size, I could readily see now why observers on the ground would call it a metal cloud, or a flying mountain.

We flew on through the afternoon, gaining only slowly on the immense craft, and by sunset we were still miles away. As night fell, we could see lights blossom aboard the other airship – what I assumed were lanterns shone in several of the main compartment's windows.

We had no lights aboard our own vessel save the glow from the firebox. I had a handful of candles somewhere in my luggage, but there was no safe way to use them in our gently swaying craft, mere feet below a gigantic bag of highly flammable hydrogen. I envied the unknown aeronauts ahead who had such comforts.

As before, Miss Vanderhart and I took turns standing watch and keeping the Aeronavigator on course. Those lanterns I coveted made it easy to maintain our bearings – there was no mistaking their yellow glow for the cold white of the stars, or for the dim orange of campfires in the jungle below.

The lanterns were doused, one by one, as the night wore on, until all but one were dark. That last lonely light, near the front of the upper deck of the main compartment, served as our beacon until well after midnight, and I was glad that our two ships were angled such that it remained visible. When at last it, too, went dark, we had to rely on the black outline of the gigantic vessel against the stars – or, as morning approached, against the brightening eastern sky.

By sunrise we had closed the gap to less than a mile – and we were not the only ones to notice. I could see men in the other airship's fore and aft galleries, silhouetted against the dawn; while it was hard to be certain, I had little doubt they were watching us.

Not long after, the other airship slowed and turned to cross our path. Miss Vanderhart noticed as quickly as I did myself, and asked, "Do you want to go on?"

"Yes, of course," I said. "We could hardly hope to approach undetected in an airship."

"You aren't concerned about their intentions?"

I hesitated before replying, "I think 'concerned' is not precisely the right word."

"What, exactly, do you guess they'll do? Surely they aren't expecting us."

"I would think they'll be as curious about us as we are about them. I expect to exchange information."

"You don't think they'll just shoot us?"

Startled, I lowered the binoculars and turned to her. "Why would they do *that*?" I asked.

"Because we have appeared out of nowhere, uninvited, and might intend to meddle in their plans. Shooting us would reduce any risk we might present."

"But that would be murder! How could they hope to get away with such a crime?"

She stared at me. "Mr. Derringer, they are in a bloody great *airship*, above the jungles of the Yucatan! Who on Earth is going to bring them to trial? This isn't New York; it's barely even Mexico. I very much doubt that the Maya Indians are going to place the crew of an *airship* under arrest!"

"I...uh..." I felt indescribably foolish as this obvious truth registered.

"I thought you were an adventurer! Surely you realize that civilized law does not apply in uncivilized lands!"

"I am...inexperienced, as yet," I mumbled.

"At this rate, you won't live long enough to remedy that!"

"Oh, but really, Miss Vanderhart, why would they shoot us? We are their potential comrades, brother aeronauts!"

She snorted. Then she glanced up. "I wonder," she said, "whether a bullet would be sufficient to ignite the hydrogen."

"What?" I glanced up, as well, at the dirty white silk envelope above our heads, trying to remember my chemistry lessons. "I...I don't *think* so," I said. "I know hydrogen is highly combustible – "

"Explosive, more like it."

"Fine, explosive, but I don't believe it to be as volatile as all that. Bullets do not generally burn their targets. If I correctly recall what I've read, I think an actual spark would be required to ignite the hydrogen."

"But a bullet would most certainly punch a hole through silk."

"Yes, it would. But I still see no reason to expect gunplay. We don't know whether they're armed at all!"

"They've flown that tremendous machine of theirs all the way across Mexico into territory where it's said any white man is shot on sight – could they *possibly* be so stupid as to *not* be armed?"

"Perhaps not," I admitted. I might have said more, but just then our conversation was interrupted by an unfamiliar voice, shouting across the gulf between the two flying machines.

"Ahoy!" it said, barely intelligible over the steady beat of our engine. "Who are you?"

I turned to see a man in a black coat standing in the other airship's side gallery, one arm raised. "My name's Tom Derringer!" I called back, at the top of my lungs. "Who are you?"

"You're a messenger?"

"*Tom Derringer!*"

As I bellowed my name again, I saw the great airscrews slowing. The other vessel was cutting its speed.

"Bring us alongside," I told Miss Vanderhart, gesturing.

"This isn't a boat," she snapped. "But I'll try." She peered ahead. "We'll need to dump some weight, though – it's higher than we are."

"That won't be necessary," I said quickly. "I just want to be close enough to speak. And I'll want the engine shut down, so we can hear. If we're under them, rather than alongside, that should serve."

She nodded and adjusted the Aeronavigator's trim. We chugged steadily closer to the immense aerial craft, and as we did it turned broadside to us and slowed. The astute reader will understand that it was very hard to judge our positions in mid-air, with nothing around us to orient us save the jungle hundreds of feet below, so I can't say that the bigger vessel was motionless, but I can say that it *appeared* to be.

As we drew near it loomed over us, and our own forward velocity decreased, until at last we came to a relative standstill perhaps fifty feet away from the side gallery, and twenty or thirty feet below it.

The crew of the aluminum airship had watched our approach. A dozen men crowded the various gallery rails, observing us with keen interest. I could not hear what was said, but I saw them pointing, talking to one another, and gesticulating. As we reached our intended position I waved, but to my surprise, no one waved back.

Most of these observers wore black uniforms of some sort, but were otherwise reasonably varied in size, shape, and coloring. One tall fellow had his brown hair trimmed in a very peculiar fashion – the sides of his head were shaven, while the central portion was brushed up into a sort of crest, reminiscent of some illustrations I had seen of the Iroquois warriors of old. Another heavily built man wore a kilt, rather than the usual uniform trousers, though I could not make out the tartan from so far away.

One man, of well above average height, and slender enough that one might be tempted to call him gaunt, stood calmly at the rail of the forward gallery, taking no part in the discussion. He wore a frock coat and topper, rather than the uniform, and held a speaking trumpet. When I waved, he lifted this device to his mouth and called, "Ahoy! Who are you?"

I was reasonably certain that his was not the voice that had asked that question before. I raised my own hands and cupped them around my mouth as I shouted, "My name is Tom Derringer! Whom do I have the honor of addressing?"

"Derringer?"

"Yes! Tom Derringer!"

"Any relation to Jack Derringer?"

It would seem that in some circles, my father's name truly *was* better known than Henry Deringer's. I found that curiously satisfying and called back, "I am his son, sir! And you are?"

"My name's McKee. What are you doing here? Where did you get that contraption?"

I felt a rush of pride at having my theories confirmed. "The Reverend Captain Hezekiah McKee from Charleston, late of Flagstaff?"

"The same. I repeat, Mr. Derringer, what are you doing here, and what is that thing bearing you?"

"This is the Vanderhart Aeronavigator! I purchased it to enable my pursuit of your own very impressive craft!"

"Indeed? How did you know that the McKee Skymaster existed?"

"I learned, sir, of your acquisition of a vast store of what I believe to be aluminum from the Lost City of the Mirage, and put that together with reports of a mysterious object seen in the skies over Phoenix. I followed you hither to see whether my guess was correct!"

"It would seem that it was," McKee replied. "Now that you are here, what will you do? Have you come to join me in my enterprise?"

"I confess, sir, that I do not know the nature of your enterprise! Curiosity in that regard is what prompted me to come."

For a moment there was no reply, and an uncomfortable silence descended. I could hear machinery puffing and whirring aboard the vessel McKee called the Skymaster, and snatches of unintelligible conversation from its crew, while closer at hand the tropical breeze hummed through the Aeronavigator's rigging. I could see McKee eyeing me thoughtfully; then he turned and whispered something to someone I could not see clearly before raising the speaking trumpet and addressing me again.

"That seems a great deal of trouble and expense to satisfy mere curiosity," he called.

"I suppose it is," I replied. "I had the resources, though, and chose to employ them in this fashion in hopes I might follow in my father's footsteps. Would you be so kind as to explain to me your purpose in building your airship and flying it to this uncivilized place?"

Once again, there was a silence. Then McKee lifted his megaphone and said, "I intend to build an empire. Would you care to join me?"

Chapter Fifteen

The Reverend McKee's Plan

At first I did not believe I had heard him correctly. You will understand that our conversation was conducted under circumstances that were far from ideal, shouting back and forth between two airships that were drifting in the wind at considerable, and slightly different, altitudes.

"Build a *what?*" I called back.

"An empire," he repeated. "With myself as the emperor. I will need a court, however, and a man such as yourself might well find a high place therein."

I blinked, then glanced at Miss Vanderhart, who shrugged in an unladylike manner. I turned back to McKee.

"Would you do me the kindness of explaining your plans in greater detail, sir?" I shouted.

"I intend, Mr. Derringer, to present myself to the Maya of Chan Santa Cruz as a divine messenger sent to lead them in a crusade. With their aid, and with the resources of this airship, I expect to conquer all of Mexico in short order – I believe President Diaz to be a pragmatic man, and I think he will accept reasonable terms of surrender. From there, who knows?"

"I don't believe I understand."

McKee turned and said something to one of his crew, then addressed me again. "I think it simple enough, Mr. Derringer. I have not been pleased with the course of history since the defeat of the Confederacy, so I hope to change it. When I was fortunate enough to visit the Lost City of the Mirage, I saw that its builders had made extensive use of a strange metal that was as strong as steel, but weighed only a fraction as much. I immediately saw that this metal could be used to build an airship far larger and more powerful than the devices that have of late graced the skies of Europe, and so I proceeded to take as much of it as I could."

"What does aluminum have to do with conquering Mexico?" I asked, honestly befuddled.

"I did not say it was aluminum, but in fact the chemists I consulted agree with you that it is, for the most part. One fellow said that the sample he assayed was an alloy of aluminum and magnesium, a combination he had not known to be possible – but whatever it is, the metal could be worked and forged, and I used it to build the Skymaster." He gestured upward. "Isn't it magnificent?"

"It is," I agreed. "But I still don't – "

"Oh, come now, Mr. Derringer. The military applications of flying machines have been known for centuries, in theory. Your own Union government used balloons to scout out our positions in the war, and the notion of using dirigible airships to bombard one's foes from above the range of artillery is obvious. It is merely the pitifully primitive state of airship development that has prevented the realization of this dream. Well, with the aid of the Lost City, I have made a gigantic leap in airship design! My Skymaster is fully steerable and can change altitude at will to a maximum height of more than two miles. Its structure is so resilient that I believe it can survive any storm short of a hurricane. It can be resupplied in flight, so that it need never land, and therefore need never be vulnerable to attack. It carries significant armament – I shan't bore you with detailed specifications, but rest assured, our firepower is sufficient to do extensive damage. We can sail untouched over land defenses, or over naval vessels at sea, and unleash the fires of Hell upon anyone below. And before you suggest that someone else might match us, as the Union matched the C.S.S. *Virginia* with the *Monitor*, remember that the only known source of metallic aluminum is the Lost City, and without aluminum or some other such material, no comparable craft is possible. Look at your own vessel – *that* is the best any foe might send against us, and it is a mere gnat beside my behemoth!"

"Your airship is indeed impressive, Mr. McKee, but a single war machine, however powerful, can scarcely hope to conquer an entire nation!"

"Of course not! Though I admit, I would not have expected a person as young as you appear to be to have realized this so quickly – I congratulate you on your perspicacity. Indeed, an empire requires loyal men to administer it and to enforce the imperial edicts. And *that*, my boy, is why I am here in the Yucatan." He waved toward the jungles below. "Down there is a land ruled by a mystical cult that believes a cross spoke to their founder and told him how to fight the Mexicans. Inspired by that vision these savages have fought fiercely and effectively for thirty years. Now, suppose that a new vision appears, a gigantic silvery vision floating high above them, directing them in attacks on Merida and Campeche, attacks where their mysterious aerial advisor will rain down fire and terror upon the Mexicans. Do you think they won't transfer their allegiance to their new god?"

In fact, I had serious doubts about this – there were many incidents in my father's journals that demonstrated that the primitive peoples of the world, however backward they might appear in some ways, were not necessarily stupid or gullible. I did not, however, think it wise to say so.

"I had thought of simply trying to take Mexico myself, by presenting the present government with an ultimatum," McKee continued, "but I believe a cohort of fanatically devoted savages will be useful. General Diaz will not betray me while surrounded by bloodthirsty Maya believers in the cult of McKee!"

"I see," I said.

"And the Maya will never reject me; they surely won't comprehend what an airship *is*, let alone think of trying to capture or destroy mine."

Again, I had my doubts. The first Indians to encounter rifles thought they were magic, but the late General Custer could testify that they had learned better in short order.

"Now, that little dirigible balloon of yours is too small and open to be of any use in battle, but it might serve a purpose in scouting or carrying messages. Would you care to place it in my service?"

I hesitated. I had no interest in aiding McKee in his mad dream of empire – and I *did* consider it mad. I did not think the Mayans would be the enthusiastic warrior slaves he wanted, nor that General Diaz would give in as readily as McKee believed. His airship might be able to stay aloft indefinitely, out of reach of any attack, but it still needed to resupply somehow; its stock of ammunition could not be infinite, and its crew would need food and water. Those ropes that hauled goods aboard would not find coal or food without human hands to guide them, and those humans could be killed or captured. Diaz could almost certainly find ways to starve the monster.

Those were the purely practical considerations, but in fact the ethical concerns were far more immediate and important. I would not be party to slaughter and enslavement, nor to dictatorship. Even if I thought McKee's scheme flawless, I wanted no part of it.

I briefly considered the possibility of feigning agreement, so that I might be taken into McKee's confidence, the better to move against him when the opportunity arose – for there was no doubt whatsoever that I intended to move against him in some fashion. I could not allow him to carry out his plans, for even if they failed miserably right from the start, dozens of innocents might die in the process.

This, it seemed, was the adventure I would undertake to launch my career – stopping a madman's attempt to conquer Mexico. My curiosity about the aluminum airship had led me, whether by happenstance or divine inspiration, to a task that needed to be done for the good of humanity. McKee had to be brought to justice, and his airship turned over to people who could be trusted to use it wisely, and I was the only one in a position to ensure that.

But first, I had to answer his question. He was waiting.

I was not suitably equipped for intrigue, I decided. I had no allies waiting to aid me, no hidden resources of any kind. I replied, "Thank you for the offer, Mr. McKee, but I think not. I prefer to avoid military and political entanglements. I would be happy to carry messages back to the States, though, should you have any to send."

I spoke in as friendly a manner as I could manage. I gave no hint of my horror at his proposed actions, not the slightest clue that I wished him ill. The offer to carry messages was intended to allay any suspicions he might have about my intentions.

"You're sure of that? The pay would be considerable."

"I'm sure," I said.

My attempt to allay his suspicions had not worked. He had already made up his mind, it seemed, along the lines of the old Colonial motto: Join or die. The moment my words reached him, he nodded once, then raised the hand that was not encumbered with the speaking trumpet and brought it down in a chopping gesture as he shouted a single word. He did not direct this word at me, nor use the megaphone, but I heard it nonetheless.

The word was, "Fire!"

Miss Vanderhart, who had remained silent throughout our conversation, shouted, "Down!" and grabbed at me before I could react to McKee's order. Together we dropped, ducking behind some of our bundled supplies, as a roar of sustained gunfire sounded from somewhere above us, a drumming roar like nothing I had heard before.

While that dive for cover had seemed to be the wisest possible course of action at the time, it turned out to be unnecessary. The bullets tearing through the Aeronavigator were passing well above us. I looked up and belatedly realized what those four half cylinders affixed to the superstructure of McKee's airship were. They were gun turrets, each equipped with a Gatling gun, and the two on our side of the gigantic vessel had opened fire on our own craft, spraying bullets at an astonishing rate. Fortunately for us, they were unable to depress the barrels sufficiently to hit Miss Vanderhart and myself in our current position – the Aeronavigator was quite close to the Skymaster, so as to facilitate conversation, and somewhat below it, while the gun turrets were near the top of McKee's creation.

Unfortunately, they were able to hit the Aeronavigator's gas-bag with devastating effect. We could hear the hissing of the escaping hydrogen even over the rattling fire of the guns.

And we could feel the effects of that loss – our little craft was falling out from beneath us. I felt a curious sensation of lightness, and the Skymaster seemed to go flashing upward out of sight.

I stared up in disbelief as the chattering of the guns continued. McKee's men were *shooting* at us, for no reason but their captain's order, and that given merely because I had declined the offered alliance. The Aeronavigator, which had carried me so far and behaved so reliably, was being torn to pieces as I watched, bits of silk and bamboo scattering on the breeze as the bullets tore through the gas–bag and its supporting superstructure.

Even in my state of stunned disbelief, I noticed that the hydrogen did not ignite, which was a blessing.

"Oh, damn it to Hell," Miss Vanderhart said, demonstrating that even after so long in her company I could be surprised by her complete disregard of society's expectations of feminine delicacy. Even as she spoke she was clambering out of her hiding place, up onto the railing surrounding the platform. I arose from my own concealment, unsure what she hoped to accomplish – perhaps she meant to dive to her death, rather than go down with our doomed machine? But that hardly seemed likely, given what I had observed of her personality during the long voyage.

That strange lightness was growing more intense, and the air was rushing upward around us – or so it felt. I knew that in fact we were plummeting downward. I glanced over the rail and saw the jungle below approaching at alarming speed. It seemed clear to me that only a miracle could save us.

"Come on," Miss Vanderhart called, as she reached up to grab the bamboo strakes along the underside of the silken gas envelope. "The steam engine is dragging us down. I'm going to cut it loose."

"What?" I said, rather stupidly. Then the words penetrated my confusion, and I grabbed a line and climbed up on the rail beside her. "What can I do to help?" I asked.

"Grab onto the struts – pull yourself up, if you can," she said, as she hooked her left arm around a strake and leaned forward, reaching into a tangle of ironmongery with her right. "And pull that handle – the red one." She took a brief pause from her task and pointed.

I saw the handle indicated and tried to discern its function, which, I saw, was simple enough; it was one end of a rod that passed through the heart of the Aeronavigator's structure, securing the framework in which the steam engine was mounted to the framework surrounding the gas-bag.

I glanced at Miss Vanderhart and saw that she was closing certain valves and opening others, working as quickly as she could. I reached for the red handle.

"Make sure you're holding onto the bamboo when you pull it," she called, her voice scarcely audible over the roar of the wind. I belatedly hooked my own left arm up over a strake, as she had.

She finished her task, whatever it was, and grabbed at a strut with her right hand. "Now!" she screamed. "Pull it now!"

I pulled, and the rod slid free with surprising ease. When it did the railing dropped out from beneath our feet; my right hand grabbed desperately for the bamboo struts as I abruptly found myself dangling over empty space, hanging from my left arm. When I was secure I looked down, and then around.

The entire lower structure of the Aeronavigator had detached from the silken balloon and was dropping into the jungle below, airscrews turning, steam engine still smoking as it fell. Our supplies and personal belongings were tumbling about the open platform, some of them coming free and scattering on the wind.

As for Miss Vanderhart and myself, we were dangling from the bamboo framework surrounding the ruined gas-bag. We were falling, too, but much more slowly – not all the lifting gas had escaped, and the larger, lighter portion of the flying machine also had much greater wind resistance, so that it was slowing our descent.

Not, though, enough to be sure that we would survive. The ground was still approaching at frightening speed.

"I don't – " I began.

"My father planned for an emergency," Miss Vanderhart said, interrupting me. "The envelope is lined with gum, designed to at least partially seal any punctures, and the entire undercarriage was built to be readily detached."

"So I see," I said, as I watched the platform and steam engine crash through the green canopy and vanish into the jungle below. I looked up at the gas-bag and swallowed. "Did he provide for *that?*"

Miss Vanderhart's gaze followed my own, and she said, "Oh, *Hell!*"

Without the steam engine's weight as ballast, the tapering cylinder above us was turning one end up, the other end down – to be more specific, what had been the nose was now pointing upward, and what had been the tail was now directed toward the earth below. This, unfortunately, reduced the air resistance, allowing our descent to accelerate again.

Miss Vanderhart said nothing more, but neither did she do nothing in the face of disaster – instead she began to pull herself upward along the bamboo structure, toward the quondam prow of our ruined craft. I saw immediately what she had in mind, and what's more, I saw that it was working – the gas–bag was shifting, righting itself to accommodate her weight. I tried to calculate whether my own weight was best positioned where it was, or whether I should move toward one end of the other. I was, I realized, a few feet aft of what had been the center – that had been the spot closest to McKee's position while we spoke. It had probably been my own weight that unbalanced the remaining structure and determined which way it tipped.

I had just reached that conclusion and decided that Miss Vanderhart would best be able to judge the proper leverage point if I did not move, when we hit the treetops.

Chapter Sixteen

Lost in the Jungle

The impact was not as damaging as I had feared – we were not striking bare ground, but the uppermost branches of the strange tall palms that made up most of the Yucatan jungle. We were not falling freely; the great silken envelope was still partially inflated with hydrogen, and the fabric itself served as a sail, slowing our descent. Even so, we were bumped and battered on the way down. The impact broke several of the bamboo strakes, collapsing the gas–bag, sending us tumbling downward. My grip gave way, and my right hand flailed wildly while my left arm slid along the bamboo and finally came free as well. I fell the last fifteen feet no longer impeded by anything but thin air – no more branches barred my path, and I was no longer clinging to the ruins of the flying machine. I had been trained in surviving a fall, so I was not seriously injured, but I landed with a thump on a bed of undergrowth, where I lay on my back, dazed.

Miss Vanderhart's hold was apparently more secure than my own. When the balloon ended its fall, hanging from the trees, she was still dangling from the remains of the bamboo frame. She was able to clamber over to one of the trees, only to discover that this particular variety of palm was ill suited for climbing, even when attired in her canvas and leather engineer's garb. She began to pick her way slowly downward and had still not reached the ground when I finally gathered my wits and managed to force myself up into a sitting position.

"We're alive," I said, looking up at her.

"No thanks to you," she snapped, looking for her next hand-hold. "Why did you say you wouldn't help him?"

"Because I did not want to help him," I replied, just as sharply.

"It didn't occur to you he would take that poorly?" she said, still climbing.

"I did not expect him to take it as poorly as *this*, no," I retorted. "Did *you?*"

"I certainly thought it was possible!" she said, as she dropped the last few feet. Unlike myself, she landed well and stayed on her feet

"You might have said so."

"*You're* the adventurer! You're the one who is supposed to know what he's doing."

I grimaced, which made a fresh scratch on my cheek sting. I was, indeed, an adventurer; I did not think anyone could deny that being shot out of the Mexican sky and surviving constituted an adventure. "At least we can confirm that bullets will not ignite hydrogen," I remarked. "I was right about that, in any case."

"I'm just glad we were too low for them to shoot *us*," Miss Vanderhart said, looking up at the tangled remnants of our flying machine. "What *were* those things? They seemed simply to *spray* bullets!"

"Gatling guns, I believe," I said. "Are you unfamiliar with them?"

She turned to glare at me. "Unlike you, Mr. Derringer, I have not dedicated my life to studying the ways men kill one another."

That stung, inaccurate though it was, but I swallowed my retort. "They use a hand–cranked system of rotating barrels to produce rapid fire. They were invented during the War Between the States, but Mr. Gatling was initially unable to convince the Union of their practicality. He has now had twenty years to perfect the mechanism, and I am given to understand they have seen considerable use in Europe and South America."

"That's appalling."

I was not inclined to argue with her assessment. "I commend your father's contingency planning. Being able to drop the undercarriage undoubtedly saved our lives."

"Father does try to consider every possibility," she said, sounding somewhat mollified.

"I am very grateful for that."

"So we are alive," she said, looking down at me through her goggles, "and the Aeronavigator is gone. Now what do you propose to do?"

"Mr. McKee has destroyed my airship," I said. "I intend to take his in recompense."

Her mouth fell open at this display of audacity, and she stared wordlessly at me.

I confess, I had said that more because it sounded grand than because I really meant it. I was playing the role of an adventurer, and at least in the stories, adventurers were prone to making bold claims of this sort. I continued, "Besides, you heard his plans. I don't believe he can succeed in building an empire, but he can certainly do a great deal of damage in the attempt. I can't allow that."

"Can't *allow* it? How can you *stop* it?"

"I don't know yet," I admitted. "But I came here seeking adventure, and I would say preventing a madman from attempting to conquer Mexico should qualify nicely. If I succeed, I rather think I'll have the credentials I need to join the Order of Theseus."

She pushed her goggles up onto her forehead and gestured at our surroundings. "Merely surviving should be enough of a challenge, I would think! Need I remind you that we are stranded in unmapped jungle without supplies, hundreds of miles from civilization, surrounded by hostile natives?"

"It may not be hundreds of miles," I said. "To the north are the great plantations surrounding Merida, and to the south is the British trading port of Belize Town." I looked up at the sun, visible through the hole our craft had left in the jungle canopy. I could see no sign of McKee's aerial leviathan, but I could judge the angle of the afternoon light. I pointed to my right. "South is that way."

"Good," she said. "Then that's where we're going." She straightened her belt and brushed bits of greenery from her clothing.

I shook my head. "No," I said. "That's where *you* are going. I regret the necessity of being ungentlemanly, but I am going to stop McKee's monstrosity from wreaking havoc. You will have to make your way to Belize Town on your own."

Her jaw dropped again, and she stared at me in open astonishment. "You're *abandoning* me here?"

"Miss Vanderhart, I sincerely regret endangering you, but given a choice between escorting you to safety or saving hundreds of innocent lives from a madman bent on conquest, I must choose the greater numbers. I have faith in your resourcefulness."

"Seriously? You would not consider escorting me to Belize Town *before* you undertake this suicidal enterprise?"

"I cannot afford the delay, Miss Vanderhart. Hundreds could die."

"*I* could die."

"Miss Vanderhart, you are no fragile blossom to be easily plucked from the tree of life. I have faith in your ability to take care of yourself."

I could see conflicting emotions warring as she considered this. I was complimenting her strength, but at the same time it might seem that I was impugning her femininity and refinement. Finally, though, she decided not to concern herself with her feelings, but to confine herself to facts. "Fragile blossom or not, Mr. Derringer, I am an unarmed woman in an unfamiliar land, and I think you bear some responsibility for having brought me here. At the very least, should we not work together to see if we can recover anything useful from the wreck of my father's machine?"

"Indeed," I said, realizing that all I had of our supplies were the clothes I wore and the binoculars that had managed to stay slung around my neck throughout the day's adventures. "An excellent suggestion. Did you note where it came down?"

At that, I saw Miss Vanderhart's expression turn uncertain for perhaps the first time since we met on that train to New York. She looked around at the surrounding jungle, then admitted, "No."

I confess I felt an unworthy surge of satisfaction at this. "I believe it's that way," I said, pointing to the northwest.

No, I had not managed to stay oriented throughout our descent, and I will say any man who could must verge on the superhuman. I had, however, noted the direction of the light when I saw the steam engine smash through the jungle canopy, and my wilderness training in the Adirondacks enabled me to calculate from that. Even so, I only knew the general direction, not the precise location.

I felt no need to explain this to Miss Vanderhart, however, as she gazed upon me with a combination of annoyance and relief. With another companion I might have hoped for an admixture of respect or even admiration, but I knew better than to expect that from her. I got to my feet, and said, "Come on."

I held out my hand, but of course she did not take it; instead she ignored it, and me, as she stamped off in the direction I had indicated. I sighed and followed, keeping a wary eye out for boa constrictors or other dangerous snakes, or for any sign of jaguars.

In the event, we saw no jaguars or great serpents. Birds, lizards, and monkeys were plentiful, and insects of every imaginable variety and of rather distressing size were everywhere, but excluding the possibility of venomous spiders or the like, there was nothing that might have posed a serious threat to our wellbeing. Although we knew the area to be at least theoretically inhabited, we saw no sign of any human presence, either Mayan or not – no tracks, no lost implements nor abandoned structures, and certainly no actual people. The possibility that they were present, observing us unseen, could not be entirely ruled out, but I thought it unlikely. *We* were sufficiently ignorant of the environment that they could have remained hidden from us, but the birds and monkeys did not seem to be troubled by any intrusion but our own, and they would surely be as familiar with the jungle as were the Maya.

It proved distressingly easy to become disoriented in the trackless green gloom of the jungle, and we wandered for almost half an hour, slapping at insects and cursing the sharp edges of assorted vegetation, without success. I had reluctantly suggested doubling back, thinking we must surely have gone too far, when I finally spotted a shaft of sunlight off to one side and realized that it must mark the spot where the steam engine broke through. I took a look through the binoculars that seemed to confirm my first impression. I called it to Miss Vanderhart's attention, and we redirected our steps.

Our first discovery assuring us we were indeed in the right vicinity was Miss Vanderhart's traveling case, lying on the jungle floor; it had burst open upon impact, scattering her belongings across a patch of moss. With a wordless exclamation, she knelt and began gathering up her possessions.

I left her to it and proceeded on.

The steam engine itself, and the framework upon which it had been mounted, had landed in a single piece, but this does not in any way mean that it was intact; the boiler had burst, and hot water was still dripping from the ruptured metal. Burning coal had spilled from the smashed firebox, and still smoldered on the damp ground several places; here and there it had burned holes in the undergrowth, but the humidity had not permitted open fires to spread very far. The framework and platform were twisted and bent into a shape vaguely resembling an old shoe.

Two airscrews were still attached to the visible end of the bent shaft; the other screw I did not see at first, but eventually located it embedded in the trunk of a tree, some thirty feet off the ground. The three screws at the other end were buried in debris, but I doubted any of them retained its original shape.

Our luggage was strewn hither and yon, and I set out to collect and sort as much of it as I could before nightfall. Miss Vanderhart, having gathered up most of her bag's contents, joined me in this enterprise.

I was very pleased to retrieve both my rifle and revolver, apparently unharmed; I did not fire them, for fear the sound of a gunshot would draw unwanted attention, but I did check them out as thoroughly as I otherwise could, dry-firing both successfully. The ammunition, too, was still there, in its battered but intact boxes.

Of more immediate use, however, was the implement called a "machete," midway between a large knife and a crude sword, that I had acquired at one of our earlier stops in central Mexico; had this been in our possession sooner, the journey from our landing site to the remains of the undercarriage would have been much easier, as a machete is ideally suited for hacking through the jungle underbrush.

A glance at the sky made it clear that we would not be doing any more traveling that day, so once I located the appropriate bundles I set about making camp. Using the stoker's shovel, which was only slightly bent, to gather smoldering coal and build a fire was easy enough, much easier than gathering firewood and finding our matches. When loading the Aeronavigator before abandoning the wagons I had used my tent to cover some of the supplies; that tent had blown off in the fall and was nowhere to be found. I suspected it might be snagged in a treetop somewhere, but at any rate it was not in sight. That meant that we had no shelter beyond what we could improvise from palm leaves and wreckage.

Food, on the other hand, was plentiful; most of our stocks had remained aboard the platform until impact and now lay strewn along one side of the ruined steam engine. We had cheese, hard tack, jerky, corn meal, beans, and even beer – surprisingly few bottles had broken. While I was sure that I could live off the land if necessary, I was relieved it was *not* immediately necessary; I preferred to devote my attention to other matters.

Thus it was that as the tropical sunset faded rapidly in the west, Miss Vanderhart and I were seated comfortably on bundles of our belongings on either side of a coal-filled fire pit, eating a generous, if not particularly varied, repast. This situation seemed to ease both our minds – it certainly eased mine, and Miss Vanderhart also appeared calmer than she had when we had discussed our plans earlier.

"Are you really going to go looking for McKee?" she asked me.

I took a swig of unpleasantly warm beer, then said, "I am."

"He stays airborne."

"I am aware of that."

"How can you hope to get aboard his airship, then?"

I had had that very question at the back of my mind ever since we reached the ground and had not yet devised an entirely satisfactory answer. I drank more beer – rather more than I actually wanted – as I struggled to phrase my reply. At last I said, "While it's true that he and his craft do not return to earth, his men do come down for supplies on occasion. I shall have to find a way to get aboard along with them during such an occurrence."

"How do you propose to do it?"

"Perhaps the element of surprise will be sufficient. I might catch them off their guard, run past them, and climb one of the ropes."

Miss Vanderhart's response was a rather rude laugh. "And climb three or four thousand feet up to the airship? Where you will be a lone man against his entire crew? Besides, won't they *see* you climbing the rope? All they need to do is cut the line and let you fall to your death."

I grimaced at the ease and thoroughness with which she had countered my idea. "I concede the matter still requires some thought," I replied.

"I should say so, yes."

"I shall have to find a way to be taken aboard unseen. Perhaps hidden in one of the barrels of food."

"Are they large enough?"

I shook my head. "I don't know," I admitted. "I have not seen them, any more than you have; I have only Mr. Herrington's description to rely upon."

"He spoke of McKee's men lifting the bags and barrels into baskets the airship had lowered."

"Indeed he did."

"I would think they would notice a man's weight."

"I suppose they would," I acknowledged. "Nor can I see just how I might insinuate myself into their supplies in the first place."

"Well, that would depend on where they're *getting* those supplies, I should think."

"Yes." I frowned. "In Alvarado, they bought salt pork, salt beef, corn meal, and coal. I would suppose they will buy similar supplies from the Maya."

"Or take them at gunpoint; remember, McKee intends to *conquer* the natives, and use them as troops in his army."

"An excellent point," I agreed. "Do you know, I think I see a serious flaw in McKee's schemes?"

"Oh?"

"To the best of my knowledge, the Maya have no coal. What will he use for fuel?"

Even in the dim glow of the coal fire, I could see Miss Vanderhart blink. "I don't know," she said. "Do you suppose he could get sufficient heat by burning wood?"

"Much as I hate to admit it, Miss Vanderhart, you know more practical engineering than do I; *would* wood be sufficient?"

"I'm afraid I can't say, not without a great deal more information about the construction of that flying monstrosity of his."

I nodded. "Perhaps charcoal would be adequate."

"It might be, yes." She shifted in her seat. "I don't really see how it matters, Mr. Derringer. I'm sure McKee has considered his situation and has some plan in place. Perhaps he intends to get his coal from that British port you mentioned – they must surely have considerable stocks of coal to supply their steamships."

"I suppose that's it," I acknowledged. "Perhaps we should head for Belize Town after all, so that I can smuggle myself aboard hidden in the coal."

"Much as I hate to give you any reason *not* to head for Belize Town, honesty compels me to say that I suspect their containers are not suited for concealment. Coal is usually poured from one receptacle to the next, rather than being transported in closed vessels."

"True," I said, frowning.

I sat in silent thought for a moment as I reviewed what McKee would need to take aboard his craft. Food, fuel, water...

Water? I had not seen anything on McKee's airship suggesting a system to collect rainwater. "He didn't buy water in Alvarado, did he?" I asked.

"Mr. Herrington did not mention it, so far as I can recall – and really, Mr. Derringer, who would *buy* water?"

That was an excellent question. In a desert like the ones around Phoenix clean water might be sufficiently precious to be bought and sold, but the essential fluid was plentiful in most settled areas, more or less free for the taking. McKee undoubtedly had some system for taking it aboard. That might provide some means of access.

Climbing the ropes openly would not work, but concealing myself in a barrel of corn meal, or a hopper of coal, or a water vessel – these were possibilities deserving further exploration.

First, of course, I would have to find McKee and his airship and see just how he actually provisioned his vessel and that was not something I could do that night. We finished our meal without further meaningful conversation, and then crawled into the crude lean-to I had devised, and went to sleep.

Chapter Seventeen

In Search of the Aerial Leviathan

Our slumber was untroubled by anything more than heat, humidity, insects, and the occasional unidentifiable noises I assumed to be the local fauna going about its business. We awoke in the morning reasonably well rested. Upon rising we set about sorting through our possessions, choosing which we would take with us and which we would abandon. With only our own legs for transport, we were far more limited than we had been while the Aeronavigator still flew.

As we worked, we argued anew about what our next step, and our destination, should be. Miss Vanderhart maintained that we should head to Belize Town and inform the local authorities of McKee's intentions, while I argued in favor of direct intervention. She pointed out that I still had no idea how I would get aboard the aluminum airship, and I might well wander about the jungle for months looking for one, while the British had artillery that might be able to shoot McKee's creation out of the sky.

I replied that the British government might take months or years to reach a decision and might decide not to intervene at all. Furthermore, the airship might well be able to stay out of range of even the best artillery.

"Then I would expect them to build their own aeronauts to pursue it!"

I sighed. "Miss Vanderhart, building a craft to match McKee's is no easy task, as you should know from your father's work. From what I have seen of it, I would say his vessel incorporates easily two-thirds of the world's supply of metallic aluminum."

"Can't anyone find more, then?"

I shook my head. "Metallic aluminum does not occur in nature, at least not in detectable quantities. The only known processes to manufacture it are outrageously difficult and expensive; I doubt the entire British Empire could afford to refine as much as McKee stole from the Lost City. By the time such a task is accomplished, McKee may well control everything from the Rio Grande to Colombia."

"Then build airships without aluminum! Yes, he took down the Aeronavigator easily, but it was not built with combat in mind. A hundred small airships could – "

I interrupted her. "It might be possible, yes," I admitted. "But think how much damage could be done before such a fleet was ready!" I frowned, as a fantastical vision of airborne battles filled my thoughts. "Also, my dear Miss Vanderhart, do we really want to encourage the militarization of the skies? Should not one part of the Lord's grand creation remain free of man's propensity for cruelty and carnage?"

"But do you really have an alternative?" she asked.

"If I can just get aboard..."

"But you have no way to do that!"

"I'll find one! They do need to take aboard food, fuel, and water; I need only find some way to conceal myself in one of those."

"And they will open a barrel of flour and find you smothered therein, or look in a cistern to find you drowned."

"Obviously, I will take measures to avoid any such inconvenience," I said.

As it happens, I was just then looking at the wreckage of the steam engine's regulatory mechanisms, the network of valves and pipes that had allowed one to control the pressure at every point in the system. "Perhaps I could devise something that would allow me to breathe while confined."

Miss Vanderhart's gaze followed my own and she began, "I could..." Then she stopped and tilted her head thoughtfully to one side.

I did not interrupt her thoughts, but returned to packing my own supplies – food, clothing, tools, and weapons. I debated whether I needed to devote any space to such personal items as my razor and shaving mirror, especially in light of my youth – in truth, I could not yet have grown a proper beard had I attempted to do so – but concluded that both had other uses besides maintaining my appearance and included them.

"You know," Miss Vanderhart said, pointing at some of the less ruined machinery, "I believe I could use the piston here as an air compressor and build a sort of pneumatic chamber that would hold a considerable quantity of air. A valve would release it upon demand, and you could place a pipe in your mouth that would transmit these releases."

"Could you?" I asked.

"I think so," she said, studying the plumbing. "It's an interesting problem." Then she turned. "Where's the toolbox?"

I smiled and pointed.

I devoted my own attention to obtaining our breakfast from our surroundings, so as to conserve our rations, while she worked. I discovered that spit-roasted lizard basted in beer is surprisingly tasty, if not particularly filling. I don't think Miss Vanderhart really noticed what she was eating, but as she did not complain, I did not concern myself with telling her. I also finished my packing, and as much of hers as I could manage without intruding on either her privacy or her work. I cleaned my rifle and pistol, as I had done regularly throughout our voyage.

I had run out of urgent tasks and was sharpening knives when Miss Vanderhart finally announced, "There!"

I looked up from the machete's blade to see her holding up an ungainly device roughly the size of a small turkey. Its body was a metal cylinder; at one end a bent copper tube perhaps a foot long protruded from a tangle of valves and straps.

"I don't know how long it will last," she said. "I don't know how much air a person consumes. However, it contains as much air as I was able to force into it – it's under more than a hundred pounds of pressure. There's a step–down system, and a secondary holding tank, so that air can be dispensed safely, rather than releasing it all at once – see here?" She pointed to something in the tangle at the top, and I nodded as if I actually understood.

"You'll need to show me how it works," I said.

"It's simple," she said.

"I'm sure it is. Thank you."

She suddenly looked up from her creation and turned to stare at me, and I thought I knew what was going through her mind. "You have, I take it, just realized that you may now have given me the means I need to board McKee's airship, ruining any chance you had of convincing me to head directly for Belize Town," I said.

She looked back at the device, and said, "Damn." Then she looked at me again. "Damn you, Tom Derringer. Now I want to see whether it works."

"So do I," I said. "Can it be tested?"

"There's no way to refill it without this," she said, gesturing at the wreckage of the steam engine. "I used the cylinder as my compressor. You can test it here, but once we move on, that will be it."

I nodded. "Show me how it works."

We spent the next fifteen or twenty minutes experimenting with her device, which seemed to work quite well – squeezing a lever caused it to spurt air in a gentle spray, and releasing the lever stopped the flow.

Of course, we had no way of testing it under water.

Miss Vanderhart was not entirely satisfied until she had made several adjustments, but in the end we were both content that it functioned as designed. She refilled it when we were finished and handed it to me. I slung it on my back, beside my pack, and together we marched off into the jungle, headed somewhat north of east, as I calculated that to be the direction McKee's so-called Skymaster had been bound. There was no further argument for heading directly for Belize Town; Miss Vanderhart now wanted to see whether her breathing contraption would work. She did, however, suggest that if our supplies ran low before we found McKee's craft we should turn south, and I agreed to give it all due consideration should the circumstances arise.

We could not see much of the sky from the jungle floor. For all we knew most of the time, McKee's airship might have been directly above us. The theory, though, was that McKee was proceeding with his scheme and flying on toward Chan Santa Cruz. We therefore wanted to locate a Maya village where a guide could be found, or a road that would lead us to the rebel stronghold.

"How do we know the Mayans won't murder us on first sight?" Miss Vanderhart asked.

"I am relying on simple human decency," I said.

She stopped dead in her tracks, startling a large lizard. "Are you serious?"

I smiled. "No, I am not," I admitted. "I may be idealistic, but I like to think I'm not a complete fool. No, I'm relying on *curiosity*. We obviously aren't Mexican soldiers, and despite your engineer's attire, *you* obviously aren't a soldier of any sort. I would think any Maya we encounter would at least want to ask us a few questions before doing us in."

She frowned at me. "You have more faith in their inquisitiveness than I do. I've encountered plenty of people with all the curiosity of a brick."

I shrugged. "Do you have a better alternative to offer?"

She considered that for a moment, then let out a sound I would categorize, if forced to venture an opinion, as a snort. This was not the first time I had heard her produce this unladylike noise. Then she turned and began marching eastward again.

We slogged through the jungle for two days before finally stumbling upon a trail, and a few moments later after finding this path we encountered a Maya hunter, who looked at least as frightened by our appearance as we were by his. Given Miss Vanderhart's attire, I cannot blame him. To our pleased surprise he had several words of both English and Spanish – more than either of us had of Maya, in any case. With extensive use of hand gestures and simplified grammar, we managed to convey that our intentions were peaceful and that we wanted to go to Chan Santa Cruz, which was, after all, undoubtedly McKee's destination.

He gave us to understand, in the same mix of words and gestures, that if we went to Chan Santa Cruz it was likely we would get our throats slit. I'm honestly not sure what he made of our reply; we were trying to say that we were willing to take that risk, but I don't think we managed to communicate anything so subtle as that. All the same, in the end he made a gesture with spread hands that was either acquiescence or his equivalent of a shrug and led us along the track in much the direction we had already been going.

Not long after that an inspiration struck. I took a rope from my pack, threw a loop around Miss Vanderhart's wrists and one about my own, then managed to communicate to our guide that he was to play the part of our captor. He smiled and threw himself into the role with perhaps more enthusiasm than I found entirely comfortable.

Miss Vanderhart made some protest at this arrangement, but I pointed out that her bonds were held with the loosest of slip-knots and could be cast aside on a moment's notice, which mollified her enough to continue the ruse.

Several hours later, after passing unmolested through a village or two, we came upon the outskirts of the Maya capital, a town of some size. I had thought we might attract attention there and be something of a nine day wonder, but in the event no one paid us much heed; all eyes were instead focused upon the sky, where McKee's airship hung.

Our guide stopped in his tracks and studied this aerial phenomenon for several minutes, then turned to us, pointed at the airship, and then pointed at us.

I shook my head. "No," I said. "It is not ours." I thought he might know enough English to follow that. I pointed at the airship myself and said, "Enemy."

He frowned, then beckoned, and tugged at the rope so hard that our wrists almost came free. Where he had heretofore maintained a leisurely pace, his demeanor was now all urgency. I hoped that he had not decided upon some reason to consider us hostile, and I checked to be sure my revolver was loose in its holster – I had not carried our false captivity so far as disarming myself. We hurried through the open spaces – I hesitate to call them streets – until we reached a structure that blended the native architecture with that of the Spanish colonial era, where our guide spoke with a feather-wearing guard. The discussion grew more heated, with many gestures and some shouting, and then finally we were led into the building and into a large room where several men were conversing.

It is odd how even in the most barbaric cultures, no matter how strange or sparse the clothing may be, one can always tell a man of importance by his dress, whether it be a fine top hat or a bright feathered cloak. Half these men were clearly men of importance, and I did my best to look respectful without being obsequious while our guide explained himself to his superiors.

One of these worthies turned to me and asked a question in Spanish better than my own. I shook my head, and replied, "Do you speak English?"

"I do," he answered, speaking with more of a British inflection than a Mexican one – a product, I assume, of trade with British Honduras. "Who are you?"

"My name is Tom Derringer," I said. "I'm from the United States."

"A Yankee?"

"Yes."

"Why are you here?"

"I came to stop the airship above your city from starting a war."

He seemed to have some trouble parsing this sentence, so I tried again. I pointed at the stone ceiling. "That airship," I said. "I came to stop it."

"Stop it? Stop what?"

I decided his English might be more limited than I had thought. "From killing."

He considered that for a moment, exchanged a few words in his native tongue with his companions, then asked, "Killing who?"

"Anyone."

He thought for a moment, then said, "Emperor McKee says he has come to help us."

I frowned. "You call him 'Emperor'?"

"He calls *himself* 'Emperor.' What does it mean?"

"An emperor is a king of kings, a man who rules many nations."

He frowned. "*Does* McKee rule many nations?"

"No – but he hopes to. Starting with yours."

"He says God has sent him and that he will help us fight the Mexicans, Diaz and his men."

I shook my head. "God didn't send him. He wants to enslave you, and then use your people to conquer the Mexicans, as well. He wants to rule you, and rule all of Mexico, and all the Americas. He will use his flying machine to help you fight the Mexicans, but for himself, not for you. When the fighting is done, he will rule you both."

He considered this, then turned and began a lengthy conference with the others. Miss Vanderhart and I stood, our wrists still apparently bound, and waited for the discussion to finish.

At last, when we were both desperate to sit down or at least lean against a wall, the spokesman turned back to us. "Why do you want to stop McKee?" he asked.

"Why should men die needlessly?" I said. "Why should he rule over anyone?"

He shook his head and demanded, "How does it benefit *you*, to stop him?"

These people were obviously not inclined to accept a white man's altruism on faith, and from what little I knew of their history I could scarcely fault them for a certain skepticism. "He intends to conquer my homeland of New York eventually. It is easier to stop him now, when he has only his airship, than when he has the Maya and the Mexicans at his back."

That made sense to him. He turned and spoke to the others, then returned his attention to me – and only to me; I had noticed that he gave Miss Vanderhart no notice whatsoever. Despite her unorthodox garb he obviously considered her merely another useless female, unworthy of his concern.

"You say he intends to rule us. Why should we not accept his help and conquer all of Mexico, and then cut his throat while he sleeps?"

"How will you do that, when he never leaves his airship?"

He gave that some thought. "Never?"

"Never. He has his men pull up everything he needs on ropes."

He glanced at the others and asked a quick question. One of the others answered, and then it was my turn again.

"How will *you* defeat him, if we allow you to try?" he asked.

"I have a way to get onto his airship unseen," I replied.

"Tell us this way."

"No."

That flat refusal seemed to baffle him at first, but after a moment he said, "You are in Chan Santa Cruz, many miles from the lands of your own people. We can kill you at any time."

"I know that." I decided the time had come to make my own position clear; I twisted my wrists against one another, and the rope fell free. I dropped my right hand to the butt of my revolver. "I came here of my own choice to aid you against McKee. Killing me would be a mistake."

He considered me for a moment, then said, "You say this."

"I do."

"Yet you do not say how you can get to the flying machine."

"Not while you are undecided whether McKee is your enemy or your friend. I know that I have told you the truth about his plans, but you do not know whether to believe him, or to believe me. I cannot tell you my own plan because one of you might tell McKee."

He turned to his companions and spoke for some time in their own tongue – a language that has rather a pleasing sound to it, really, a sort of rolling staccato, but which was completely and utterly incomprehensible to us. When he had finished several of the others replied, each in turn.

This discussion continued for several minutes, and when it finally concluded, our interlocutor turned back to us and said, "You will stay as our guests for now, until we have seen more of Emperor McKee's actions. If you give me your word you will not try any treachery, you may keep your guns, but there will be guards at your door. If you harm them, or attempt to elude them, you will be killed."

I glanced at Miss Vanderhart, but she offered no comment. I turned back to the Mayan gentleman and said, "I will abide by your generous terms. You have my word I will not harm our guards, or attempt to escape them, so long as they do not try to harm *us*."

"That will do." He waved a hand, and four men – presumably our guards – stepped forward and took our arms. We were led away to our quarters, a modest room with a single straw mattress – our captors had made an obvious but incorrect assumption about our relationship. I assigned Miss Vanderhart the bed, of course, and took up my own place in one corner with a folded poncho as my pillow.

We had seen no evidence that any of our four guards spoke English, but Miss Vanderhart leaned close to whisper, "I hope you have a plan to get us out of here."

I smiled. As my father's journals had made clear, much of adventuring was an improvisational enterprise. "Not yet," I said, "but I'll think of something."

The resulting expression on her face was quite indescribable. I leaned back against the wall and closed my eyes, as much to keep from laughing as to help myself think.

Chapter Eighteen

Our Stairway to the Heavens

We remained in our cell – for there could be little doubt, despite the lack of locks or bars, that it *was* a cell – for the next two days. Meals were brought to us – the food was unfamiliar, but quite palatable – and most of our other needs were met. I had lost most of my journals and writing implements, but still had a notebook and a pencil stub in my pack that allowed me to record something of our experiences.

On the third day the Maya official who had interrogated us before came to visit us.

"There is a village," he said, without preamble. "Two hours' walk from here. The men of the village refused to give Emperor McKee's men food that they demanded. The flying machine pulled them back up on ropes, and then the machine descended until it was no higher than the treetops. Then it fired on the village with spinning guns. The bullets tore men and women and houses to pieces. Eighteen men and four women died. Twenty-three others were injured. The village is in ruins. Now Emperor McKee has come to us here in Chan Santa Cruz, and he does not apologize, he offers no payment for his crime. He says that now we have seen what his machine can do. He asks us, do we not want to turn it against the Mexicans?"

"I am very sorry for your losses," I replied. "If there is anything we can do to aid the wounded, we would be happy to help."

He seemed surprised by this answer. He did not speak for a moment, then said, "That is not why I am here."

"I know that, but my heart goes out to those people."

"I...thank you. My uncle was one of the men who was killed."

"I am sorry. May his soul be at peace."

He seemed to sag for a moment, then straightened up. "You said you could stop Emperor McKee."

"I think I can, yes."

"Then do it. We will not stop you. We will not help you, either – we do not want to draw Emperor McKee's anger."

"Of course!" I lowered my head. "I understand completely. Thank you."

"Go. You are free." He stepped aside, opening a clear path to the door.

"Miss Vanderhart?" I called. "Let us be on our way."

"I'm coming," she said. She had been collecting our belongings while we spoke; now she handed me my pack and held our improvised air dispenser ready.

It took another few moments to finish our packing, and our host stood watching silently as we did so. As we gathered the last few items, I asked him, "Has anyone seen the flying machine take on water?"

He hesitated, then said, "Yes. Several days ago a hunter saw them lower a great barrel into the river."

"Where?"

"Not far from here. I can show you."

"That would be very much appreciated." I slung my rifle onto my shoulder, checked to be sure my revolver was secure in its holster, then stepped toward the door. "Lead on, sir."

He led. We followed him out of the building into the streets, such as they were, of Chan Santa Cruz, where many of the Maya turned to stare at us – those who were not already staring upward. A quick glance confirmed that McKee's airship was hanging above the town, perhaps a thousand feet up, its Gatling guns clearly visible – apparently McKee wanted to make sure no one in Chan Santa Cruz forgot his little demonstration, and he had not withdrawn the weapons into their turrets. The Skymaster's shadow lay across the town, darkening the buildings.

"Do you think he can see us?" Miss Vanderhart asked, tugging her goggles into place as she stared upward.

"If he has a telescope and cares to look I'm sure he could spot us," I said, "but I cannot think he would recognize us. He must surely believe us to be dead; how could he think we would survive that fall?"

"It was not so difficult as all that," she replied.

"If he had thought we were still alive, I think he would have made an effort to finish us off," I said.

She looked up at the airship, shuddered, then said, "I fear you're right." She kept her gaze focused ahead thereafter, as our guide led us out of the town and past fields of corn, along a broad, well-trodden path.

In less than an hour we had reached a fair-sized river, both its banks thick with overhanging trees, the cries of birds and monkeys echoing from the blue-green water. "That way," our guide said, pointing upstream. "There is a pool. Our hunters take game there, when the animals come to drink."

"A watering hole," I said. "Excellent!"

"It's probably the only fresh water they can see from the air," Miss Vanderhart said – the first words she had spoken since leaving the town.

"It might be, at that," I agreed. "Certainly the closest. Come on!" I turned aside, ready to plunge into the underbrush.

She hung back. "Are there no roads to this watering hole?"

Our guide had ignored her presence as completely as he could until now, but at those words he turned to glower at her. "No," he said. "Animals would not come to drink if a road led there."

"Oh," she said, in a voice much smaller than her usual. "I see."

"Come on," I repeated, pushing aside a leaf the size of my shirt.

Reluctantly, she followed me. We had only gone perhaps three steps into the jungle when she realized our guide had not accompanied us and put her hand on my shoulder. I turned to look in time to see him give a gesture of farewell, then turn and head back toward town.

"He isn't coming with us?"

"I'm sure he has other matters to attend to," I said.

"More important than destroying McKee's airship and avenging his uncle and the others?"

"That, Miss Vanderhart, is *my* job, not his. Now, let us be about it."

"What if we encounter some of those hunters, though? Won't they assume we've escaped, and try to recapture us?"

I opened my mouth to speak, then stopped. Her point was a good one. I turned back.

"Excuse me," I called after our erstwhile captor.

He paused and turned to regard us. I took a step back toward him, and called, "What if we meet some of your people in the jungle?"

He gazed silently back at me for a moment longer, then sighed. "Tell them this," he said, and spoke a sentence in his own tongue.

I tried to say it back to him, and he smiled unpleasantly at my awkward attempt – obviously, I had said something else entirely. He repeated it.

I tried again, but after half a dozen repetitions I had still not entirely mastered it. He was clearly growing exasperated when Miss Vanderhart stepped up beside me and recited the sentence perfectly.

He blinked at her, then smiled, much more pleasantly this time, though there was still something about it I did not care for. "Yes," he told me. "Your woman must speak for you." He seemed to find this unduly amusing. Before I could protest, he turned and strode away.

I turned to contemplate my companion. "It would seem," I said, "that you have a better ear for languages than I do."

She lifted her nose. "Is that so very surprising?"

"No, I suppose not," I admitted. "Perhaps you can teach me this password he gave you as we walk."

With that, we resumed our trek through the jungle toward the watering hole, and Miss Vanderhart did her best to comply with my suggestion. I did, in fact, eventually learn the sentence adequately, but not well enough that I can record it here.

"It might be useful if I knew what it meant," I griped, as I shoved aside a vine as thick as my forearm.

"It says...well, I don't know all of it, but part of it is his name, and there's something about elders or chiefs sending us somewhere."

I stopped to stare at her; she stared back. "You understand Maya?" I demanded.

"No, of course not," she said. "But I picked up a few words listening over the last few days. Didn't you?"

"No," I said. "I did not." The possibility, I confess, had not even occurred to me.

"Well, that was silly," she said. "I thought you were a trained adventurer!"

"I thought so, too," I said. Then I shook my head and resumed the march through the jungle along the riverbank. Clearly, I still had a great deal to learn about my intended occupation. It seemed that my training had not caused me to *think* like an adventurer. Perhaps only experience would do that – if I *survived* the experiences.

The walk took longer than I had expected, and I was beginning to wonder whether we had somehow followed the wrong branch of the river, when we finally pushed through a thicket and found ourselves facing the pool we had been seeking.

Miss Vanderhart shoved branches aside and stood beside me. "There it is," she said. "Now what?"

"Now we prepare your breathing apparatus, and then we wait."

"Wait for what?"

"For McKee to replenish his water supply."

"Very well," she said. "And how long will that be?"

"I have no idea."

We stood silently, side by side, for a long moment as she considered this answer. Then she demanded, "You don't *know?*"

"How could I possibly know?"

"I thought... I thought you might have calculated the frequency somehow, estimated how long he could go between refills."

I shrugged. "Even if I had, I don't know when he last took on water; our friend only said 'several days,' which is inconveniently unspecific."

"So we could be waiting here for *weeks*? What are we supposed to eat?"

"Oh, I doubt very much it will be weeks. I doubt it will be more than three or four days. Carrying any great volume of water would add so much weight that even that aluminum monstrosity could not maintain any great altitude."

"That's true," she admitted. She looked up, as if expecting to see McKee's airship appear at any second – as indeed it might, though I doubted we could be *that* fortunate.

A thought struck me. "You do not need to accompany me, Miss Vanderhart," I said. "Indeed, should you choose to leave now and head for Belize Town, I would not fault you. You have done more than your share to aid me. You came with me to fly the Aeronavigator, which is no more; you have no further obligations here, and I would think you would be eager to return to the bosom of your family."

She glared at me. "You think I want to go hiking through the jungle alone?"

"That fellow who directed us here might be able to provide an escort."

"And why would I trust him?"

"Why did you trust *me*?"

"It's hardly the same, Mr. Derringer."

"If he wished you ill, he had plenty of opportunity to inflict it these past few days."

"I know that! I don't mean...I'm sure he's a fine fellow, but he's...damn you, Tom Derringer! I've accompanied you this far, I might as well see it through."

"It's likely to be dangerous."

"I would have to be a complete fool to not realize that, Mr. Derringer, and I trust you do not think me a fool."

"I most certainly do not." I hesitated, then said, "We have only a single air supply."

"We can share it."

"Then you are determined to go with me, rather than heading for civilization?"

"I am."

I met her gaze, then nodded my acceptance. "Perhaps we should ready our air supply?" I suggested.

She gestured at my burden and said, "I think it's as ready as it will ever be."

"Then could you give me a hand removing it from my back?" I said, trying not to sound annoyed.

"Oh," she said. Then she stepped forward and helped me disentangle the device from the straps securing my pack, my rifle, and my gun belt. A moment later we had the ungainly thing on the ground between us, where I eyed it uncertainly. Using that contraption to breathe underwater had seemed very clever when we created and tested it, but I was beginning to have my doubts. It was heavy and awkward, and relying on something we had never tested in its intended environment for something as basic as air was definitely not as appealing an idea now as it had been in our first flush of enthusiasm.

"Now what?" Miss Vanderhart asked.

"Now we wait," I said, and with that I sat down upon the riverbank and looked up. The watering hole was large enough to leave a good-sized hole in the overhanging foliage, and I looked up through that opening at the cloudless blue sky of a tropical afternoon.

There was no sign of Reverend McKee's aluminum airship.

Miss Vanderhart settled to the ground beside me, and we waited.

We spent the next several hours swatting at oversized insects, with occasional interruptions to avoid passing snakes. I was reminded once again how much of adventuring was stupendously boring – it seemed, judging by my experience so far, that adventurers spent far more time either riding peacefully or sitting around waiting for things to happen than in any other pursuit.

I did undertake one useful task while we waited – I once again cleaned first my Colt revolver, and then my Winchester, and then wrapped the pistol in oilcloth, since it looked likely, if our scheme was to go anywhere, that I would need to take them underwater with me at some point, and I was unsure what effect immersion would have on firearms. I had heard that Mr. Colt's otherwise fine products were prone to rust if not kept clean and dry. I had grave reservations about how effective oilcloth would be as protection, but saw no better option.

I did not wrap the rifle, as I did not care to leave us unarmed in a jungle where snakes or big cats might find us. I trusted that the mechanism would survive a brief swim, and the cartridges were warranted waterproof.

Shortly before sunset, as I was reassembling the rifle, we had occasion to employ our Mayan password – as advised, I left it to my companion to speak the sentence to the hunting party that had discovered us. They seemed at least as startled to hear a white woman speak their language as they had been to find us there in the first place, but after a few whispered words among themselves they stole silently away, moving through the jungle with a stealth and ease I envied. I could travel unheard through the forests of upstate New York, but the jungles of the Yucatan were another matter entirely. This encounter distracted me, interrupting the familiar routine of rifle maintenance, though it was not until later that the effects of that distraction became significant.

The sun set, and as I looked up at the golden-streaked clouds of the tropical twilight I wondered what would happen if the airship came to resupply under the cover of night. What if we slept through the entire operation? What if we could not see well enough to slip into the water vessel? We knew little of the vessel's nature; the Maya had described it as a great barrel, but was that accurate? Was there an obvious way to gain entrance?

What if the openings by which it was filled were not large enough to admit us? That possibility had never occurred to me until that moment, but as I gazed up at heaven's glory it suddenly seemed an obvious issue. McKee had probably not worried about intruders such as ourselves, but had he considered the risk of unwanted fish or vegetation in his water supply? Our entire scheme might be ruined by so simple a matter.

I said nothing to Miss Vanderhart, but my heart sank as the light faded from the sky above us. I wondered whether there was any point in even staying where we were.

My gloomy thoughts were interrupted by Miss Vanderhart asking, "Are we going to sit up all night, or will we get some sleep? Should we take shifts?"

"Yes," I said, glad to have a simple question with an obvious answer. "I'll take the first watch; you sleep whenever you feel the need, and I'll wake you for your turn."

She nodded, slapped at an insect, then stretched out on the bank. "I'm hungry," she said.

I glanced around. There were almost certainly a hundred things we could eat in the surrounding jungle, but neither of us knew what they were, and choosing at random might well poison us. I shrugged. "So am I," I said. "At least we have water."

She sighed, then scooped water from the pool with her hand.

That was the last we spoke for what I would estimate to be at least an hour. Miss Vanderhart dozed intermittently; every so often she would awaken enough to slap an insect. I sat upright, watching, but as the darkness grew ever more complete that grew ever more frustrating. It was not long after sunset that all I could see around us was blackness, save for the hole overhead where the star-strewn panoply of the tropical heavens gleamed. I stared up at it, trying to identify the constellations, but succeeded mostly in giving myself a sore neck.

The jungle's inhabitants were invisible in the darkness, but by no means silent; we could hear countless buzzings and scrapings, and an occasional screech or howl or whistle. I was uncomfortably aware that I would have very little warning should a jaguar decide we looked tasty and that an unexpected moment of relative quiet was more likely to indicate a big cat's arrival than any sound the cat itself might make.

But then a new sound intruded, very faint and far away, a sound too deep in pitch to be made by any insect I knew of, and too steady and rhythmic to be entirely natural for any other creature. I held my breath and listened.

When I was sure what I was hearing, I reached out and shook Miss Vanderhart's shoulder.

"What?" She stirred. "Is it my turn already?"

"No," I whispered. "Listen."

"Listen to what?" she said, pushing herself up on her elbows.

"Steam engines."

In an instant she was crouching beside me, staring upward. I reached for the breathing apparatus.

The airship appeared not as the gleaming monstrosity we saw in daylight, but as a darkness blotting out stars, with a few tiny spots of yellow light along either side. It slid out from one side of the opening above the pool, perhaps two hundred feet up, blacking out more and more of the heavens. It was visibly slowing, even as it encroached on our view of the sky.

I quickly rummaged through my pack until I found a screwdriver, which I tucked into my hip pocket just in case I might find some use for it in prying at an opening somewhere. I checked to be sure my pistol was secure in its oilcloth wrapping, and that my rifle was slung on my shoulder.

That was when two arc lights came on, shooting brilliant white light down on the jungle behind us. "Quick!" I said. "Into the water!" I suited my actions to my words, grabbing my weapons and the breathing device and dragging them with me.

To her credit Miss Vanderhart did not question or hesitate, but followed me immediately in slipping into the water and crawling down the bank until we were submerged up to our necks. She adjusted her goggles as we settled into position, and I found myself wishing that I had a pair – while their primary purpose had always been to protect her eyes from sparks or steam, I thought they might be very useful in the water.

The arc lights' beams swept across the treetops, turning the jungle behind us into a brilliant kaleidoscope of black shadow, white light, and green leaves, and then reached the water. I took a breath and ducked down and was pleased to see Miss Vanderhart do the same. I paddled myself backward slightly, hoping the disturbed water would make it harder for the light to penetrate the water. There were certainly plenty of animals around that might have been startled by this super-scientific intrusion and would have responded by diving into the river; if anyone aboard the Skymaster saw movement, they would have no reason to assume a human cause.

Then both arc lights were directed toward the pool, their glare almost blinding me, though we were just outside the beams. The huffing of the ship's engines ceased entirely, and we could hear rattling chains, metallic banging, and shouting voices, though I could not make out a word of what was being said. I reached for Miss Vanderhart's wrist below the river's surface to reassure her, but she shook off my touch. We waited, once more.

This wait was far shorter than the last. It was no more than ten minutes before a final deafening clang rang out across the jungle, and the airship's great water-scoop descended swiftly toward us.

Our stairway to the skies was before us.

.

Chapter Nineteen

A Dark, Wet Journey

Whenthe water vessel passed into the light of the arc lamps it gleamed blindingly bright. I had expected it to be black iron, but that had been foolish of me; like the airship itself, it was made entirely of that strange silvery metal called aluminum. It fell almost to the surface of the river but at the last possible instant was caught up short by a network of chains, and I was able to get my first good look at it.

It was, as the Maya had told us, essentially a barrel, a bulging cylinder, but made entirely of metal, rather than wooden staves. It was roughly half the size of a Pullman car, supported by chains big enough to secure the largest steamer to a dock. Four of those chains were connected to the circular rim at one end; a fifth was attached at the opposite end, and at the moment that fifth one hung slack, a few of its links trailing in the water, while the other four supported the barrel.

The size was impressive, but given that the Skymaster not only carried a good-sized crew but was driven by steam engines, not really excessive. Those engines would surely consume thousands of gallons in a day's operation, far more than the men would need for drinking and washing.

I heard more shouting overhead, and the water vessel slowly descended another four or five feet, until its base was well below the surface - but at that point its motion changed, and I realized that it was now floating, as any empty bucket, regardless of size, might.

Then we heard a very distinct clank, followed by the huffing of an engine, and that fifth chain began to withdraw, pulling upward into the night sky. And when all the slack had been removed, the gigantic barrel began to tilt, as the chain pulled the bottom out to the side. Clearly, the vessel was going to be filled in exactly the same fashion as an ordinary bucket; McKee and his engineers had not bothered to devise anything needlessly complex when a perfectly viable solution had existed for millennia.

That almost certainly meant that the top of the barrel was open, and when it tilted far enough, water would rush in and fill the vessel. I felt a rush of relief that it appeared so simple, and that the device was not filled through some arrangement of sluices or pipes that would have blocked our entrance. We were crouching in the water perhaps a third of the way around from where that open end would strike the surface.

I raised my head far enough out of the water to expose my mouth. "Come on," I whispered, as I started toward that opening.

Miss Vanderhart took a look upward, blinking in the glare of the arc lights even with a hand shading her eyes, then ducked back down and followed me.

The water grew deeper faster than I realized – but then, it would have to, if they were to fill that immense container effectively here. In order to reach the vessel we would need to swim. Accordingly, I ducked my head, pushed off from the bank, and sent myself shooting forward, a foot or so beneath the surface.

At least we did not need to fight a current; indeed, as water began pouring into the barrel, we were sucked forward, toward it. The churning water and the vivid glare from the arc lights quickly reduced visibility to almost nothing; the world ahead of me was a mass of shining, seething bubbles, white and green and brown. I did not even see the mesh cover on the barrel until I slammed into it.

Fortunately it was my hand, and not my head, that struck first, so I remained fully alert as I struggled to make out what I had encountered. Even as I did, I hoped that the foaming chaos around me hid me from any crewmen overseeing this operation from above.

For a moment I thought my entire scheme was going to be defeated by an entirely predictable and sensible bit of design aimed more at fish than at foes like myself – though there were no pipes or sluices, there was a sturdy aluminum mesh covering the barrel's open top. In fact, this mesh was partially responsible for the churning bubbles that made it impossible to see exactly what I faced, as it acted as a strainer, breaking the flow of water.

Unable to get a clear picture of the situation in the baffling tangle of light, darkness, and foam, I felt my way along the barrel's rim. I was not entirely sure what I was looking for, but when I found it I knew it instantly. I was running my hand along the turned metal that secured the screen when my fingers struck a metal rod in a simple bracket.

A slide bolt.

Blinking, coughing, disoriented, and half drowned, I still recognized a bolt when I felt one. Quickly, I pried at the knob, turned it into the slot, and slid the bolt back. I was not entirely sure what I was releasing, but whatever it was, it could only be to our advantage to open it.

The latch the bolt had secured flapped free, and something began banging; I grabbed at the moving edge and heaved. The rushing water was working against me, trying to push the panel I had opened back into place, but at last I was able to throw it back on its hinges, and I was immediately swept through a hatchway into the interior of the great water vessel, where I banged against the metal side, caught myself, and got to my feet.

I was standing in water to my waist that was rising rapidly. I could clearly see the situation; the arc lamps brilliantly back-lit the foaming torrents spilling through the great screen.

Indeed, the entire open end of the barrel was covered with that sturdy aluminum mesh, but in one spot a hatchway, much like any ordinary hatch in a ship's deck, stood open. The hatch cover was jammed back against the mesh, held by the pressure of the incoming water. Rungs were set into the side of the vessel below the opening.

It only made sense that there would be a hatch; after all, McKee's crew would need access to the vessel's interior on occasion. They probably cleaned the inside regularly; those rungs would let them climb down into it easily. And who could foresee any need to secure it with anything more than a simple slide bolt? Fish would not be able to work even the most primitive of latches.

But there was something else pressed against the mesh beside the hatch cover, a figure silhouetted by the arc lights – Miss Vanderhart. I could see her struggling, and even thought I heard her gasping over the roar of the rushing water and the clanging of objects in the pool bumping against the vessel's sides.

Miss Vanderhart!" I bellowed. "There's a hatchway! To your right, at knee level!"

She heard me, but did not seem to understand – hardly surprising, under the circumstances. She turned to peer through the screen into the vessel's interior, but I could not tell if she saw me in the darkness.

I struggled through the rapidly rising water to confront her and held a hand directly before her face, pointing to the hatchway and gesturing for her to dive to it.

She seemed reluctant to obey; where she was her face was largely out of the water, allowing her to breathe, while the hatchway was now a foot or more below the surface, but eventually she took a deep breath and plunged in the direction I had indicated.

I was waiting for her and pulled her into the vessel as quickly as I could. A moment later we were both standing upright inside the barrel – but the surface beneath our feet was sloping more steeply with every passing instant, as the incoming water weighed down the bottom of the bucket. What's more, the water that was only now reaching my chest was up to her neck and rising rapidly.

I untangled the air supply she had devised for us and held it out to her. She stared at it for a moment, then shook her head. "Not yet," she said, struggling to keep her chin above water as she spoke. "It's going to take them awhile to haul this thing back up to their ship. We can't afford to waste any."

I saw immediately that she was right and nodded, rather than trying to make myself heard over the swirling water – though in fact, now that the vessel was partially filled, the water's noise was lessening. I watched as Miss Vanderhart laced the fingers of one hand through the mesh and pulled herself upward, further into the air that still remained in the vessel.

A moment later the water reached my own nose, and I let my feet rise from the metal beneath us as I leaned backward into a dead man's float – hoping, as I did, that the name would remain purely metaphorical.

Not long after that the entire vessel was full and had tilted until the open end was the top, almost horizontal – and a few inches underwater. The two of us were floating pressed against the mesh, holding our breath as I readied our improvised air pump. We had agreed that if the device did not work, we would climb out through the still–open hatch and dive for safety, abandoning the attempt to board the Skymaster this way. I hoped very much that it would not come to that.

It had been decided that I would go first; I placed my mouth over the valve and squeezed the lever.

I cannot adequately describe the sensation of air jetting into my mouth; I spluttered, gasped, and almost choked, but I persevered, and after a few seconds had mastered the technique. I nodded, made a thumbs up sign to Miss Vanderhart, then passed her the device.

She grabbed it and shot air into her own mouth hard enough to jerk her head back and send her coughing and spitting in a most undignified manner. She adjusted quickly, though, just as I had, and managed to fill her lungs.

She had just passed the device back when, with a rattle and a slither, the chains around the upper rim jerked taut, and the entire vessel swayed, then began to rise, bursting up out of the pool. We were, along with several thousand gallons of water, being hauled up to the airship. All we had to do now was to remain out of sight until the tank was aboard and unguarded.

I reached up and heaved the hatch cover closed; it had been closed when the vessel was lowered and should therefore be closed once it was raised. I could not see an easy way to work the bolt from inside, but I doubted so fine a detail would be noticed, and besides, I was not eager to lock ourselves in. That done, I took Miss Vanderhart by the arm and gestured toward the bottom of the barrel.

It was at that moment, before I could see her response, that the arc lights went out, plunging us into virtually total darkness. It was very fortunate that I had been touching Miss Vanderhart at the time; I was able to guide her, with gestures and gentle tugs. Together we sank to the bottom of the vessel, where we settled onto the metal surface.

We sat there, facing each other but quite invisible to one another, in silent, stygian darkness deep under water, passing the breathing apparatus back and forth every few seconds, working the lever by feel. It was a very strange experience and not a pleasant one.

We could feel the vessel's upward movement, and every so often we would hear a resonant, echoing clang as the tilting-chain bumped against the side, but otherwise our senses were almost useless. I found myself thinking how fortunate it was that McKee had chosen a tropical land as his target; in more temperate climes we might have been risking hypothermia, staying submerged so long, but the water here had been as warm as a well-heated bath, and while I could tell that it was starting to cool, we were, as yet, in no danger in that respect.

I was beginning to worry that our air would run out – we had, after all, no way of measuring it – when new sounds intruded, and a faint glimmer of light appeared far above us. I passed Miss Vanderhart the breathing machine, then looked up. I thought I could make out the golden glow of a lamp, a tiny dot of light far away; I could hear rustling and sliding and thumping sounds, though I did not have enough information to interpret them.

It seemed that we had reached the airship.

I glanced at Miss Vanderhart, and now I could see her face. Her hair had come undone and was drifting around her in a cloud, her nose and eyes were red, and she looked utterly miserable, but she was alive. She took a pull of air, sending a stream of bubbles upward, and stared back at me.

I held a finger to my lips, an obviously stupid gesture I immediately regretted, but I could think of no better way to convey that we were to remain concealed a little longer.

There were more noises – clanging, banging, thumping, scraping – that concluded with a single loud impact that sent the water around us swirling and made my ears ache. After that, I could no longer feel any movement.

That single light above us burned steadily, no longer moving. There were more noises – rattles and hisses, mostly – but none as loud as before.

Then that lone light went out, and silence and darkness descended upon us as we sat in the bottom of the tank, passing the air supply back and forth.

I was beginning to think it might be safe to ascend, to finally get out of the water, when I took the air supply, worked the level, and received only the slightest vibration, and no rush of air.

We had run out. If we were to avoid drowning, we had to get out of the tank *immediately.* I stood, flung the breathing apparatus aside, reached out, grabbed Miss Vanderhart's arm, and tugged her upright. I groped for the rungs, but my companion had grasped the situation immediately and was already swimming upward.

I followed her, praying that no one had checked the latch on the hatch cover.

Fortunately, no one had; the hatch opened easily, and I only remembered at the last instant to catch it before it clanged against the screen. We thrust our faces up through that opening, out of the water, gasping desperately as we struggled to fill our straining lungs. After spending so long submerged the air felt strange, and when I dragged myself up onto the screen my entire body felt weirdly heavy.

Water ran from my clothing and hair and pack in streams and splashed through the mesh; I hoped no one was in earshot. The utter darkness suggested that no one was in the immediate area, but sound might easily travel through the metal walls and floors. In fact, now that the water was out of my ears, I could hear the huffing of the airship's steam engines and other indefinable hummings and hissings. Something that sounded like a pump was chugging away nearby.

I shuddered as my body adjusted to my changed environment, then turned and groped in the darkness for Miss Vanderhart's hand. "Let me help you out," I whispered.

Her fingers closed around my wrist with surprising strength and I heaved her out onto the screen beside me. We lay there in the dark for a long moment, coughing, letting the water run from our clothes, and letting our skin and lungs re-acclimate themselves. She tugged off her goggles and shook them.

"That was stupid," she said at last. "It's a miracle we didn't drown."

A chuckle escaped me. "You were the one who built the breathing device."

"And I shouldn't have done it. That was insane."

"I'm an adventurer. Insanity is part of the job."

"It must be." I could hear her moving, but I could not see what she was doing. "Now what?" she asked.

"Now we find a way off this thing, and see where we are."

"You make it sound simple."

"Well, it probably is," I said. "I can climb one of those chains and see where it goes."

"You'll probably fall to your death."

"Oh, I don't think so." I was already staring into the darkness, trying to see our surroundings, but could only make out vague shapes. I pushed myself up on hands and knees and made my way to the edge of the water vessel, then began inching along until, in fairly short order, I found one of the chains.

It was not drawn tight, but neither was it completely slack; it had a moderate amount of give to it. I got to my feet, intending to climb it – and hit my head on something hard. I suppressed a pained outburst, then reached up to feel what I had struck.

It was a metal surface. I felt it out and concluded that we were under a catwalk that ran directly across, about five feet above the top of the water vessel. What's more, my hand encountered something that I realized was an Edison lamp. A sort of petcock projected from one side of its mounting, and I risked turning that. The light blazed to life, blindingly bright after the deep darkness we had just experienced, but our eyes adjusted quickly. I looked around.

We were in a large, metal-walled, cylindrical chamber; the water tank filled most of its volume. As I had surmised, a catwalk ran across the room approximately five feet above the screened top of the water vessel; about seven feet above *that* was a smooth metal ceiling. The four chains that were secured to the top of the vessel were wound onto huge drums on either side of the catwalk, with formidable machinery attached; I guessed that the drive-belts we could see there were connected directly to the airship's engines. The tank itself, now that I could see it clearly when it was not moving, I estimated to be about fifteen feet in diameter, and the surrounding chamber was perhaps twenty-five feet across. Some of that five-foot ring around the great bucket was taken up with complicated plumbing; when I leaned over the side I could see that half a dozen large hoses had been screwed to valve fittings in the tank's sides. Securing those would explain most of the noises we had heard after the vessel was brought aboard.

With only the single Edison lamp to illuminate this space much of it was still lost in shadows; I looked around and spotted several more lamps. Tracing the wires, I concluded that they were operated by a single set of switches mounted to the wall at one end of the overhead catwalk.

At either end of the catwalk ladders were bolted to the walls, allowing passage down to the floor around the base of the tank. There were also doors at either end of the catwalk, beside the ladders, and I could see two more doors on the lower level, one near the foot of each ladder. All four were closed.

I had no idea where any of them led, but the most important thing was that they led *out*. I pulled Miss Vanderhart to her feet, pointed at the nearer end of the catwalk, and said, "Come on."

Chapter Twenty

Aboard the Flying Fortress

I hoisted Miss Vanderhart up onto the catwalk, then pulled myself up after her, and together we made our way to the door. When we reached it I held a finger to my lips, then put my ear to the wooden panels – the door appeared to be made of balsa wood, which was logical, given the need to minimize weight, and that there was no need for great strength.

I heard nothing but the now familiar sounds of engines and pumps and saw no light beneath; I turned the knob.

The door opened onto another catwalk, a strip of metal flooring between two metal railings. That much was plain enough, but I could not make sense of the rest of what I saw. There were no metal walls to be seen, but a foot or so beyond the railings on either side were great expanses of what appeared to be grayish-white cloth covered in some sort of webbing, as if we were looking into a long, narrow, unlit tent hung with fishnets, one where the sides all seemed to bulge inward, and none quite reached the ground. What was a place like this doing on an airship? That cabin I had seen slung beneath the gas–bag of McKee's craft was large, but still, I had expected it to be filled with small rooms, narrow corridors, assorted equipment, and busy crewmen. How could it contain a space like this?

The only light came from behind us, spilling past us through the open door, which did not make it any easier to interpret the strange vista before us. I looked around for some other source of illumination and spotted a glass-and-wood box with a knob on it much like the one I had turned to work the lamp on the underside of the catwalk, mounted to the wall beside the door we had just opened. I reached around and turned the knob, and another Edison lamp blazed to life inside the box, pouring light through the glass.

With that, I could see what lay before us.

We were not in the airship's cabin at all; we were above it, inside the gigantic aluminum gas-bag itself. The water tank was too tall to fit entirely inside the cabin – and indeed, since much of the water would be used in the steam engines, which were all above the cabin's roof, it was only good sense to give it access to the gas-bag. One would not want to place all that weight *too* far up in the airship's structure, as that would unbalance the craft, but placing it so that the top extended into the gas-bag was perfectly reasonable.

However, that gas-bag was not the simple tin of hydrogen I had assumed it to be. Instead, there were dozens, perhaps hundreds, of separate balloons inside the great aluminum chamber, each one roughly spherical and perhaps eight feet in diameter and secured by that netting.

That made a great deal of sense, now that I thought about it; in fact, looking about, I realized it was a very sophisticated design. There were significant safety advantages; if one or two or three of those balloons were pierced, it would diminish the airship's lifting capacity, but it would not send the whole thing plummeting to earth, as our own Aeronavigator had fallen when its gas-bag was shot up. What's more, I could see pipes and valves and pumps that I judged would make it possible to pump hydrogen or air in or out of the balloons, changing pressure as desired, thereby modifying the airship's buoyancy without any need for ballast and without constantly manufacturing or bleeding off hydrogen. These could surely also be used to adjust the craft's trim, keeping it level, which would be a significant concern aboard a vessel this size.

And the Edison lamps made more sense than ordinary lanterns in this environment – yes, they produced heat and might even spark on occasion, but still, they were surely safer than any sort of open flame in the presence of so much hydrogen. I wondered whether *all* the lights we had seen from the Aeronavigator were Edison lamps, or only those in this vast collection of caged balloons.

I could not see the full extent of the array of gas–bags, of course; I could see about forty feet of catwalk, with elaborate plumbing and bulging off–white balloons lining either side and above, but little else. At the end of that forty feet was a metal staircase, leading in both directions; I guessed that the downward stair opened into the cabin somewhere, while the other led up to the engines and gunners' compartments.

Miss Vanderhart followed me onto the outer catwalk, glancing warily around as she did; whether she realized where we were or not, I could not immediately ascertain. She had tucked her goggles out of sight somewhere and had let her hair down to aid in drying, so that she looked more feminine than her usual wont, and the glow of the electric light enhanced the effect. She leaned forward, by my shoulder, and whispered, "Now what?"

"Now we find some way to destroy this craft," I replied, turning to face her.

She stared at me for a moment, then said, "We're *on* this craft."

Nettled, I answered, "I know that."

"We've already survived one airship crash; do you really want to go for two?"

I glared at her. "Yes, Miss Vanderhart, I do. That's what I came here for, and if you had been paying the remotest attention you would know it."

"I know you want to stop McKee, but I hadn't realized that necessarily involved destroying his ship. If I *had* known you planned that, I might even now be on my way to Belize Town."

"If I leave it intact, some other would-be emperor might take up where McKee left off." I shook my head. "No, it's too dangerous to exist. We need to bring it down, and if at all possible find some way to ensure that the aluminum can't be used to build another one."

"Destroy the aluminum? The actual metal? How do you propose to do that?"

"I don't know," I admitted, as I studied the corridor. "For now, I'll be satisfied bringing down the airship before McKee can use those Gatling guns against anyone else."

"I have no objection to bringing it down if you can do it without killing us," Miss Vanderhart said. "But can you?"

"I don't know," I said, turning my gaze to the balloons. "I am rather more optimistic about it now than I was a few minutes ago, though."

"Why?" she asked.

For answer, I reached for the knife on my belt. I found it somewhat the worse for its long submersion – it did not slide easily from its sheath, the soaked leather grip felt wrong in my hand, and I could see the blade was wet – but it still cut well enough when I slashed at the nearest balloon with it.

The rush of gas was expected, but its effects were not; I had not realized what a face-full of hydrogen would do. Yes, hydrogen is tasteless and odorless, but it isn't breathable, and there may have been other noxious gases mixed in; I began gasping as my lungs found themselves unexpectedly flooded with this unusable substance, and my throat, already much abused by our stay underwater, tightened painfully, choking me. My eyes closed involuntarily, watering badly.

When I could open them again I found Miss Vanderhart staring up into them from mere inches away, which was, in its fashion, almost as disturbing as the choking had been. "I'm all right," I said, but my own voice betrayed me, emerging at a much higher pitch than my usual.

"What are you trying to *do?*" she demanded.

"Bring down the airship," I replied, as I straightened up. I gestured at the balloons, and in particular at the collapsed remnant of the one I had ruined, which now looked like nothing more than a pile of bed linens on their way to the laundry. "If I destroy these one by one, we should descend gently as the vessel loses buoyancy."

She looked around, comprehension dawning. She glanced back at the boxed light.

"The box must be to keep sparks from igniting the hydrogen," I said. "Of course, an ordinary lamp's flame would be *much* too dangerous."

"Of course," she said. Then she glanced along the passageway toward the stairs. "But why isn't anyone guarding this area?"

"Why would anyone need to guard *anywhere?*" I asked. "We're on an airship, hundreds of feet above the ground; there's no way anyone could get aboard without McKee's permission."

She grinned at that. "Of course." She drew her own knife – a rather different implement from my own. I carried a general-purpose Bowie knife. Miss Vanderhart had an engineer's knife that appeared to be designed for scraping and prying, rather than cutting. Still, it had a decent point. Learning from my experience, she kept her face well clear as she slashed the balloon across the catwalk from the one I had deflated. It took two blows – whatever material the balloons were made of had to be tough enough to hold hydrogen, after all, and the netting was also something extraordinarily strong – but her second strike pierced the fabric.

Together, we began walking toward the stairs, cutting the balloons on either side as we went. We had destroyed half a dozen when we both heard the rapid thudding of footsteps on the stairs ahead of us – someone was running up the steps from below.

"It would seem our activities have been noticed sooner than I expected," I said. I sheathed my knife and swung my rifle off my shoulder. Miss Vanderhart stepped behind me. I brought my weapon to bear just as a head appeared in the stairwell; I quickly took aim between the new arrival's eyes. "Stop right there!" I shouted.

The man stopped, eyes wide.

"Hands up!" I called.

He raised his hands.

"Now, come up the steps slowly! Keep your hands where I can see them!"

He obeyed, giving me several seconds to look him over and consider the situation.

He was a young man, lean and muscular, with a somewhat peculiar appearance, and I realized I had seen him before, from a distance – this was the fellow I had seen from the Aeronavigator who had shaved the sides of his head. That odd crested hair of his was stuffed into a black cap, so that I had not spotted it immediately. He wore a black uniform jacket of unfamiliar design, trimmed in gold braid – presumably the self-proclaimed Emperor McKee's livery. The jacket was none too clean, however, and a canvas strap over one shoulder supported a well-worn, soot-blackened bag of tools, indicating that this was a workman or engineer, not a soldier.

When he had reached the level of the catwalk I gestured with the rifle, indicating he should stop. "Who are you?" I demanded.

"Oliver Austin, engineer's mate," he replied.

"What are you doing here?"

"We lost some lift, so I was coming to see what the problem might be." Keeping his hands up, he jerked his head toward the ruptured balloons and collapsed netting on either side. "I'd guess that was your doing?"

"It was," I acknowledged. "Reverend McKee shot down my airship, so I intend to take *his* down." That was by no means my actual motivation, but I thought it would convey a desirable impression. Men working for McKee would certainly understand revenge. "How did you know you had...had lost some lift?"

He looked baffled, as if I had asked how I knew the sky was blue. "We lost altitude, when we hadn't compressed anything."

That was simple enough. I had known that our actions would be obvious in time, but we had scarcely put a dent in the vast supply of hydrogen, and *I* had not felt any change in the airship's behavior. I had not expected the crew to be monitoring the situation so closely in the middle of the night. I cursed myself for that oversight. I had the feeling I had forgotten something else, something at least equally important, as well.

On the other hand, here was a chance to learn more about my foes. "How many men does McKee have aboard?" I asked.

"Thirty, maybe? I never counted," he said. "That's not my business."

"What *is* your business?"

"Well, Jim Tolbert and Mr. Cavendish and I, we keep the machinery running – the steam engines, the gas lines, the gun turrets, the coal burners, all of it. The other fellows, they do the piloting and steering and shooting and see that we've got the coal and water and food we need, but the three of us make sure everything *works*."

"Mr. Cavendish is the ship's engineer?"

"That's right."

It struck me that this Cavendish might be a useful man to see. "Where is he now?"

"Asleep in his bunk, I'd think – it's the middle of the night!"

"Ah. And you take the night watch?"

"You've got the way of it."

"Are most of them men asleep, then?"

"Well – yes, I suppose they are."

I smiled. "Well, far be it from me to disturb them," I said. "How many are awake?"

"There's myself, and Toby at the wheel, and the two lads on watch – I don't know who's got that duty tonight, as I was in the pilothouse with Toby. Little Bertie's up in the coal bunker, I believe. And of course, Mr. McKee keeps whatever hours he pleases, so he might be about."

"That's all? Who was it brought the water tank on board?"

"Well, I oversaw that myself, of course, and Henry and Blackie and Dutch crewed with me, so I suppose they might still be up and about. If I know Dutch, they're in the wardroom passing a bottle around, and when the bottle's empty they'll go sleep it off."

I nodded. "So they're probably still awake, as well. Anyone else?"

"Not as I know of."

"Good." I tried to think what to do next. I was more and more certain I had forgotten something absolutely vital; I shifted my grip on the Winchester as I tried to think what it could be, but nothing came to me.

I had hoped we could do enough damage to the balloons to knock the airship out of the sky before anyone noticed our presence, but Mr. Austin's appearance had ruined that plan – or had it? As yet, no one *else* knew we were here. I was about to suggest that Miss Vanderhart might resume our assault on the balloons, while I held the engineer's mate at bay, when a small bell jingled.

"What does that mean?" I asked Austin.

"That's the signal to open the speaking tube," he said. "I'd guess Toby wants to know what I've found."

I had not noticed the existence of a speaking tube. "Where is it?" I asked.

He pointed upward. "Next landing, by the coal bunker."

"And Bertie is in the coal bunker?"

"He should be – either in the bunker, or feeding one of the hoppers."

"Will he answer, then?"

"He might."

I did not like that; it seemed more and more likely that our presence aboard the airship would soon come to the attention of others. I glanced around, looking for inspiration.

The little bell rang again. I heard movement somewhere ahead and above, and the murmuring of a human voice.

"Is that Bertie?" I demanded of Austin, keeping my voice low.

"Sounds like," he said.

"He's using the speaking tube?"

"That'd be my guess."

"Who's he talking to? Toby?"

"Well, how would I know? Listen, who *are* you, anyway? What are you doing here? Why did you cut up the gas cells? How did you get on board? Why are your clothes all wet? Can I put my hands down? My arms are getting tired."

"I'm Tom Derringer..." I began, but I was interrupted by a voice from above.

"Oliver! You down there?"

Austin gave me a wide-eyed glare and spread his raised hands, plainly wanting me to tell him what to do.

I didn't see any way to keep my presence secret any longer. "He's here," I called back, "but he's my prisoner."

That resulted in a long moment of silence that ended when Bertie, still invisible among the grayish balloons above us, demanded, "Who the Hell are *you?*"

"My name's Tom Derringer," I said. "I've come to put an end to Reverend McKee's little scheme."

"Jack Derringer's boy?" Austin asked.

I gripped the rifle more firmly. "Yes," I said.

"I always heard he was a little feller, but you're almost as tall as I am."

"I take after my mother in that. Now, Mr. Austin, are you armed? Do you have a pistol in that bag of yours?"

"Hell, no," he said. "I'm an engineer, not a cowboy or a soldier. I've got a good knife and a couple of hammers, but no guns. I'm not going to give you any trouble, Mr. Derringer; that's not my job."

"You won't mind if my associate takes a look?" I jerked my head toward Miss Vanderhart.

"Please yourself."

Miss Vanderhart needed no detailed instructions. She marched up to Austin, carefully staying out of my line of fire, and began rummaging through his tool bag. As she did, I asked, "What about Bertie? Is he armed?"

"No more'n I am, most likely. Of course, there's a pair of Gatling guns up there, in the aft turrets."

"He can't use those inside the airship, though; he'd rip the balloons here to bits and bring the whole thing crashing down."

Austin snorted. "That would be some damn fool engineering, letting that happen!" he said. "No, he can't swing the Gatlings around even if he was stupid enough to try it – which, sir, Little Bertie ain't. But even if he was, they're mounted in traveling frames that won't let them shoot anywhere but out the gun ports."

"So he can't turn them on me."

"He surely can't."

"There's no one else up here? Everyone else is down in the cabin?"

I heard a click behind me. Austin grinned and lowered his hands. "Looks like that's not how it is after all," he said.

"*I'm* here," a deep voice said from behind me, a voice I thought I recognized as the one that had shouted across empty space to me just before the Aeronavigator was shot down. "And yes, Mr. Derringer, I'm armed."

Chapter Twenty-One

I Meet Captain Hezekiah McKee At Last

I spun around, swinging the rifle with me, and found myself staring directly at a man I knew at once, from descriptions, newspaper etchings, and our previous long-distance encounter, to be Hezekiah McKee. Instead of his frock coat and topper he wore a cap and jacket similar to Austin's, but impeccably clean and with somewhat more gold braid, unburdened by any tool bag. He stood framed in the open doorway of the chamber that held the airship's water supply. He was pointing a large, rather old-fashioned, but deadly-looking revolver directly at me.

I, however, was pointing my Winchester directly at *him*.

"Reverend McKee," I said.

"I prefer 'Captain'," he said. "Or 'Emperor'."

"As you please, then, Captain. What brings you up here at this hour?"

"It's my ship, Mr. Derringer. I go where I please."

"Yes, of course, but this is hardly as pleasant a place for a stroll as that open gallery of yours. Surely there was something that prompted you in this direction?"

He smiled. "Surely," he said. "When I saw that the Skymaster had descended a hundred feet or so without my orders, when taking on fresh water had already forced us down to a lower altitude than usual, I called in at the pilothouse to inquire as to the reason. Mr. Fotheringay, our pilot, told me that he had sent Mr. Austin up to check on the problem, but had as yet received no report. I told him to call on Mr. Oppett, up in the coal bunker, to see if he had any word of Austin's whereabouts or the nature of our problem, and while he did that I ascended to the forward gangway to do my own investigation." He gestured toward the bulkhead behind him. "I heard voices aft and came through the hydrochamber, moving as quietly as I could. And here we are."

Mr. Oppett, I supposed, would be Bertie. I glanced around. "This would be the aft gangway, then?"

"Very good, Mr. Derringer. If you survive this we might make an airman of you yet – but I think it very unlikely you'll have that opportunity. Yes, there are two stairs from the cabin into the lifting chamber. The aft stair leads to the engines, the coal bunker, and the aft gun turrets, while the forward stair provides access to the forward gun turrets, the altitude regulators, and the main stores. The hydrochamber lies midway between them, to simplify load balancing."

"I see."

"And now, sir, if you would be so kind as to tell me how you survived the destruction of your flying machine and how the Devil you got aboard my ship?"

"Ah," I said. "I don't believe giving you that information would be wise."

"Whereas *I*, now that I have a look at you, don't think it's necessary for you to explain the latter. You stowed away in the water scoop, didn't you? I should have considered that and guarded against it, and it's not an oversight I'll make twice. But you must have stayed submerged for some time; how did you breathe?"

Since having the Aeronavigator shot out from over my head I had given the subject of honesty some thought, especially while sitting in our cell in Chan Santa Cruz, and I had concluded that truthfulness was overrated. "I studied with Tibetan mystics as a boy," I said. "They taught me ancient mystical techniques that allow me to stop my heart at will, or to hold my breath for hours at a time."

He grimaced. "You're scarcely more than a boy *now*," he said. "Did your female companion also study in Tibet?"

I had forgotten Miss Vanderhart's presence when devising my lie. "I taught her myself," I said.

"How very convenient. I think I'll have the water scoop searched, though, just in case; I think I might find some sort of breathing tube. Or perhaps it's still on your person? Or hers?"

"Why are you asking me questions, Captain, if you are not going to believe my answers?"

He smiled the most astonishingly unpleasant smile. "I would not be too hasty to convince me our conversation is useless, Mr. Derringer – if that is indeed your name. The only reason I didn't shoot you immediately was that I would like to know more about how and why you are here."

"However that may be, Captain, I would think that the rifle I have pointed at your heart might discourage you from shooting me; I doubt I will perish so swiftly I won't be able to return fire."

"Ah... Captain?" asked a voice from behind me.

"Yes, Mr. Austin?" McKee replied.

"Would you mind if I were to get out of the line of fire here before you two start shooting one another? Also, could I just remind you both that these gas cells are full of highly combustible hydrogen?"

"A point well taken, Mr. Austin," McKee said. "But I think we saw, when Mr. Derringer's little flying toy went down, that bullets won't ignite the gas."

"Well, they didn't *then*, Captain, but that doesn't mean they never will. We're in an enclosed space here, and that might make a difference."

"I'll keep that in mind, Mr. Austin. In any case, please do go down to the pilothouse and tell Mr. Fotheringay of the situation here and see that the men standing watch are informed, as well."

"Aye aye, Captain." I did not dare turn to look, but I heard footsteps descending the metal stair behind me. I also heard Miss Vanderhart coming closer, and felt her breath on the back of my neck.

There was a moment of silent tension as McKee and I stood, eyes locked on one another and guns pointed at each other's heart; then McKee said, "Now, as I was saying, the only reason you are still alive, Mr. Derringer, is that I want some answers. Make them satisfactory, and I might permit you to live."

"As one of your crewmen?"

He laughed outright at that. "Good heavens, no! Do you think me *that* much of a fool? No, you turned down my offer, and that was your one and only chance. I could never accept a man who refused to join freely; a conversion at gunpoint cannot be trusted for a second. But if you coöperate, I might be convinced to put you aground alive – unarmed, but alive."

"Once again, Captain, may I remind you that I have a rifle pointed at you? I believe my weapon is significantly more accurate than yours."

That disturbing smile was back. "You aren't going to shoot me."

"Oh? Why not?" Even as I asked, though, I had a sudden suspicion he might be right, though he could not have guessed the reason.

"You haven't the stomach for it," he said, and the disdain in his voice was so palpable I was sorely tempted to pull the trigger then and there. I did not, though, because I now doubted whether it would have any effect. I had realized what had been troubling me, nagging at me, for some time now.

I had cleaned the rifle at dusk – and I did not remember reloading it afterward. Those hunters had interrupted my routine just as I finished reassembling and dry-firing the weapon, and I had no recollection of putting any cartridges into the magazine after their departure. I wasn't *sure* I hadn't loaded it – but I wasn't sure I *had*, either. It seemed to feel a bit lighter in my hands than it should, now that it had dried out some, but that might have been my imagination.

"If you think the rifle won't fire after submersion, I think you underestimate Mr. Winchester's work," I said.

"Oh, I think it would fire – if you had the gumption to pull the trigger. I don't think you do. I've been through a real war, boy – you probably weren't *born* yet when I shot my first Yankee – and I can tell when a man's got the fire to kill. I don't see it in you."

My jaw tightened, and I raised the barrel of my rifle ever so slightly.

"What's more, boy, I don't think you're stupid. Your father certainly wasn't – idealistic, yes, but not stupid, from what I've heard of him, and I did have a chance once to speak with a fellow named Sweet who claimed to have known him. You know that you're alone here, where I have two dozen men eager to protect me – or if I've misjudged you completely, to avenge me. The only way you get out of this alive is to tell me what I want to know."

I felt Miss Vanderhart's hand on my back; I shifted my position slightly, into a more traditional shooting stance, which had the advantage of swinging the holster on my belt back, out of McKee's line of sight.

I'm not sure he would have noticed anything in any case. His eyes were directed at my own, with the unwavering gaze of a serpent; undoubtedly he thought that I would betray any intention to shoot him there, and he did not intend to miss it.

I'm not sure whether I had been responding to her signal, or she was taking the hint I gave, but once I had turned, I felt Miss Vanderhart pull my wrapped Colt from the holster, just as I had hoped. *That* gun I knew to be loaded, with bullets in five of the six chambers as was my custom; now, once she had unwrapped it, we needed merely contrive some way for me to swap weapons.

"Ask, if you're going to," I said.

"Perhaps I should wait until my men arrive. You may be more coöperative when surrounded."

"Oh, I don't think so."

"Very well, then. Tell me, who hired you?"

"No one," I said. "I told you that when we spoke before."

"You hold to that outrageous story?"

"It's the truth." I felt a length of oilcloth brush against my leg as it fell to the catwalk, and I heard a faint click, as if Miss Vanderhart was turning the revolver's cylinder to bring a live round into position.

"You bought yourself that sorry excuse for a flying machine and chased me across the entire length of Mexico on a *whim?*"

"Yes, I did," I said. "I'm a wealthy man, Captain McKee, and able to freely indulge my whims."

"It seems a very *peculiar* whim, Mr. Derringer. Are you quite sure you weren't encouraged in this rash enterprise by some older gentleman? Gabriel Trask, perhaps?"

I had no idea who this Gabriel Trask might be, but I was not going to reject the gift. I wanted to misdirect McKee in any way I could, but had not had the means to devise a plausible lie – until now. "How did you know?" I asked. "He told me you'd never figure it out."

The expression on McKee's face in response to this was fascinating; he was obviously furious and trying to hide it, but there was more to it than that – disgust, maybe? Condescension? I really wasn't sure what I was seeing.

"Trask," he said. "Of course."

"He didn't *hire* me, as such," I said.

"Of course not. That would be much too direct for a scheming scoundrel like Gabriel Trask. I suppose he offered you a reward of some sort? Some service his corrupt cadre of spies and assassins could provide?"

"Something like that," I said, trying to make it sound like a reluctant admission. "Captain McKee, perhaps there has been a misunderstanding. Might we put down our weapons and discuss this like gentlemen?"

I made this suggestion not because I really thought we had anything to discuss, but because it had become clear there was no other way I would emerge safely from this standoff. McKee's henchmen would be arriving at any moment. My rifle might not be loaded, while McKee's revolver undoubtedly held half a dozen bullets. It appeared I had a much better chance of talking my way out than shooting my way out.

He stood for a moment, clearly considering my proposal, then shook his head. "No, Mr. Derringer. I think we'll just wait for my men to arrive and then tie the two of you up. I think I'll find whatever you might have to say more believable once you see that you have no alternatives other than coöperation or death."

"And if I decide I'd rather see you and myself both dead than allow myself to be captured?"

"You won't do that. You're a young man, Mr. Derringer, with your whole life ahead of you. You don't want to die for the simple mistake of listening to that bastard Trask and believing his lies – and they *are* lies, I assure you. He never delivers on his promises, not really."

This was getting interesting – who *was* this man Trask, and what history did he have with McKee? But I could not afford to be taken prisoner; there was no reason to believe McKee's promise to let me live if I coöperated.

"Why should I believe you, instead of him?" I demanded, raising the rifle's barrel to point between McKee's eyes. *Had* I loaded it, after all? Perhaps a single shell in the breech?

"Fine," McKee said. He raised his pistol, pointing the barrel upward, and cocked the hammer. "If you're so certain, then go ahead and shoot me."

I hesitated for only an instant. This was my chance! While some part of me screamed that this was murder, I knew that it was justice. McKee and his men had slaughtered twenty-two Mayan villagers, and if I permitted him to continue he would plunge all of Mexico into war. Praying that my habits and training had not failed me, I pulled the trigger.

There was a click as the hammer fell on the empty chamber.

His eyes widened, and for a moment he stared at me, shocked. Then he threw his head back and laughed.

While he was thus giving voice to his amusement, I quickly reversed the rifle and took a swing at his head with the stock.

Alas, he was more alert than I expected; he ducked, and brought his pistol back down to point at my face.

"It would seem I misjudged you, young man," he said. "You had the backbone to shoot, after all – but not the ammunition! Or has the mechanism rusted, perhaps? Fool. I've had quite enough of you. Drop the rifle. Now." His finger tightened on the trigger.

I expected to die, then and there, and I resolved to go down fighting. I would not close my eyes and meekly await death. If I had to join Ashton Darlington and Ichabod Tunstall and the rest of Mr. Arbuthnot's list of unsuccessful adventurers, at least I would play my role to the end. I lifted the rifle by the barrel, readying another swing.

A shot rang out, the sharp report almost deafening; the sound echoed from the stretched fabric of the gray-white balloons that still surrounded us. I waited for the bullet's impact.

It didn't come. Instead McKee's own eyes widened, and the pistol tumbled from his hand as he looked down at the blood spilling from his chest. Then he raised his head again, and his mouth opened, but no sound emerged.

Then his knees buckled, and he crumpled to the metal floor.

Chapter Twenty-Two

Polite Captivity and Gentle Interrogation

I turned to see Miss Vanderhart standing behind me, my smoking Colt clutched in her trembling hand. She had fired under my arm and struck McKee in the center of his chest. "Is he dead?" she asked.

I considered taking the gun from her hand, but decided against it. Yes, she appeared stunned by her own action, and the hand holding the revolver was anything but steady, but it was not at all clear she would give the weapon up without a fight. Instead I said, "Point that thing somewhere else, and I'll check."

She pointed it somewhere else, a random direction off to her right. I dropped my rifle and knelt by McKee - or rather, beside McKee's corpse; I could feel neither heartbeat nor breath, and his eyes were wide open and horribly blank. He was gone.

The suddenness and ease with which the Reverend Captain Hezekiah McKee had left this world struck hard at some part of my soul, and I found myself trembling just as hard as was Miss Vanderhart, even though I had not been the one to fire the fatal shot. My stomach churned, and I thought for a moment it might betray me completely, but I was able to keep my gorge down, and kept enough of my wits about me to pick up the dead man's revolver.

I was just rising to my feet when footsteps came thundering up the metal stair; I turned to face the new arrivals, struggling to devise an explanation that would stave off further bloodshed.

The figure who emerged from the stair was a stranger, though I was fairly sure I had seen him before – he wore a kilt, as had one of the men at the rail when the Aeronavigator was shot down, along with the airship's now familiar black livery jacket. He was heavily built and held a pistol, one more modern than the one I had just retrieved, pointed upward – not, I was pleased to see, at me. I could quite possibly have gotten the drop on him, and the possibility of shooting him did occur to me, but I was in no hurry to shed more blood. Furthermore, my father's journals had provided plentiful evidence that it was, in general, easier to talk one's way out of a tight spot than to shoot one's way out.

"What happened?" he demanded, speaking with a Scottish accent.

I considered various possible answers, truthful and otherwise, and arrived at the one that I thought most likely to avoid further hostilities. "He tried to force himself on Miss Vanderhart," I said. "She fired in self-defense."

She turned to stare at me in open-mouthed astonishment, and I was grateful that the new arrivals – a second man was now ascending the stair behind the first – could not see her expression, which was quickly shifting to outrage.

"I don't think she meant to kill him," I added quickly. "She may not have intended to shoot him at all."

"Shoot...he's dead? Captain McKee?" The accent might have been that of Aberdeen – I had had some instruction in identifying local accents, but cannot claim great expertise, and at that moment I was not especially concerned with his origins.

"I'm afraid so," I said. "But I'm no doctor; if you think there's still a chance to save him..." I let my sentence trail off, unfinished.

The man gave me an uncertain glance, then lowered his gun and stepped past me to examine the corpse. I made way as best I could on the narrow catwalk, keeping my own newly acquired weapon pointed skyward.

More men were coming up the stairs now, coming to stare at the tableau we presented. None seemed to be taking any particularly aggressive attitude, and I only saw one other, the second to arrive, who was visibly armed. Oliver Austin was among them, and at least one other also gave the impression of being another engineer, rather than any sort of fighter.

The first man had knelt by McKee's body, much as I had, and checked for a pulse, then for breathing. He found neither. He thumbed back an eyelid, noting the complete lack of response. Then he stood and turned to the others. "He's gone," he said.

"Now what, yer Lairdship?" someone called from the stairs.

"Who killed him?" asked a late arrival.

"The girl," the second man answered.

"You sure?"

"Check the guns," I said. "Hers is the only one that's been fired."

I heard someone mutter, "Self-defense, the man said."

Miss Vanderhart had finally come to a good understanding of the situation and cried out, "He came at me! I didn't know what to do!" Then she burst into tears.

Perversely, that outburst seemed to lighten the atmosphere immensely. I threw my arm around her and drew her close, letting her cry on my chest.

"Why'd she have a gun in the first place?" someone asked, and I turned on him, glad to have a target for my own fury – which was not, I must confess, as false as I had meant it to be; I had been holding my emotions in check for some time, throughout our submarine adventure and the confrontation with McKee, and given this outlet they were more than I could control. Fear and frustration turned to rage.

"You shot us down in a jungle full of bloodthirsty savages!" I shouted, and I could feel my face reddening. "What kind of man would I be if I didn't give her some means to defend herself? Little did I know that when she needed it, it would be against a fellow American!" I managed to bite off any further words, and instead embraced Miss Vanderhart more tightly. Her tears were soaking my shirt as she continued to sob; clearly, her distress was not entirely feigned, any more than was my anger.

"What do we do with 'em, Mr. Watt?" someone asked.

"I'll have to wake Lieutenant Entwhistle," the man in the kilt. "He's next in command."

"Is there somewhere we could sit down?" I asked. "Away from that?" I nodded toward the corpse.

The man considered, then said, "Bill, take them to the after salon."

Bill, it appeared, was the other armed individual. "Come on," he said, with a jerk of his head. "This way."

We were escorted down the stairs to a comfortably furnished parlor, where Miss Vanderhart draped herself upon a settee, her peculiar engineer's attire looking almost comically out of place, even without her goggles. For my own part I took a few minutes to gaze out the windows at the tropical night, with the stars above us and the black jungle below, then found a place on a music bench and began idly picking out tunes on the rosewood piano. I was never much of a pianist, but learning a few basics had seemed a reasonable thing to do, especially after reading in my father's journals how he had once used a harpsichord to send cipher messages to Darien Lord without their foes ever noticing a thing. No one attempted to disarm us, which rather surprised me. I suppose that if anyone thought of it, they decided it was unnecessary – we were outnumbered, outgunned, and as I had just confirmed at the window, hundreds of feet above ground, with nowhere to go if we attempted to shoot our way out. Bill stood guard over us, but seemed pleasantly casual about it.

We had been there only a few moments when I heard an odd chattering, and looked up from the keyboard to see Miss Vanderhart sitting upright, her hands in her lap. She was trembling. I abandoned the piano and hurried to her side. "Are you well, Miss Vanderhart?" I inquired.

"*No*, I'm not well!" she snapped. "I just killed a man!"

"Yes, you did," I said. "But he was a butcher who ordered the destruction of an entire village, a would–be conqueror, guilty of who knows what crimes in years past. Surely, you cannot regret his death."

"I can regret *killing* him!" she retorted. "He was alive, and then he wasn't, and I..." She looked down at her hands. "I did that. I feel sick when I think about it."

I hesitated, unsure what to say. I could hardly fault her for taking a man's death seriously; indeed, if she did *not* suffer pangs for what she had done, I would suspect her heart to lack normal human sensitivity. Still, this did not seem the ideal time and place for such a reaction.

I wondered whether, had it been I rather than she who shot McKee, I would be feeling such remorse.

At any rate, I could think of no way to help and sat beside her in useless silence for a moment before retreating once again to the piano bench and leaving her to contemplate her actions without my interference.

I would estimate we waited almost half an hour in all before a tall, cadaverous individual stalked in and introduced himself. Four or five somewhat more familiar faces followed him into the room; I was sufficiently tired that I was not sure whether the party now included every living soul we had encountered aboard the aluminum airship, but it was certainly the majority of them.

The tall stranger, however, was the only one who spoke. "Lieutenant James Apollonius Entwhistle, late of the C.S.A.," he said. He did not salute, but his arm twitched, as if he were fighting the impulse to do so. "And who might *you* be?"

"I might be the bloody Prince of Wales," I said, "but I'm not. My name is John Thomas Derringer, Junior, of New York, and my companion is Miss Betsy Jones."

"That's not the name he gave for her upstairs," Bill interjected. "He called her something Dutch."

"It's Vanderhart," she said. She appeared to have entirely recovered from her earlier distress. "Betsy Vanderhart. Mr. Derringer was attempting to protect me. My father has enemies."

"Thank you, Miss. Is his name really Derringer?"

She glanced at me, then said, "So far as I know, yes. I've never heard him use another."

Lieutenant Entwhistle nodded. "Connor Watt has told me something of what happened up in the lifting chamber, but let me see if I understand the situation. The two of you were aboard that funny little airship we shot down a few days ago?"

"We were," I admitted.

"Why? What were you doing there?"

I sighed. "I bought the machine from Miss Vanderhart's father so that I might track down the mysterious object sighted over Phoenix, an object that turned out to be this airship that we are all presently aboard. Miss Vanderhart accompanied me to teach me how to operate and maintain her father's creation."

"Then you snuck aboard our airship when we refilled the main water supply?"

"Yes."

"Why?"

"Captain McKee had downed our craft; I intended to return the favor. I had not expected him to discover us and to attempt to assault Miss Vanderhart."

"About that – it seems rather out of character for the captain." This was greeted with murmurs of agreement from the little knot of men observing our conversation.

I glanced at Miss Vanderhart, then back at the lieutenant. "He lunged at her and grabbed for her blouse, and we both certainly perceived that as an affront to her modesty, at the very least. If his intentions were otherwise, he should have made that plainer. I flung myself between them, but too late – Miss Vanderhart had already fired the fatal shot."

"Was the captain armed?"

"With this very pistol," I said, displaying the weapon I had retrieved.

"Ah," Lieutenant Entwhistle said. "No wonder Mr. Watt failed to discover it. That's the same gun that Captain McKee carried in the war; he kept it with him at all times. How do *you* come to have it in your possession?"

"Why, he dropped it when he fell, and I picked it up. I would be happy to deliver it to his heirs." I proffered the weapon, but the lieutenant did not take it.

"Why didn't you hang on to your own rifle? At least, I presume that was your weapon we found?"

"Of course it was," I said. "I flung it aside as a gesture of good will. And if you think I came aboard planning murder, I suggest you check the magazine – it wasn't even loaded. When I held it on Mr. Austin I was bluffing, plain and simple. His appearance had caught us by surprise. We had intended only to slash enough of those balloon things to bring this airship gently to ground."

He stared at me for a moment, then sighed. "Even if I believe you – and I admit your account does seem consistent with the facts – is there any reason I should not simply shoot you both out of hand?"

"Aside from common human decency, you mean?"

He smiled unpleasantly. "Aside from that."

"Well, I have been wiring regular reports of my progress back to New York, so that my approximate whereabouts and circumstances are known; if you kill me, I would like to think my friends would make some effort to avenge me, even if the authorities do not. As for Miss Vanderhart, her father is a professor of engineering at Rutgers University, and he has done a fair amount of work for the federal government; I think there are a good many powerful people who would take umbrage at her murder."

He considered that at length, then said, "So with Captain McKee dead, what are your intentions toward the rest of us?"

I shrugged. "I *have* no intentions toward the rest of you. I hold Captain McKee solely and entirely responsible for the destruction of the Aeronavigator, and his fate has been taken out of my hands. What are *your* intentions? What do you plan to do with this flying machine?"

Lieutenant Entwhistle glanced at his compatriots. "That hasn't been decided," he said.

"I'd like to make some comments on that, if I may."

McKee's crewmen exchanged glances. "Go ahead," Entwhistle said.

"I hope you weren't planning to continue with your late captain's original scheme. The Mayans are unlikely to coöperate. They took us prisoner, you know, and told us something of what was going on. They did not take kindly to your people shooting up that village. If that carnage was meant to convince them of McKee's divinity, I'm afraid it failed. Instead they set us free, and helped us get aboard, in hope that I would indeed be able to bring down your vessel. Besides, if McKee was supposed to be a god, his death is not going to fit the narrative well – not unless he returns to life, and if he does that, *I'll* be convinced of his godhood."

At least one of the men blushed at this blasphemy, and the Scotsman gave a snort, but I continued, "*My* advice would be to fly this thing to Belize Town, in British Honduras – it's only a hundred miles or so south of us, on the coast. I'd guess the British governor there would be interested in buying it from you, or perhaps hiring you as mercenaries. I'd think Her Majesty's government might be interested in signing up some aerial privateers."

"British?" Again, the men looked at one another. "Privateers?"

"That's...that's a very interesting suggestion, Mr. Derringer," Entwhistle said. "Were you thinking of joining us in this proposed career of piracy?"

"Me?" I managed a weak laugh. "Good heavens, no! I just want to go home to New York. I'd very much appreciate it if you could put me ashore - or rather, aground - in Belize Town, where I ought to be able to book passage thither."

"Lieutenant," someone asked, "can we trust him?"

"Trust him to do what?"

"To not double-cross us. He might tell the authorities we shot those Indios, or sic McKee's family on us, trying to claim the airship."

"Why would I do that?" I asked. "What's in it for me? And if I did, why would the British care that you shot a bunch of savages on the other side of the border? How would McKee's heirs enforce a claim? How could they prove McKee ever owned this thing in the first place? Possession is nine points of the law."

"He's got a point there," Austin said.

"I'm not sure about this privateering idea," another man said.

"Then just sell the ship's metal," I said. "Do you have any idea what aluminum is worth on the open market? This thing probably contains two-thirds of the world's entire supply; if McKee hadn't been more interested in power than in money, he would have taken the aluminum straight from the Lost City to the assay office."

"Now, *that's* an idea!" Austin replied.

"Lieutenant, can we trust this man?"

"He didn't shoot me when he had the chance," answered the man who had first found us with McKee's corpse.

"He's been peaceful as a mouse waiting here," Bill added. "Spent most of the time playing the piano."

"What about the girl?"

"What *about* her? She's just a girl under that silly outfit."

"She did shoot the captain."

"In self-defense!"

"So she says."

That brought a moment of uneasy silence, broken at last when someone asked, "Shouldn't we do something about that?"

That provoked another awkward silence; clearly, nobody really wanted to take the initiative in dealing with Miss Vanderhart's act of homicide.

Throughout this exchange I had held my tongue, in the conviction that anything I might say was more likely to do harm than good. Defending either Miss Vanderhart or myself would be an invitation to argue with us. I waited.

Finally, the Scotsman - Mr. Watt, I assumed - defiantly announced, "I believe her. It's not *my* problem if the captain got himself killed. It's not as if we all loved him like a father - I don't think there's a one of us hasn't complained about the way he treated us. I can't say I'll miss him."

Some of the others exchanged sheepish glances at that, and I judged that McKee had indeed not been beloved of his men.

"Should we wake up the rest of the crew, perhaps, and see what they say?" someone suggested.

Watt shook his head. "With the captain gone, the lieutenant's in charge; it's up to him."

"We'll discuss it with them in the morning," Entwhistle announced. "For now, I think it's high time we got some rest."

By the expressions on the other men's faces, I judged that to be the wrong thing to say. Most, perhaps all, of the others had been on the night watch to begin with. Only Lieutenant Entwhistle had been rousted out of bed. No one, however, seemed inclined to argue. The crowd began to dissipate.

"Wait a minute," Bill protested. "What about them?" He jerked a thumb toward Miss Vanderhart and myself.

The lieutenant paused in the doorway. "Keep an eye on them," he said.

"Shouldn't they be locked up somewhere?"

"Why?" Entwhistle asked. "We're four hundred feet up; they aren't going anywhere."

Bill had no answer for that; he stood in disgruntled silence as the others departed.

When there were once again just the three of us in the salon, he glared at us and said, "Don't give me no trouble."

"Of course not," I said.

"Give me those guns."

I handed over McKee's revolver and watched as Miss Vanderhart reluctantly surrendered my own pistol.

"And that knife."

I drew my Bowie knife and presented it, hilt first.

He did not demand Miss Vanderhart's engineer's knife; I assume he had not noticed its existence amid her clutter of tools. He placed our guns and my knife on a table at his elbow, then flopped into the chair beside it, his own pistol still in his hand.

I settled back on the bench, then turned to the keyboard and tried to pick out a half-remembered Bach fugue.

Chapter Twenty-Three

The Fall of the Aluminum Airship

Looking out the salon window I could see the first traces of pink in the eastern sky when Bill finally dozed off. I had been playing lullabies as quietly as I could for the past hour or more, humming along with the piano, in hopes that boredom, exhaustion, and the calming effects of music would overcome his sense of duty.

At first I had more or less meant what I told the lieutenant. I was tired after our adventures, and McKee's death had disturbed me - not, it may be, as much as it had disturbed his killer, but I was nonetheless unsettled by my first close encounter with violent death. I had thought that perhaps eliminating McKee was enough, at least for the moment, and that leaving the aluminum airship intact might not be so *very* unfortunate.

The more I thought about it, though, the more the idea of leaving this flying monstrosity fully functional troubled me, and the less I trusted McKee's men to free Miss Vanderhart and myself. As I had sat at the piano, playing whatever piece came to mind, I had gradually come to the conclusion that we did need to completely destroy the Skymaster, just as I had told Miss Vanderhart when we first came aboard. I had devised a few possible approaches, most of which began with escaping from our guard immediately; anything that waited until full daylight, when the rest of the crew would be about, would be far more difficult.

I had therefore casually switched my playing to the most calming, soporific tunes I could recall, and had, after longer than I had hoped, achieved the desired result.

Now the trick was to capitalize on his slumber before anyone else woke up. Moving as silently as I dared, I retrieved my revolver – I had more faith in the familiar weapon than in McKee's antique – and crept toward the door.

I noticed Miss Vanderhart's eyes were following my every move. I held a finger to my lips. Alas, that did not have the effect I had hoped for; rather than staying quietly in her seat, she rose and, with a single quick glance at our guard, followed me.

When we were out the salon door and moving down the passage toward the stairs, she whispered, "Where are we going?"

"To destroy this airship," I replied.

"We're still *on* the airship!" she pointed out.

"I'm well aware of that."

"If you slash more of the gas cells, they'll notice again, just as they did the first time."

"That would be why I am not going to use that method," I retorted.

"Then what *are* you going to do?"

"I am going to light a match in the lifting chamber," I told her.

"But the hydrogen! It will explode!"

"That's exactly my intention," I said.

"We'll be killed!"

"That is *not* my intention."

"How do you plan to *prevent* it?"

"We, Miss Vanderhart, will be off this ship by the time of the explosion. At least, I hope we will."

"*How?*"

"Suppose you were to remove two of those balloons and leap over the rail of that aft gallery holding one of them, while I followed with the other – what would happen?"

She blinked. "I...I don't know," she said. "One might not be enough – and how would you get it out?"

"You, Miss Vanderhart, are the engineer here – how would *you* get it out?"

"I don't...well, hydrogen is compressible, but I don't... wouldn't it be easier to cut a hole in the side, and go out that way, rather than trying to get the gas cell down the stairs?"

"Would it?"

"I think so, yes." Then, more certainly, "Yes, it would."

"Good! Can you cut a hole, then?"

"I don't know. What is that gray stuff? It isn't all aluminum, isn't it? I've never worked with aluminum."

"I don't know what it is, but from what we saw before, only the frame appeared to be metallic aluminum. The sides appeared to be fabric."

"We can probably cut that," she said.

"Let us hope so."

We proceeded up the stairs, out of the cabin and into the great lifting chamber, which was now dark and deserted. We were just reaching the catwalk where we had encountered McKee when Miss Vanderhart said, "All the others will die, though, won't they? The crew?"

"In all likelihood, yes."

"That's... that's murder."

"So was what they did to those Mayan villagers."

"That doesn't make it right."

"No, it doesn't." I could have made further excuses, or suggested that McKee's crew might survive the crash, but I decided there was no need. I was willing to accept the responsibility of killing these men - or at least, so I told myself.

The thought did trouble me, though. We had taken another few steps when I blurted, "You didn't hesitate to kill McKee."

"I should have, and in any case, he was holding us at gunpoint!"

I did not reply; I had no sensible retort, and in any case I was looking for the switch that would turn on the Edison lamp.

"Why don't you just let them fly to Belize Town, as you suggested?" she continued. "They don't seem to mean us any harm."

"Because, Miss Vanderhart, I do not want to leave a mechanical monstrosity like this airship loose in the world, not when there's no possibility that others can be built to stop it."

"Can't you *warn* them? They could lower themselves on ropes, the way they do when they fetch supplies."

"If I warn them, they might find a way to stop me." I did consider the possibility, though. *Was* there a way to stop me? Would they think of it, if there were? After all, it would not take much to set all that hydrogen ablaze; now that I was out of the cabin and into the lifting chamber I could make some very convincing threats.

My hand finally located the lamp case and found the control. I turned it, and light blazed forth.

McKee's body had been removed, but his blood was still smeared on the catwalk. The half-dozen balloons - or "gas cells," as the engineers seemed to call them - that we had slashed still lay limp and empty on either side, while dozens more filled the surrounding space. Miss Vanderhart stepped past me, then knelt by an undamaged one, examining the fittings that connected it to the pipes that supplied it with hydrogen.

"I can tie this off and cut it free," she said, "and we can hold onto the silk netting. But one for each of us won't be enough. I'll need at least two, I'd estimate, and you'll want three or four. One wouldn't even do as much as we managed with the Aeronavigator's gas bag after it was shot."

"All right," I said.

"I'll need tools and probably some cord – though I suppose I can cut that from the netting. I'll particularly need something to cut through the side – I doubt I can do *that* with just a pocket knife."

I nodded.

She hesitated, then asked, "Why can't we just go down the ropes and escape? Why do we have to destroy it? I think we've demonstrated that it's not as invulnerable as McKee thought."

"But they *know* how we got on board, simply because we were still soaked when they found us; we wouldn't be able to do it again."

She frowned, and then repeated, "I'll need tools. More than the ones I have. Wrenches, for these gas fittings."

I looked around for anything resembling an equipment locker, but saw nothing promising. I didn't remember seeing one in the hydrochamber, either, though surely the crewmen had used *some* tools in attaching the various water lines after bringing the scoop aboard. Perhaps they had carried those away again when they were done.

"There are probably some up near the engines," I said, pointing.

"I'd think so," she agreed.

"Little Bertie Oppett is probably still up there in the coal bunker." I drew my Colt. "But I doubt he's armed." I started toward the stairs.

"Don't hurt him!" she called after me.

I did not bother to reply. I had no particular interest in harming anyone, but neither did I intend to be balked in my efforts to bring down this aerial leviathan. My foot hit the first step – and I heard a bell jingle. I paused. I heard Little Bertie's voice as he opened the speaking tube and called into it.

I hesitated only briefly, then continued up the stair.

I had not seen this part of the airship before – and in fact, it was not easy to see now, as the gas cells pressed in on all sides. The narrow stair rose perhaps fifteen feet through the array of hydrogen balloons and then debouched onto a platform with no fewer than six other exits. Catwalks led through the gray gas-bags directly to either side; I guessed those went to the gun turrets. Forward there was nothing but a rail, where gas cells pressed in. Astern, however, was a wooden partition, with a walkway at either side and a ladder leading upward; I guessed these led to the three engines that propelled the flying machine through the heavens. Pipes extended alongside all three that I supposed provided water for the steam engines.

Next to the ladder was an open door, revealing the interior of what could only be the coal bunker. A boxed Edison lamp, like the ones we had seen below, illuminated a room blackened with coal dust, revealing a system of chains and buckets that presumably distributed fuel to the three engines. Behind this was a vast coal bin, very nearly full. Assorted shovels were leaning against a wall.

Standing near the door, half-hidden by the frame, his back to me, was a boy, not even my own age, whose attention was focused on a gray metal tube that emerged from the wall at roughly head height. This, obviously, was Little Bertie.

He turned at the sound of my footsteps. His eyes widened, and he shouted, "He's here!"

"Indeed I am," I said, stepping into the room and aiming the gun at his face. I looked around and spotted a well-stocked tool bench, but tried not to let him see my interest in it as I said, "Now, I want you to tell whoever's on the other end of that tube that we are going to blow up this airship – my partner is preparing to do so even now, and I'm sure you know enough about hydrogen to know it won't take much to destroy the entire thing. If anyone tries to interfere, we'll simply torch one of the gas cells, and I expect that will set them *all* off and bring us down that much sooner. If you men want to survive, you'll lower those ropes you use for hauling up supplies, and you'll all get off this flying deathtrap before it turns into a gigantic fireball."

"He's got a gun!" Bertie shrieked into the speaking tube. "They're going to blow up the ship!"

I could not make out the response, but apparently Bertie could. "I don't *know* how many there are!" he said. "I just see one, but he says his partner is setting charges right now!"

"Tell him," I said, pulling back the hammer on my pistol for dramatic effect, "that you have eight minutes to get off this ship or die." I picked eight, rather than five or ten, to enhance the impression that a countdown was already underway and could not be stopped.

Bertie relayed my message and added belatedly, "...And if you try to stop them they'll set it off *now*."

Again, I couldn't hear the reply, but Bertie answered, "How should *I* know?" He turned and addressed me. "Are you planning to kill yourselves?"

I grinned as maniacal a grin as I could manage, and said, "As our lord has commanded us."

Bertie shuddered, then shouted into the tube, "He's *crazy*! Yes, they're planning to die!"

"Close the tube," I said, gesturing with the gun.

"Bill said you jumped him and knocked him unconscious," Bertie said, as he jammed a cork into the tube.

It seemed Bill had not admitted to dozing off. "That wasn't me; that was Fred," I said, to further confuse the issue. "Now, get down those stairs and off this ship!" I stepped aside, gesturing with the gun again, and he dashed past me, clattering down the metal steps as if all the demons of Hell were after him.

I followed, at a more leisurely pace, after I had gathered up a few tools I thought might be useful.

I found the lower catwalk empty, but Miss Vanderhart had apparently heard my approach; she called from somewhere off to starboard, "Over here!"

I tried to follow the sound of her voice, but she had crawled through the massed gas cells by a route where my larger frame did not readily fit. I wrapped my fingers in the netting and clambered off the catwalk into the maze of fabric and cord, but could not get very far. "Where are you?" I called.

"Over here!" she repeated, but she had apparently recognized my predicament and was making her way back through the gas cells. A moment later her face emerged, and she smiled at me. She had not retrieved her goggles, and I could see that her eyes were bright with excitement. Her hair was tangled and dirty, her face smeared with grease and dust, but she seemed pleased with herself. "I don't know what that outer skin is made of, but it's not as tough as I feared," she said. "I should have a large enough hole in a few minutes."

"Good," I said. "But we may need to hurry. I took your suggestion and warned the crew. If they decide to try to stop us instead of fleeing, we'll want to get out of here quickly."

"Oh," she said. Then she saw the tools in my arms, and smiled again. "Give me that!"

She snatched an implement I did not recognize and vanished back into the lightless tangle of cloth and silken mesh. I struggled to follow, plowing through the gas cells, hoping that my movements would not strike a spark and kill us all.

A moment later a sudden burst of light and air washed over me, and I saw open sky ahead of me. By the soft gray color of that sky it was still early morning, not yet full daylight.

"Now I just need to rig harnesses," Miss Vanderhart said, as she knelt amid the balloons, hacking at the silk netting.

I stared out through the hole she had cut in the vessel's side, and the insanity of what we were about to attempt caught up with me. I could see jungle far below us, stretching out toward the distant horizon, and while the angle was such that I could not accurately gauge our altitude, I knew it had to be well over a hundred feet – probably the full four hundred Lieutenant Entwhistle had claimed. If these improvised balloons failed us, we would plummet to our deaths. Or if I misjudged the explosion, we might be cooked by flaming hydrogen.

"Keep at it," I said, as I pushed my way back toward the catwalk.

"Derringer!" someone called – from some distance away, so I continued my crawl through the gas cells. I did not answer.

"Derringer!" the voice came again. "This is Lieutenant Entwhistle! Are you there?"

"Of course I'm here," I shouted back, annoyed. "Where *else* could I be?"

"Why are you doing this?" Entwhistle called. I thought his voice was coming from the stairs.

"Because this machine is too dangerous to leave intact!" I bellowed back. "Why are you still aboard?"

"Because I think you're bluffing! I think you want the airship for yourself!"

I snorted as I tumbled out onto the catwalk. "What in blazes would *I* want it for?"

"The same things as any other man!" the lieutenant called.

I looked around and spotted the oilcloth that had been wrapped around my pistol. I snatched it up, then fished in my pocket for matches, hoping that inundation had not ruined them all. "I don't want *anyone* to have it," I called. "Are the others with you? Because I'm not bluffing about blowing it up."

"They're all climbing down the ropes," he said. His voice was definitely coming from the stairwell. "I'm the only one here to call your bluff."

I wondered whether that was true, or if he merely intended to make me lower my guard while someone came around behind me, as Captain McKee had.

"Ready!" Miss Vanderhart called.

"Coming!" I called back. Then I shouted to Entwhistle, "This is your final warning – get to ground *now!*"

"Listen, we can share it!" he cried. "You'll need a crew – you can't fly it by yourself!"

"Last chance," I said, as I began climbing back through the gas cells, the oilcloth in one hand and a box of matches in the other. The box, I noticed, was much the worse for wear, the pasteboard softened and distorted, but dry.

"You *need* me!" Entwhistle called. I heard his footsteps on the stairs.

I pushed through the final line of cells and found Miss Vanderhart leaning out into space, both hands clutching a tangle of silken cord that was wrapped around her forearm. One end of this rope was wrapped around one of the metal beams that made up the airship's frame, while other end rose up out of sight, beyond the opening in the vessel's skin. Another, larger bundle was lashed nearby.

"That one's yours," she said, pointing at the larger bundle. "I hope it's enough." Then she tugged her own bundle free of the beam and allowed herself to be pulled out through the side of the airship.

I hurried forward and stared out, to see her dangling from a triad of gas cells and slowly descending toward the jungle below. I looked up, and saw a bundle of five cells awaiting my own escape. Apparently she had revised her estimates of the necessary lift.

"Derringer, where are you?" Entwhistle called from behind me – from closer than I liked. Cursing his stubbornness, I quickly wrapped the oilcloth around the beam next to my ropes, and fumbled out a match. The ruined box claimed these were waterproof, but I had had my doubts about that, and indeed, it took three strikes before a flame leapt up. I held it to the dangling end of the oilcloth rag until the flame spread. As soon as I was certain it had caught I grabbed the ropes, wrapped them around my arm as Miss Vanderhart had, then tried to pry them loose from the beam.

Miss Vanderhart had tied them more securely than I had thought, and as my fingers plucked at the silk I could not help staring at the flame spreading up the oilcloth, growing larger, licking closer and closer to the surrounding gas cells...

And then all at once the rope came loose, and I was jerked out through the side of the airship so abruptly that I thought my arm might tear from its socket. I grabbed at the cords, looking up at my five balloons, trying to gain some sort of control.

I was perhaps fifty feet from the vessel, just beginning to feel my motion steady, when the aluminum airship exploded.

Chapter Twenty-Four

The Journey Home

The explosion was not as loud as I had expected, but otherwise the fireball was as spectacular as anyone could have asked. Orange flame blossomed in all directions, turning the gray of early morning into a vivid blaze of color and light. Although I was dangling from a cluster of balloons with very little control of my situation, I had by chance rotated enough that I was almost facing the Skymaster when it erupted, and it appeared to me that those flames came within a few feet of me. I felt a blast of fiery heat on my cheeks; the wind whipped through my hair, and I, along with my supporting balloons, was flung backward – and then pulled forward again, as the burning hydrogen, so much lighter than the surrounding atmosphere, swept upward, sucking in air to fill the void it left behind.

The great rounded cylinder of the lifting chamber disintegrated; when the burning gas had cleared enough for me to see it, there was nothing to see but twisted girders and scraps of flaming debris, the entire mass plummeting toward the ground.

The great cabin was more nearly intact, and I glimpsed half a dozen ropes dangling below it, collapsing from straight lines into wild scrawls on the morning air as gravity ceased to draw them taut. Three of them, I think, still had men climbing down them; I fervently hoped that the jungle canopy would break the fall for those unfortunates and permit them to survive, and that the other crewmen had all reached ground safely before the blast.

Lieutenant James Apollonius Entwhistle, I knew, must have perished instantly.

And as I watched the wreckage falling, for the first time it occurred to me that there might be innocents *below* it, in a position to be crushed by that immense mass. I hoped there were not, or that the trees would protect them.

The sound of the ruin's impact reached me a fraction of a second after I saw it strike. It seemed as loud as the initial explosion. I saw trees crumple like matchsticks, and a cloud of green leaves and brightly colored birds fountained up around it. The leaves scattered on the wind and fell back; the birds gathered speed as they rose and fled in all directions.

And then the skies were empty, save for myself – but where was my companion? I saw no sign of Miss Vanderhart. Grabbing at the tangled cords that supported me, I twisted myself around, looking for her.

At last I located her. As is only natural for creatures such as ourselves, who live out our lives on the surface of the earth, I had been looking at my own level, and I only found her when I lowered my gaze. She was still safely suspended from her three grayish-white balloons in their gray silk net, but hung well below me and off to the west. I could see that she was descending slowly toward the jungle below.

Whereas I, I realized with some concern, was rising; it would seem Miss Vanderhart had either overestimated my weight or underestimated the buoyancy of my five gas cells. The sun's rays might also be heating the balloons, causing further expansion, though I cannot say with certainty that was a contributing factor. At any rate, I was ascending, and I did not want to be. I had the cords wrapped around my left forearm; I kept my left hand clamped on them while I reached my right down to draw my Bowie knife from my belt.

It wasn't there. My captors had removed it, and I had not taken the time to retrieve it when we recovered our guns and left the salon. I cursed my own lack of foresight and looked up.

I knew the balloons would not keep rising indefinitely; not only would they reach equilibrium as the air thinned, but in time the hydrogen would leak out. The gas is of so fine a structure that it will eventually leach out through any even slightly permeable container, and while I did not know the exact nature of the treated fabric that these gas cells were made of, I did not believe it could be utterly impermeable.

But would the air still be enough for me to breathe when the bundle of balloons reached its final altitude? Would the gas bleed off enough to lower me to the ground before I died of thirst or exposure? I did not care to gamble my life on these questions. I reached up with my right hand and began to claw my way up the tangled cords, trying to get at one of the balloons.

I honestly don't know how long it took; I was so focused on my task that I lost all sense of time. It seemed like forever, but the sun was still low in the east, and the jungle below did not look much more distant, so I suppose it was only a few minutes before I was able to get my fingers on the tied–off stump where Miss Vanderhart had detached one of the balloons from its controlling network of pipes and valves. She had looped a length of silken cord around the fabric to close it off. I picked at the knot and found it hard and tight – Miss Vanderhart might be a mere girl, but she clearly knew how to tie a knot as well as the most experienced seaman. I fumbled at it, wishing I could use both hands but not daring to loosen my left hand's grip on the cords that kept me from plunging to my death.

I never did untie the knot; instead, the length of cord pulled off the balloon's mouth entirely and fell, still knotted, from my grip. Thus freed of its confinement, hydrogen gushed from the opening, and one of my five supports collapsed in on itself.

My gradual ascent ceased abruptly, and with a small jerk I began to descend.

Content with my situation for the moment, I looked around until I once again spotted Miss Vanderhart, who had reached the level of the highest treetops and seemed almost to be dancing along the jungle canopy, propelling herself from one point of contact to the next, the buoyancy of her balloons allowing her to make leaps of thirty or forty feet at a time. She was, I noticed, heading due south – toward Belize Town.

A very sensible young lady was Miss Vanderhart. I could not help smiling at the sight of her golden hair gleaming in the morning sun as she sailed from tree to tree.

I tried to maneuver myself toward her, but I had no control of my direction. Rather, I was entirely at the mercy of the winds. A gentle westerly wind was blowing – the morning sea breeze, I suppose, pushing me inland. I was descending quickly now, though, and I hoped I could emulate her means of locomotion. I waited impatiently until my feet began to brush the highest treetops, by which time Miss Vanderhart was almost out of sight to the south and east.

That stunt of hers, I discovered, was far more difficult than it looked; I did not dance along the treetops so much as stumble, twirling madly on the cords like a top on a string. I would like to think that my awkwardness was due in part to the lesser lift of my reduced cluster of balloons, but whatever the reason, my progress was slow and clumsy compared to hers and moved not in a straight south-easterly line, but in a zigzag path of fits and starts.

In the end the only reason she did not vanish in the distance was that she looked back, observed my struggles, and came back for me.

With her assistance I was able to make better progress. It took some tricky maneuvering to gather our supporting cords, but we did at last link ourselves together and proceeded southward across the canopy for some time, our balloons united in a single cluster, our arms about each other's waists as we made prodigious leaps across the jungle's roof together.

At last, though, well into the afternoon, we grew sufficiently tired and hungry that we decided the time had come to abandon our bizarre mode of transportation and resort to more ordinary methods. We caught ourselves on a tree and released Miss Vanderhart's balloons, letting them soar away into the empty sky.

Mine, however, we retained to assist us in our climb down. They tangled in the branches occasionally, but all in all made our descent much easier, as we did not need to move from limb to limb over distances no greater than we could reach.

When we reached the ground we were in a situation that was far from desirable – alone in the jungle with almost no supplies, no transportation, and no clear idea where we were – but all the same, we were relieved and optimistic. We had accomplished the task I had set out to accomplish, destroyed a menace to peace, and had survived the experience without serious injury. We had done things I do not believe anyone else had ever attempted – that strange hydrogen-assisted bounding across the jungle canopy had been a terrifying and exhilarating experience. What's more, it had almost certainly taken us several miles south of wherever the surviving crew members of McKee's Skymaster had landed, and well away from Chan Santa Cruz, so that we did not expect to encounter any particularly dangerous human enemies. We had my revolver and I had somehow, throughout everything, retained a box of cartridges in my pocket, so we were not defenseless. I still had the rest of the box of matches, it seemed – I must have stuffed it back in my pocket without thinking, purely out of habit. A few tools were still attached to Miss Vanderhart's blouse and belt, as well. We knew that somewhere to our south, probably no more than a hundred miles away, was an outpost of civilization where we could expect a reasonably hospitable reception.

It was hardly an ideal situation, but we were satisfied, and set out toward Belize Town.

It took us nine days to reach that pleasant little port, nine days in which we learned that well-cooked snake is surprisingly tasty, that hostile Mayans prefer to retreat when confronted with a cocked pistol, that certain insects have *very* unpleasant but not life-threatening stings, and that one can stumble across stone ruins, barking one's shin in the process, in the most unexpected places.

After the fifth day we did come across other Honduran villages before reaching Belize Town itself, in each of which we found at least one or two people who spoke English. Thus we were able to barter our labors and our few remaining possessions for food and an opportunity to wash ourselves and our clothing, so that when at last...well, I would like to say when we marched into the British colonial capital, but "staggered" would be closer to the truth. At any rate, when we arrived in Belize Town our appearance was not *completely* barbaric, so we were allowed into the telegraph office, where I wired my mother to inform her that we were alive and well, and in need of funds.

She obliged us by wiring a considerable sum that same afternoon, enabling us to take up lodging in the town's best hotel, which was surprisingly comfortable, and to do a great deal to restore our wardrobes. Miss Vanderhart and I negotiated a sum that would serve as her pay for piloting and maintaining the Aeronavigator, and I added a bonus on top of that that she seemed to consider reasonably generous. I paid her from my mother's gift, so that she was able to attend to her own needs rather than relying on my charity or troubling her own family for support.

Another week saw us recovered from our travails and boarding a steamer to New York, by way of Havana.

During our stay in British Honduras and throughout the long journey home, Miss Vanderhart was troubled by the killing of Captain McKee. She said that she relived that moment in her dreams almost every night, and also suffered from nightmares where the late captain appeared alive once more, pursuing her and demanding vengeance.

For my part, I found myself hoping that Lieutenant Entwhistle had somehow survived, though I knew it to be impossible. I knew that I, like Miss Vanderhart, had killed a man, and although I did not suffer the torments she did, nonetheless the pangs of remorse did darken my disposition.

I also worried a great deal about what we had left behind. What had become of McKee's men? No word had reached Belize Town at the time of our departure. What had, and what would, become of the wreckage of the aluminum airship? Several tons of metallic aluminum, a large majority of the world's supply of that material, rested somewhere in the jungles of the Yucatan. Another aerial conqueror might follow in

McKee's footsteps, or perhaps treasure hunters would scavenge the remains and put the aluminum to other uses – perhaps even more nefarious than McKee's.

I resolved that I would, if necessary, fund and lead an expedition to recover the downed flying machine, to prevent it falling into the wrong hands.

Aboard ship I tried to maintain the emotional distance between us, as I had during our voyage aboard the Aeronavigator, so as not to take any unfair advantage of our position, but it grew more difficult as time passed. We had been through a great deal together, and we were no longer employer and employee; further, Miss Vanderhart was no longer occupied with her engineering duties. Still, I was careful to always treat her with appropriate reserve, and never to presume upon our shared experiences.

Although we had not yet forgotten the deaths we had caused, when at last, weeks later, we stepped ashore on the island of Manhattan, our spirits had largely recovered. We were both cheerful enough and made our way together to the railroad depot. There I accompanied her as she arranged passage to her home in New Brunswick, and I saw her off.

"Farewell, Miss Vanderhart," I said, as she stepped aboard her carriage. "Thank you for your invaluable service."

"Thank you, Mr. Derringer," she said with a smile. "Now that our professional association is at an end, I would be pleased if you would call me Betsy. After spending these last few months in your company, I concede that you are indeed a gentleman, a good-hearted man, and not quite such a fool as I thought."

I smiled. "And I would be honored, Betsy, if you would call me Tom. You are as valiant as anyone, man or woman, I have ever known, and should you ever find yourself in my home town, I hope you will come visit and meet my mother and sister." I took her hand and kissed her fingers, and then released it and stepped back. She waved and vanished into the car.

I waited until the conductor called "All aboard," then turned and left the station. I was not going directly home; indeed, I was not sure I would see my home again for quite some time. My concern about the airship's wreckage had only grown with the passage of time, and I intended to waste no time in investigating what might have befallen that wreckage, and what I could do about it. I hailed a hansom cab and gave the address of the Pierce Archives.

My arrival there created something of a stir; apparently my mother had kept Mr. Arbuthnot and Mad Bill Snedeker informed of my progress, and they had in turn let it be known at the Archives and the meeting rooms of the Order of Theseus what I was up to. I was greeted with a smattering of applause, and several individuals came to shake my hand or slap me on the back. I was invited to join a party for dinner that evening, so that I might regale them with my adventures, and I accepted.

First, though, I managed to get Dr. Pierce alone to make my inquiries. I explained the nature of my concern.

He waved a hand in dismissal. "You need not trouble yourself, young Mr. Derringer. That aluminum presents no danger to anyone."

I frowned. "On the contrary, Dr. Pierce, I think you misjudge the situation. That area is not so very remote – "

"No, no," he interrupted, holding up a hand to silence me. "I am sure that you are right, and that the aluminum can be salvaged. However, things have changed in your absence. Recovering the wreckage would not be worth the trouble."

"Why *not?*" I demanded, astonished. "We are speaking of several *tons* of aluminum!"

"Because, sir, a Mr. Cowles is reported to have devised an entirely new method of processing aluminum that has completely changed the situation. Aluminum is no longer a mere laboratory curiosity, Mr. Derringer. Cowles is now able to supply it, in an admittedly impure form, in any quantities desired at a very reasonable cost, and a dozen companies are said to be experimenting with various industrial uses for this marvelous metal. Other researchers are engaged in efforts to refine his process, or improve upon it, and given the remarkable technical ingenuity of our time I have no doubt they will succeed. Anyone seeking to build an aluminum airship on McKee's model can now do so without salvaging anything, from either the Lost City or the Yucatan jungle."

I stared at him for a moment, unsure whether to laugh or curse.

It seemed I would not need to return to the Yucatan after all. My adventure was complete as it was. In fact, I thought for a moment it might have been altogether *unnecessary* – but no. McKee could have cut a swathe through Mexico and done immense damage before anyone else could match his accomplishment and set an aerial fleet against his Skymaster, and I had prevented that disaster.

On a personal level, I had achieved my goal of following in my father's footsteps and becoming an adventurer. Judging by my reception at the Archives, I would have no trouble joining the Order of Theseus now, should I choose to do so. I was under no *compulsion* to do so, however; I was free to go home to my mother, if I chose – or free to set out upon some new adventure.

I could, if I wanted, go to New Brunswick and set about wooing Betsy, for despite her lack of proper feminine delicacy I could not imagine a more worthy companion. There was no longer any need to maintain a professional distance between us.

I had had a good taste of the adventurer's life, the life my father had lived for so long and that my mother had experienced as well, the life that I had thought so utterly irresistible for so long. I had tasted it and discovered it did not suit my palate, and my temperament, as well as I had expected. I had learned that adventuring consisted of days, or weeks, or months of tedium and discomfort leading up to mere minutes of excitement, that the excitement was more likely to be terror than exhilaration, and that success usually came not from forthright action, but from subterfuge and deception. I had discovered that the death of anyone, even a foe, was a saddening thing. I had had my adventure, had had my triumph, and now I had every right to retire, to return home and once again live quietly on my inheritance. I could take up any career that caught my fancy; I did not *need* to follow in my father's footsteps.

But on the other hand...

"Well, then, Dr. Pierce," I said. "What can you tell me about Gabriel Trask?"

– THE END –

Author's Note

I am aware that the Cowles electric smelter did not in fact go into production until 1886 – in the history *we* know. Let us just say that Dr. Pierce had extraordinary sources of information.

About the Author:

Lawrence Watt-Evans has been a full-time writer for more than thirty-five years, with about fifty novels and well over a hundred short stories to his credit, as well as assorted essays, poems, comic books, and so on. His story "Why I Left Harry's All-Night Hamburgers" won the 1988 Hugo for short story, as well as the Asimov's Readers Award. He lives in Takoma Park, Maryland, with his wife and the obligatory writer's cat.

His website is at www.watt-evans.com.

Made in the USA
Monee, IL
24 November 2021

82815000R00148